# HATE THE AIR:

## THE ABBREVIATED LIFE OF SHEA KENNEDY

**RM JOHNSON**



Published by MarcusArts, LLC

**Also by RM Johnson**

My Wife's Baby
Bishop 3
Bishop 2
Bishop
Keeping the Secret 3
Keeping the Secret 2
Keeping the Secret
Deceit and Devotion
No One in the World with E. Lynn Harris
Why Men Fear Marriage
Stacie and Cole
The Million Dollar Demise
The Million Dollar Deception
The Million Dollar Divorce
Do You Take This Woman
Dating Games
Love Frustration
Father Found
The Harris Family
The Harris Men

# HATE THE AIR:

THE ABBREVIATED LIFE OF SHEA KENNEDY

RM JOHNSON

MARCUSARTS LLC—ATLANTA, GA

# 1

Mom had held a position high in the World Health Organization as a researcher, and had been called to D.C. to find a cure for whatever had people dying in the streets. At that time, the latest estimate on the news was that millions of people had died from the air just two weeks after the first casualty. Back then Mom seemed gone more than she was home—flying to D.C., and all over the rest of the country.

When she was with us at dinner, Dad would ask if Mom had found out anything: if anyone had. "When will people stop dying?" he'd ask.

Mom would stare down at her food, picking at it with her utensils, obviously not there: in D.C. most likely. She'd look up. "I don't know, Ben. Just keep wearing your mask. All of you. Better yet, don't go outside."

"You know I can't do that," Dad said. "People depend on me."

Mom smiled sadly, tossed around a few grains of rice with her fork. "I know that. I know."

All that responsibility ate at her. I knew each time she heard word of the death toll rising—that was every minute of every day—she would fault herself for those deaths. All of it wore her down. She wasn't the same, moving about the house wrapped up in a blanket of depression.

One night at dinner, after returning from D.C. that same day, she reported again to Dad, me and my 19 year-old, sister Sloane, that the researchers assembled weren't able to figure exactly what was causing the deaths, or how to stop them.

Sloane stared at me, prodded me with a soft, under the table shin kick, then nodded toward Dad.

I looked at him, ready to ask the questions Sloane apparently was afraid to, when Dad said to Mom, "You going to tell them, Cynda, or do I have to?"

They obviously had talked: Mom telling Dad something she thought was too mature for our ears. She appeared small and tired in her chair:

shoulders slumped, eyes sunken, lids hung low, her dark brown hair frizzy and pulled back in a ponytail held by a little green rubber band.

Dad, bearded and broad-chested, his skin the color of an old penny, stared at her downturned face, his fist wrapped so tight around the handle of his steak knife, the veins on the back of his hands were fatly inflated like gummy worms.

"Cynda," Dad pushed again. "You can't just keep this a secret."

"It's not definite," Mom finally spoke, her voice apologetic, as if she were to blame. "It's not confirmed."

"Tell them anyway. Our children have a right to know everything you've found out."

Mom looked up at us. Gently set her knife and fork down on the plate of her mostly untouched dinner, closed her eyes and nodded as though convincing herself that what she was about to do was the right thing.

"There were just dead ends," Mom said, exhaustion and frustration in her voice. "We knew it was respiratory, we knew it was in the air. We knew that in the victim, it killed the lungs, rendering them inoperable. Twenty years ago, lung and bladder cancer, respiratory illness, even death, were all on the rise due to high levels of particulate matter—sulfate, nitrates, ammonia, sodium chloride and black carbon. It was the fault of the larger, industrialized regions, Europe, China, and of course, the U.S.," Mom said. "Before you kids were born, it was decided we needed a fix: a cure for a problem that would only get worse, that would kill more and more people till one day the earth's air would not be suitable for any living thing to breath. So two decades ago, a remedy to the world's air pollution problem was created: a "miracle additive" was how they regarded it.

"But it wasn't safe like they thought, was it?" Dad said, anger making his voice tremble.

I glanced at him, noticed his eyes narrowed at Mom like it was her fault, like she had something to do with all of this.

"No, it wasn't," Mom said, defeated, as though accepting the blame. "Two weeks ago when people started dying, it was approximately twenty years after the initiation of the miracle additives." No longer staring down at her hands, but blankly in front of her, Mom said, "The reason why so many—tens of millions of people have died in just two weeks, and why we haven't noticed negative affects until now is that the fatal effects of the additive are cumulative."

"I don't understand," Sloane whispered, sounding a frightened as I felt.

Turning to Sloane, Mom said, "After inhaling the additive for twenty years, the lungs die. No warning, no signs, the lungs just cease to operate, and then...and then the individual dies."

Frightened, my head filling with numbers, I did the math, stared at Dad, then Mom, expecting to see them start to cough, then choke, as I've seen others do, grab their throats, fall to the ground, roll around, kicking, their backs arching, as their faces turned from red to blue to a morbid purple.

"That means," I said, choosing my words very carefully so there would be no misunderstanding, "...those who haven't already died over the age of twenty, are going to die just like everybody else?"

Mom nodded. "I'm afraid so, sweetie."

"But..."I glanced at Dad, then back to Mom. "You and Dad are over twenty, right?"

Mom chuckled sadly. "That's right. We are."

"And what about...the rest of us?" Sloane eyes were shiny-wet with impending tears. "What about all the people under twenty?"

"Sloane, sweetheart," Mom said. "We aren't sure about—"

"No, Mom! Tell us," Sloane demanded, sensing that Mom was attempting to protect us from the truth.

"There hasn't been conclusive evidence that—"

"Cynda," Dad said. "They have a right to know. We raised them strong. They can handle it."

"What happens when *we* turn twenty?" Sloane asked, tears spilling down her cheeks.

Mom averted her stare, forced it back on us then wiped her own tears from her eyes with the butts of both her palms. “If a cure isn’t found by then, all the evidence suggests that sometime before or after you each turn twenty…you and Shea will die too.”

Coming out of my thoughts, I was doing sixty miles an hour down Sycamore Avenue. I noticed the door of a house swinging open, when yesterday it was closed. I squeezed the handbrake on the old Harley Davidson, whipped a U-turn, steered the bike into the driveway of the two-story house and climbed off.

The grass outside had grown knee high thick with weeds and spotted with trash. Visible just behind the glass windows of the house were iron bars and heavy drapes.

The sky overhead was dreary and full of clouds. I stood in the center of the driveway, looking up and down the street. It was deathly quiet around me: no sound of traffic, lawnmowers running, or kids screaming as they played, like before the air turned. I pushed my goggles up, readjusting the bandana—the attempt most of us made to protect ourselves from the air—over my nose and mouth.

“What do you think, boy?” I said still looking up at the house.

The question was for my partner, Tornado, a five year-old German Shepard: ninety pounds of muscle, he wore a vest and harness from his Police dog days. He was dark brown with a black saddle, paws, muzzle, and superhero mask of dark fur around his eyes. He had a splash of white in the center of his breast: an inverted triangle that I thought, at ten years old, looked like a tornado.

I checked his tether to the sidecar. “Make sure no one makes off with our wheels, okay boy.” He licked my hand and whined as I started cautiously up the walkway and climbed the stairs. I stuck my head inside the house. “Anyone in there?” I could barely see anything for the thick, dark curtains pulled over all the windows; it was nearly pitch black inside. I told myself not to slip, not get jumped, get caught of guard and killed. The possibility now was always in the back of my head.

I eased the Walther handgun my father gave me from my shoulder holster, pulled my flashlight and clicked it on, pointing them both at the space in front of me. It was something he had taught me, knowing how much I wanted to follow his path—to be like him.

One morning years ago while Dad was getting ready for work, I pushed open the bedroom door, slipped into his room, hoping to catch him polishing his shoes for work, but instead, saw his gun belt hanging from the bedroom chair. I slid the weapon from its holster, held it with both hands toward the bathroom door. When Dad stepped out in his uniform trousers and undershirt, I tried to pull the trigger, but was not strong enough.

"Pow! You're dead, Daddy!" I said, wondering why he didn't smile, fall to the floor, splay his arms and legs, laughing. He rushed me, snatched the gun, and wrangled me to him as though saving me from a burning building.

I had gotten the "Don't-you-ever-touch-this-again!" lecture, followed by the "Don't-you-know-how-dangerous-guns-are!" speech.

Sitting on his lap, I watched him eject the wheel of the revolver and empty the bullets from the gun.

"We can't ever let your mother know this happened, understand?" Dad said, holding me around the waist on his lap. "She'd have both of us locked up." He paused, looked up as though figuring something. "If you're really that interested in guns, you should learn the proper way to use them."

"You'll teach me?" I asked, excited.

"How old are you again?" he said, like he didn't know.

"Nine." I said, hoping that was old enough for whatever he planned to teach me.

A week later, sun shinning dimly through the dark green skins of a half dozen beer bottles Dad had carefully stacked on our fence, he watched as I focused my attention over the site of a handgun, my finger locked around the trigger.

Over the previous week, he had taught me how to hold and aim, how to holster, dismantle, clean a gun and put it together again. I picked that stuff up fast. But as I stood in the yard trying to shoot the weapon, it felt as though the trigger hadn't moved in years; it wouldn't budge.

"Fire the weapon, Shea! Do you need me to show you how again?" Dad called from across the yard.

"No Dad!" I said, determined not to fail him.

One eye closed, looking again down the site at the green bottle furthest to the left, I pulled back the trigger, squeezing until I felt the little metal sliver would slice through my finger. The gun popped, kicked in my hands, staggering me back two steps in the mud. At the same time the bottle shattered with a high-pitched tinkle in the distance. I smiled turning to Dad, hearing him laughing, seeing him running toward me, his arms raised.

"You did it!" He grabbed me up, twirled me in circles. I was happy. What I had done made him proud, and I wanted him to be proud of me like that everyday for the rest of my life. So every evening at dusk, the sun dropping behind the high trees, I stood in our huge one-acre backyard, in that muddy or dusty patch—depending on the weather—knocking off bottles from the fence.

After three months I had gotten to the point where I'd become a crack shot. That's what Dad started calling me—a "crack shot!"

At not yet 10 years old, I could snatch the gun from the old leather holster, and in seconds, get a bead on those bottles, slicing them all in half. I'd stand there, gun held out before me smoking after shattering six bottles, sparing not a single bullet.

No more cheers from Dad after my displays of marksmanship, he'd stand in awe then slowly walk to me, chest held out, prideful.

"If anything ever happens to me, I know you'll be fine," Dad said on one of those days, hugging me. My face pressed to the belly of his red and black flannel shirt, I wondered what he meant by that. Nothing would ever happen to Dad. It would've been hard for anyone to convince me that he would ever die: but impossible to prove that when he did, I would be to blame.

I stepped into the open door of the house. I saw no signs of a break-in: the living room hadn't been ransacked: no furniture upended, cushions knifed open, legs torn off end tables, or lamps broken like cracked egg shells on the carpet. It was the opposite: books lay neatly on the coffee table, burned down candles sat beside them, pocket change: pennies, dimes and a quarter were spread nearby. The kitchen was clean: no trash overflowing in the corner pail. But the cabinet doors hung open. Inside of them there was nothing.

I climbed the stairs, stopped in the second floor hallway, surrounded by four doors, all of them closed. I reached to open one, heard movement behind another, spun and with a grunt, kicked it open. The shadow of a boy rummaging through drawers whirled around, and in the splash of flashlight, I saw the gun as it was turned on me.

"Don't do it. I'll shoot!" I cried, my voice tense, high pitched, terrified. The

flashlight beam bounced around his body and face, the thing trembling uncontrollable in my hand. He wore dark pants, a sweater and a ski mask pulled over his head.

"Whatever you have, put it down now!" I demanded.

"Who are you?"

"Sheriff!" I said, trying to sound authoritative.

"Legacy?" He scoffed.

"Freakin sheriff!" I said, again, jabbing my gun at him. "Put it down now or I'll—" before I could finish, I felt an excruciating pain shoot through my skull, shudder down my spine, dropping me to the floor. Movement around me, I felt someone step over me, wrench my gun from my hand. My flashlight lay somewhere on the floor, casting a tall, oblong, light circle in the corner of the room. Within it stood the stretched shadow of the boy who had knocked me over the head from behind. He grinned, pulled his bandana down, revealing yellow crooked teeth.

"You about to say you was gonna shoot my friend?" The boy asked, pressing the side of his gun to my head.

I raised my palms, expecting to die, and thinking how disappointed Dad would've been if he could see me now. "Please," I begged.

"It's a little late for that," he said, grinning wider, dragging the tip of the gun down my face, pressing it against my cheek so hard I cried out.

"Stop!" The boy I had snuck up on, said. "We're not here to kill. Food is all we need. Besides, she's the sheriff."

The boy with the ugly grin looked harder at me. A glint of flashlight caught the point of a star on my badge. He reached down to snatch it. I grabbed his hand before he could tear it off of me, fought him for it, was ready to die before I let him take it.

"Leave it!" the boy wearing the black mask ordered.

He came up behind Yellow Grin, yanked him off of me, pointed his gun at me, while holding out his palm to his partner, gesturing for him to hand over my gun. He ejected the magazine, the bullet in the chamber and pushed both into his pocket, then threw my gun across the room. He handed the bag of stolen goods to his creepy friend and told him to take it outside.

I stared at the boy through the eyeholes in his mask, watching him, wondering if he'd kill me.

"Mother or father was a cop? Probably your hero, and you're trying to do what they did," he said, his gun still on me. "Right?"

My heart pounding, I couldn't speak, could barely breath.

"Things are different. No more heroes. Just people gagging in the street, and people who *gonna* gag in the street. Leave this place like everybody else, before you get yourself killed."

He shoved his gun in the waist of his pants, turned, left me on the floor, shaking, terrified of moving until I heard the downstairs door slam shut. I rolled on my belly, shimmied across the carpet, grabbed my flashlight then found my gun.

Downstairs, I stepped out on the porch, shielded my eyes against the piercing sunlight. Tornado barked frantically at me as though he knew I had acted stupidly—almost got myself killed trying to defend an empty house.

"Shhh, boy. Shhh!" I told him.

I climbed on my bike, kick-started the engine, about to pull off, when the realization that I had almost died hit me hard. Tears came to my eyes and with both gloved fists, I started hitting the bike's dented gas tank, screaming as Tornado barked louder. "Why would you leave me with this? Why would you think I could do it? Why, Dad?" I cried.

I hammered the tank over and over until my hands ached, finally lowering them on the dented metal. I stayed like that, stretched over the bike until I could stop crying.

Tornado had gone silent, too. I looked at him. He stared back, his head tilted to a side as if to say, now that you got that out of your system, can we please go?

I smiled a little, wiped my face and sat up straight on the bike. Glancing upward, I said, "Sorry Dad, for acting like a little girl. Won't happen again, okay."

I pulled down my goggles, toed the Harley into gear then sped off.

# 2

I pulled up to the curb in front of my home: big mustard colored yellow one with white trim and a front porch that stretched the width of the house and around the corner. Identical in design, but different color houses stood on both sides, across the street and for a mile down in each direction from mine. They were all but vacant now. Most of the people who survived the air turning four months ago had already journeyed to the capital. It was the trip my sister, Sloane and I, were going to take in two days.

I undid Tornado's tether and allowed him to leap out of the sidecar. He walked, sniffing grass that used to be meticulously cared for and neatly manicured. Now it was overgrown, full of weeds and yellow daffodil blossoms.

"You gotta go?"

The dog glanced over his shoulder like I had no business asking him that now, knowing his bathroom breaks came every four hours: 8 A.M., noon, 4 P.M. and four hours after that, at 8 P.M. I glanced at my watch, saw that it was only 7:42 in the morning.

"Really? We can't just take care of this now, save us a trip back out here?"

Tornado ignored me and climbed the porch stairs. I followed, and at the door, fished the length of leather cord from out of the collar of my t-shirt, pulled up the keys to the iron security gates on the front, back and basement doors. I unlocked the gate, then the heavy solid wooden, inside door, after taking a sec to calm down after the scare I had back in the vacant house. Sloane had enough to be concerned with regarding the planning of the trip. I didn't need her worrying about me dying on patrol.

"We're home," I called, Tornado brushing by my leg, running to the back of the house, searching for my sister.

The main level of our house was open and spacious with oak wood floors and huge windows on every wall. The windows used to allow massive amounts of sun in, now they were barred and boarded up for security, covered with blinds or curtains for privacy; we had to burn candles much of the time just to see.

I climbed the stairs to my room, needing to get out of my work gear till it was time for my next patrol. I pushed open my door and stepped into a room that was pretty dark inside, save for a strip of sunlight painting the ceiling. It snuck through a space in the planks that had been nailed over the outside of my bedroom windows.

I pulled off my gloves, unclasped my belt, held it where the badge was fastened, rubbing my thumb over the raised markings on the metal sheriff's pin.

I looked in the mirror, trying to assure myself that I was capable of doing the job my father entrusted me with. I wouldn't make a mistake—a lapse in judgment, an error in execution, a screw up that would cost a life.

I woke up from a nap in enough time to take Tornado for his noon walk. Sloane was doing more packing when I came back in the house. She wore hiking boots, a wife beater tee, a drop leg thigh holster, her Glock handgun strapped to one leg, a hunting knife tied to her other. I could see the sinewy muscles in her lean arms jump as she worked. Her skin was almond colored, her hair was shoulder length, kinky and curly, and was pulled back with a rubber band,

She was an inch or two taller than my 5'6". We were both athletically built—swimmer's bodies, I heard people say. I don't know who we had to thank more for them, Mom's good genes, or the pushups, chin-ups, and the miles and miles Dad had Sloane and I run since we were little.

"How was patrol this morning?" Sloane asked, looking up from one of the many boxes she was packing on the dining room table. They sat stacked on top of almost every piece of furniture, flaps hanging open like hungry mouths waiting to be fed with the cans of food, rope, bottled water, flares, paper and all the stuff stacked beside them.

"Uneventful," I lied, avoiding eye contact, knowing Sloane could tell when I wasn't being totally honest. I walked across the room where a large road map hung on the wall, a squiggly red Sharpie line designating the course we intended to take to D.C. It was a trip the President of the United States asked us all to make, a trip that might change the course of our history because of the pages of research our mother had left behind: her attempt to find a cure for what was killing everyone.

After she died, government men wearing dark suits and mirrored glasses took her laptop and desktop computers, and all other material linked to her research. But since Mom never trusted back ups of any kind: disk drives, her hard drives, or the cloud, a month later, Sloane and I were not surprised to find papers buried deep in her closet. After thumbing through the hundreds of printed and handwritten notes, we realized they were copies of everything she had found out about what turned the air. There were mathematical and scientific equations, autopsy reports, all sorts of measurements and calculations. It was stuff Sloane nor I would never understand, but realized might possibly lead to a cure if the information was gotten to the right people in D.C. It was our job to make that happen.

"So no problems during patrol? You sure?" I heard Sloane ask, pulling me out of my thoughts.

"Yeah, same as always."

I kept my eyes on the map, staring at the almost two hundred miles we had to travel to the capital. I turned, looked about the room, thinking about all the wonderful times my family had here.

"Hey, you okay?" Sloane asked, sensing my mood.

"We'll never see this place again, will we?"

"No. We won't."

"You won't miss it? I mean, you ever think we should just stay?"

Sloane stopped sealing a box with packing tape. "We lost Mom while in this house...Dad, and I lost Cam. I don't wanna die here, too."

Cam was Sloane's fiancé. He was a good guy, tall with sun-bleached hair, and a smooth, freckled smiling face—a deep dimple in his chin. He loved our family just as much as Dad and Mom loved him. Three nights a week, Sloane would invite him over for dinner where we'd all laugh and talk and joke, and afterward, Cam would help Sloane and I wash, dry and put away the dishes.

One year older than Sloane, he was her sweetheart since her junior year.

A month ago, he pulled me into the backyard, dug in his pocket, fished out a ring box and cracked it open for me to see what was inside.

"Well, wow, Cam!" I said, marveling at the single carat solitaire diamond, sparkling like crazy in the sun. "You could afford that stacking UPS boxes?"

"I had been saving before the air turned," he said, proudly looking up at me. "I'm going to ask Sloane to marry me. I know it's not a good time, you're mom passing, and then with what happened to your dad, but..."

"It's the best time, Cam," I said, grabbing his arm and giving him a squeeze. "There could be no better time."

The wedding was held the following Saturday at the big Catholic Church three miles from our house in the city center. We told everyone in the neighborhood. We asked them to pass the word. We were surprised at the turnout. Many of the people at the wedding were our friends from elementary and high school—the ones that hadn't left for D.C. There were people from other neighborhoods, folks I had seen at the mall, or the post office, but had never formally met before. Some wore masks or bandanas: most wore nothing, believing less in the ability of the filters to protect; so many bodies had been seen lying dead on the streets, masks covering the blue skin of their faces.

Still, it was a nice gathering. I figured with the deaths occurring, seemingly every few minutes of every day, along with the looting and the violence and the loss of hope, people needed a distraction: an event like this to remind them of how life used to be. They needed to be reminded that what was best about our lives was still with us.

The wedding ceremony was beautiful. Cam wore a suit jacket over his t-shirt and jeans. Sloane wore jeans, a top, hiking boots, and a beautiful white lace wedding veil I bought her from the only wedding dress store still open at the time. The Legacy operator, a sixteen year-old daughter of the owner who had been taken by the air, smiled gratefully when I handed her the crumpled, dirty bills from my cargo pockets, and told me her mother would be happy to know that people were still marrying despite the end being near.

The young man who presided over the ritual was once the very youthful preacher's assistant, with thick, dark eyebrows and not a strand of facial hair, but was now the town's Legacy preacher and operator of the church.

Standing beside my sister as her lady of honor, I watched Sloane wipe away joyful tears, then turn to look out on the crowd of easily a hundred people.

Speechless, not having seen a truer example of the toll the air took on the population of our small city until that moment, I spotted no one appearing over the age of 20. On that otherwise joyous day, I realized that very soon, anyone much older than my sister and I, would be dead.

Cam officially moved into our house hours after the ceremony, helping to fill the hole of despair that opened up with the passing of my parents. It was good having him there, and we felt a little more like the family we once were. Sloane was happier than I'd ever seen her, and we were hopeful about the future, even though we knew the deaths: people falling to their knees in bathrobes and slippers, dying in the crisp cool of morning, or while walking their dogs, their frightened pets dragging their leashes, barking manically at their dead owners, would never stop.

But we had each other—the three of us. And although lonely every now and then, watching Sloane and Cam cuddle on the living room sofa, I couldn't have been happier.

Over a late breakfast of scrambled eggs, waffles and orange juice, Sloane said that the two of them had very important news they wanted to share. Sloane reached over and grabbed her husband's hand. "You wanna tell her, baby?"

Cam smiled. "No, you do it."

Sloane excitedly turned to me. "We're pregnant, Shea! We're having a baby!"

How was that supposed to work? I sat there thinking, trying to bring a smile to my face. I had seen pregnant women with big round bellies dead in the park: I'd helped to burry a few of them. I've even seen a Legacy doctor try to deliver an infant via C-section on a McDonald's floor, while the mother was gulping and gagging, drowning in the air. Both mother and baby died. But who was I to steal this blessing from my sister, this moment of happiness, when everything had turned to crap.

"That's wonderful," I said, doing my best to sound excited and hopeful.

Two days later, I walked in the house after patrol and found my sister on the floor, screaming, holding Cam's head in her lap, his lifeless body, stretched out in front of her, after being taken by the air.

Almost one month to the day after the wedding, we held Cam's funeral in our backyard. It was attended by only a few; unlike the wedding, we notified only a handful of people, and did not encourage them to inform anyone else.

Dressed in the suit jacket and jeans he was married in, then wrapped cocoon-like in a stark white comforter, it took four of us—Sloane at his head, me at his feet, his closest friends supporting his sides—to lower him gently into the ground.

Silently, and seemingly dumbstruck with the possibility that this could ever happen, we blanketed Cam with the soft earth we had dug up the day before: some of us using shovels, other's on our knees, using our hands. Sloane, tears streaming down her face, appeared unsteady on her feet. She looked as though she was about to fall in the hole with her deceased husband. Concerned, I watched her drop her shovel, then run off. I caught her just inside the house, on the back porch, crumpled to the floor. I dropped down with her, held her tight and let her cry.

The next afternoon, I had gone to the flower shop, hoping they were still open, but not surprised to see that they were closed, the door padlocked from the outside. It hadn't mattered; the glass plate in the door's frame had been busted out.

I stepped through the wooden edging, onto the broken glass inside the shop and picked the least wilted bunch from what had not been looted already.

At home, I walked out the back porch door, surprised to see Sloane knee deep in a rectangular ditch.

"What are you doing?" I asked.

She sunk the spade of a shovel into a mound of dirt, looked up at me, wiping a forearm across her sweaty, dirty brow. "What does it look like?"

It looked like she was digging a grave beside her husband's, a grave I hated to think, she might've intended for herself. I walked closer, held out the flowers to her.

"Thought they might help."

"Put 'em over there," Sloane said. "If you wanna help, grab a shovel." She freed hers from the mound of dirt and started at the ditch again.

"I'm not gonna help dig a grave for my sister who isn't dead yet," I said. "That is what you're doing, right?"

"You act like it's not going to happen."

"You don't know for sure that it is."

She stopped her work again, looked up at me from over the bandana tied tightly just under her eyes. "Stop avoiding the inevitable, Shea. Tell me the last time you've seen someone walking around older than me. Weeks? A month? Cam died three months after he turned twenty. He never wanted to talk about the possibility, got upset whenever I did, so I stopped, then got so used to believing the lie we told ourselves, that I couldn't believe it when he actually died. I'm not going to lie to myself anymore."

"So what now?"

Sloane sunk the shovel in the dirt again. "Nothing left here for me...for us. We go to D.C. like the president asked. We go to D.C. like we should've done a long time ago."

"Shea! Did you hear me?" Sloane asked. She was taping up another box, staring at me from across the living room.

"What?" I said, returning from the past. "I'm sorry. I must've—"

"I said, we're definitely leaving here, so get the idea of staying out of you your head. Now have you found out for sure how many people are going with us?"

Over the past couple of weeks, we tried to convince the few people still around, to go with us to D.C. Only a couple of my friends had agreed. While Sloane did most of the packing and planning, it was my job to find more kids to accompany us.

"Still only two so far, but..." I said, making air quotes around the next word I spoke. "Homecoming is tonight at the mall. There'll be a bunch of people there, so..."

"Fine. Talk to them. Let them know we leave from here day after tomorrow. And if they don't show, they don't go."

## 3

I raced past stalled cars on the side of the road, abandoned months ago. Trash lined the streets, the windows of stores were busted out; a group of kids, wearing rags over their noses and mouths, hands stuffed in their pockets, walked casually down the street, as though most of our parents hadn't recently died the unthinkable deaths the air caused.

I pulled up onto the sidewalk in front of my friend, Beth's house. She and I were both seniors before the air turned. We had the same English Lit and Physics course and had known each other since freshman year. The air took Beth's parents just days apart from each other, Beth happening to be by each of their sides when they went, bawling, screaming for help, begging them not to die, unable to do a thing, while they gagged, gurgled and choked to death.

She took their deaths pretty bad. It seemed, April, Beth's 11 year-old younger, tougher little sister, handled the grief better than Beth, who had been really depressed and not quite right since. That was the reason I was there; I hoped taking Beth "shopping" with me for a homecoming dress (I would rather pull out one of my own teeth with a pair of pliers than shop) would help lift her spirits.

I rang the doorbell and glanced over my shoulder, always wary of something bad happening. The front door opened and I spun around, startled, to see April. She had red hair and pigtails and looked like the picture on the Wendy's Hamburgers sign. A black, skeleton jawbone bandana was pulled up over her nose.

"Kinda jumpy, huh?" April laughed, holding open the security door.

I pulled down my bandana and walked into a neatly kept living room. There were two chairs, a coffee table, out-of-date magazines on top of it. On the covers were teen heartthrobs: Taylor Swift, Justin Bieber, Selena Gomez: folks who were no longer teens, and for that reason, no longer alive.

April locked the doors then came around, pulling down her bandana, smiling at me, holding out a fist. I bumped it with my own.

"How's the law enforcement business?" April asked. "When you gonna let me be your deputy? I keep telling you, no sheriff can go with without a deputy."

"You're right. We'll have to talk about that sometime. Where's your sister?"

April stuck a hand on her narrow hip. "Like you have to ask."

"Kendall's?"

"Didn't come back from yesterday."

"She left you here all night by yourself?" I said, walking to the front window, peering out between the shades.

"I can take care of myself," April said behind me.

"I know you can. But I don't want you here by yourself. It's dangerous. You're coming with me."

We rolled right up to the door of Macy's and parked on the sidewalk. Cars sat eerie and unmanned in the parking lot: doors open, gas caps gone, windows smashed, wheels stolen from the axels, fuel long ago siphoned from the tanks.

April climbed out the sidecar and asked, "Whose throwing a Homecoming dance?" as though it was the stupidest idea in the world.

"My classmates," I said, pulling the key from the ignition as I climbed from the bike.

"Why?" April asked, walking toward the mall building.

"Who knows? Nostalgia, I guess. People want things to be the same when there's no chance of that ever happening. I agree, it's pretty stupid."

"Then why you going?"

"Recruit for the trip."

"And maybe because you believe what they believe?" April said, walking backwards in front of me, so that she could face me. "That there's a chance things will go back to the way they were?"

"There's no chance of that," I said.

April hunched her shoulders, seeming to accept my answer, turned around then ran up on the walkway and picked something up off the ground. "Ooh, an iPhone six!" She wiped at the cracked glass screen with a gloved hand.

"Put that down. It's worthless," I said. "It's no longer a phone, or a fashion accessory. It's garbage."

"But I—"

"Toss it, April," I said, walking past her.

I heard her sigh and drop the phone where she found it.

We stepped through the metal frame of the door: glass broken out, jagged shards pulled from the edges to make entry and exit of the store less hazardous.

April yanked down her bandanna so she could speak. "The dresses are over here," she said excitedly, hurrying into the dark, vacant store.

The perfume and cosmetics counter was on our right, purses to our left. Twenty feet past that, a sign reading SHOES dangled at an angle from only a single metal wire. Clothes and merchandise were strewn across the floor, mannequins lay bald, stripped naked, staring up, unblinking at the ceiling, missing arms and legs, frightening, smiles on their faces.

Seconds later I heard April's boot heels against the tile floor, running toward me, she held two dresses: one white, the other baby blue.

"Found these. There's not a lot that hasn't been picked over already, but these are pretty nice. Although this one," she said raising the blue one, "was on the floor, it's not very dirty."

I stood in a full-length mirror trying on the dress she brought me over my jeans and a black wife beater tee; I had to take off my shoulder holster in order for April to zip it up.

She stood off to the side like an aging fashion designer, fingering the balls of a long, ugly string of pearls she found and wrapped twice around her neck. "The blue, definitely the blue," she said, waving a finger at the gown I was wearing. "You don't wanna go to the dance all decked out in white like you're getting married."

"The blue it is," I said, not caring either way.

April came from behind and unzipped me. I pulled the dress over my head, balled it up, stuffed it in my bag, and put back on my shirt and holster.

I shouldered my backpack and started toward the light of the exit doors.

"You scared about making the trip?" April asked, following.

"Nope."

"Really? People died out there trying to get to the capital."

"How you know that?" I said, stepping over pairs of soiled women's slacks and business suit jackets. "No one who's left has ever come back."

"I hear things. You're not scared?"

I stopped in the middle of where the lingerie section used to be, looked back at April. "We're gonna be fine. So no, I'm not scared, and you shouldn't be either."

"I'm not. I can take care of myself."

"I know you can, April," I said, turning and starting back toward the door.

"Seriously! I can. Want me to prove it?"

"Sure." I said, giving her my attention one last time.

"You promise you won't be mad if I show you how?"

"Show me now, or you're walking home," I teased.

April bent down, raised the leg of her jeans to show a holster strapped around the ankle of her boot. A 22. caliber handgun was stuffed in it. She pulled it out, waving it around.

"Hold it! Hold it! Keep that pointed down!" I shouted, hurrying over and disarming her. "Where did you get this thing?" I asked, discharging the magazine to see that it was fully loaded.

"You promised you wouldn't take it."

"Does Beth know you have this?"

April shook her head.

"She should," I said, giving me one more reason to be angry with Beth. "How'd you get it?"

"Found it," she said, her eyes turned down. "About a block from my house. I was cutting through somebody's yard and saw someone lying in the grass. I thought he was just, like, chilling out or something. But when I walked up to him, he was...you know...dead."

"So you took this off of him?"

"You're the one who keeps telling us how dangerous it is out here."

That was true.

"I told you I can protect myself now. I could even help protect you," April said.

I shook my head, happy that the girl was still alive. "You know how to fire this thing?"

"What's to know?" April said, doing the hand on the hip thing again. "You pull the trigger and a bullet comes out the little hole in front."

"'Little hole in the front.' Really? Okay," I said, shaking my head, stuffing the magazine in my jeans pocket and handing her back the gun. "Re-holster this. You're coming with me, and I'm going to give you your first shooting lesson."

"Woo-hoo!" April yelled, raising her fists over her head.

## 4

I dropped April back home after showing her the basics of how to shoot a weapon. When I pulled into my driveway, I couldn't help but notice the vehicle that was parked beside the house across the street. It was a school bus, one of those short ones, spray painted camouflage: splotches of brown, green, black and tan.

I walked in my house, slamming the door behind me. "Sloane!"

"Coming," my sister answered, stepping out of the kitchen, sipping from a bottle of water, Tornado following behind her. "You find a dress?"

"Yeah. The bus across the street—who's is it?"

"Well let me see the dress," Sloane said.

I took off my pack and held the bag out to her. "Now who does the bus belong to?"

Sloane took my pack, smiling as she unzipped the bag, pulled out the dress and held it up. "Ooh, my little sister's gonna be so cute," she joked.

"Sloane! C'mon...the bus?"

"—in Greg's driveway?"

"Yes!"

"If it's in Greg's driveway, who do you think it belongs to?"

No way! That was impossible. Greg had up and disappeared two years ago without as much as throwing up a middle finger...and we were supposed to have been best friends. "Greg? Greg is here?"

Sloane nodded, smiling wider.

I ran to the window, parted the curtain, peeked out across the street to make sure he wasn't out there, standing in the middle of our front lawn: t-shirt too small, jeans too big, pushing up his Coke-bottle glasses on his nose so he cold stare up at the house like he used to as a love-struck 14 year-old.

"Gruesome Greg didn't come over here looking for me, did he?" It wasn't nice, but that's what all the kids in our high school used to call him because of the acne that spotted his face and the braces that imprisoned his teeth. I never called him that, but was only doing it now because my best friend broke my heart by vanishing without a word.

"Nope," Sloane said. "But I bumped into him when he and his friend drove up."

"Girl or guy?" I asked, trying to hide the tinge of jealousy I felt.

"Guy. And uh...don't think you can call him Gruesome Greg anymore."

"Really? So call him what now?"

"Go out there and see for yourself. You can finally give him the apology you owe him."

"I'm sure he's forgotten all about that," I said, still holding back the curtain, trying to glimpse any movement around or inside the house; all I saw was candlelight and shadows behind one of the living room windows.

When I looked back over my shoulder, I was startled to find Sloane standing in front of me, this crazy look of compassionate concern screwing up her face.

"C'mon, Shea. What harm would it do?" Sloane reached around me, grabbed Tornado's leash off the front doorknob and jiggled it. Tornado woke from wherever he was dosing, came running full speed toward us, sliding across the floor, skidding to a stop at our feet. "It's time for the dog's walk anyway," Sloane smiled.

Outside, I glanced across the street to see that the back door of the bus was open, as was the front door of Greg's house. Movement from behind the bus startling me, I lost my grip on Tornado's leash. He darted away, raced across the street, and lay down at the feet of a boy I hardly recognized. Rolling around in the grass, paws up, tongue hanging out the big smile on his face, my dog allowed the young man bearing the faintest resemblance to the old Greg, to rub his belly like Greg and I used to when we were kids.

Staring at the boy, I understood why Sloane said Greg should no longer be called Gruesome. The glasses were gone, the braces, as were the pink-rimmed pimples that speckled his face: there was only smooth, supple looking skin, the color of creamy Jiff peanut butter. His dark hair was wavy on top, and neatly tapered as though he had just stepped out of a Legacy barber's chair. The early teen chub that had softened all his edges had also melted, leaving him lean, angular and chiseled around the cheeks, jaw and shoulders. His arms were carved and taught—a fat vein ran down the center of either of his biceps. Both his wrists wrapped with wide, leather bands—the kind Hercules and Sampson wore in the old black and white movies.

I stopped, stood on the sidewalk a couple of feet in front of my dog, the toes of my boots touching the edge of the overgrown lawn. Boxes of different sizes sat in the driveway, stuff I figured Greg was loading or unloading. He paid me no attention, just continued rubbing Tornado's belly, asking, "You like that, boy? Do you?" as Tornado rolled around happily, like Greg had never disappeared.

"Guess he missed you," I found the nerve to say.

Not looking up, Greg said, "Dogs don't betray you like some people can."

I absorbed the insult, not know what to say to it.

"Good seeing you again, boy," Greg said. He patted Tornado on the head, and both he and my dog got to their feet. Greg walked by me as though I wasn't there, grabbed a box from the ground and took it over to the open bus door.

"You been okay?" I asked, trying to make conversation.

"Living, unlike most everyone else." He pushed the box under a seat of the bus with a grunt, turned, finally facing me with beautiful dark brown eyes, although he stared at me like he couldn't stand the sight in front of him.

"No mask?" I asked through the fabric of the bandanna covering my mouth.

"They don't work. We're all going to die anyway," Greg said, glumly. "Besides, why do you care? I'm not Markham Jennings, remember?" He walked away without giving me a chance to answer.

I was happy he hadn't punched me in the face, like I guess he might've had the right to do, considering.

A second later, another guy appeared. He was tall and nearly as handsome as Greg. He had long, dark blonde, rock star hair, deep blue eyes, and sun-stained skin. He bounded down the stairs of the house carrying two boxes in his arms.

"Excuse me a sec," he said scooting past me, setting the boxes in the bus, shoving them under a seat as Greg had.

He turned around, wearing no protective filter either, showing a line of straight white teeth. A glint of recognition in his eyes, he wagged a finger at me. "Nope, don't tell me. Shea Kennedy, right?" He said like we were already midway into the guessing game. He pulled off his glove and held a bare hand out for me to shake.

"That's right," I said, shaking. "What's your name, and how do you know me?"

"Oh, Daniel. I'd recognize you anywhere."

"But we've never met, have we?"

"Greg and I were college dorm mates before...you know. He had your picture hanging over his desk."

Totally caught off guard, I said, "Really?" I turned away so Daniel couldn't see the smile spreading across my face. "Whose bus? And what third grade class did you steal it from?" I asked, taking slow steps alongside it, noticing the windows that had been broken out and replaced with pieces of plywood, and the half dozen bullet holes peppering one of the quarter panels, just over the back wheel well. "What happened here?"

Daniel said, "Someone tried to jack us, take the bus and our stuff, I guess. If folks aren't careful out there, they can be robbed, beaten and probably worse," Daniel smiled as though there was zero cause for concern. He glanced down at my badge. "But you know that already, Ms. Legacy Sheriff."

"I guess," I said.

"So you ready for this trip to D.C.? I'm stoked. Super excited! We're gonna have the best time."

"We?" I said, surprised.

"Yeah, were going with you guys?"

Inside the house, I slammed the door behind me and stormed over to my sister who was on the sofa, thumbing through a magazine.

Sloane said, "What'd I tell you? Greg's a cutie now, isn't he?"

"He's the same Greg as always, but his friend told me that you asked them to go to D.C. with us."

"I didn't ask them," Sloane said, walking past me. "Told him we were going and Greg wanted to tag along. I told him it probably wasn't such a good idea, knowing the history between you two. But he kind of insisted."

"Really? 'Kind of insisted'," I said, finding it hard to believe he'd want to be anywhere near me, knowing what I had done to him. "Did you tell him it didn't matter what he wanted? We have enough people going with us already."

"No Shea, I didn't tell him that, because we don't have enough, and like we both know, the more people we have, the safer we'll be. Even if one of those people happens to be Greg."

Sloane left me standing in the middle of the living room. I made sure she was gone, then went back to the window, parted the curtain and snuck a peek out, careful not to be seen by Greg. He continued lugging boxes from the bus into his house. Why did he come back? Was he staying? Catching me off guard, Greg turned suddenly, looked at my house and spotted me. I thought to hide, fall to the floor in embarrassment, let the curtain drop, but it was too late. I stared back, unable to ignore the hurt still in his eyes. Sadly, there was no need to guess where it came from. He had mentioned Markham Jennings, the cutest boy in our high school: six foot tall, dark hair, chiseled cheekbones and hazel cat-like eyes that would have a girl tingling all over, if she were lucky enough to have had him glance her way. He was captain of the football and basketball teams, and I, as well as most girls in my school, would've done anything short of robbing a bank or betraying a best friend just to date him. Greg was well aware of my crush, because I never stopped bringing the boy up, falling all over Greg as though on the verge of fainting whenever Markham walked by. I was sure Greg got sick of it, but he was my best friend, so he put up with the foolishness until I allowed it to go too far.

At the window, I raised a hand, waving to Greg, hoping that he'd give me the tiniest sign: a smile, a wink, a yawn; he could've spit in my direction, and I would've taken that as him, at least welcoming the possibility of communication. Instead, he turned as though he hadn't seen me, and carried the box he held into his house.

## 5

That night, wearing the dress April had picked for me, I parked the Harley by the Macy's entrance as I had earlier. Balloons and streamers were now taped to that door as well as a huge poster board. "HOMECOMING—Main Entrance!" was scribbled in huge, red marker letters, across it.

I had combed my short-cropped hair and put on a little lip-gloss and eyeliner. I felt ridiculous, like a child dressed for Halloween as Barbie Doll. I followed a path through Macy's, illuminated by tiny cup candles, spaced every four feet apart, on the floor. Someone had swept up in there from earlier. The festivities were being held outside of the department store, in the food court. I could hear music—the hum of bass and echo of treble—loud conversation and laughter funneling toward me.

In the food court, there were twenty or thirty kids, all around my age—most of them I knew, a few I didn't. Some sat, some stood, others danced lazily about, their faces lit by candles set on top of dining tables, trash cans and counters of all the fast food restaurants we used to frequent: Taco Bell, Subway and McDonald's.

Three guys strummed guitars, one rhythmically slapped the bottom of an overturned mop bucket, while a blonde girl named Susie—a music major—her hair twisted into dreads, sang a Rihanna song that was popular not long ago. They sounded good. The place looked better than I imagined, but I knew having a good time wasn't possible the moment I looked across the court and saw Kendall pointing at me, whispering something into my friend, Beth's ear. Two more girls hung by their sides, all of them balanced on super high-heeled shoes, wearing dresses much nicer than mine. They had done more to their hair than just pull it up in a bun; their faces were done up too: heavy eyeliner, raccoon-like mascara, loud red lipsticks, blush, and false eyelashes. They each had a cell phone clamped to the belts of their dresses. Even though they were no longer of use, with no electricity and no phone towers working, a lot of people excitedly picked up the worthless devices from the ground, collecting them. Most threw them into drawers for safekeeping, but some chose to display them like a nice watch or sparkly bangle.

As I walked, I saw the popular kids, noses turned up, looking down on those of us considered the losers, the loners, and weirdoes. Greg was believed to be one of the weird ones then, and through association—me being his best friend—I was labeled one too.

I cared less what people thought of me now, but two years ago, I wanted nothing more than to be accepted by the girls I thought to be the coolest in our school. That meant being befriended by Kendall Ross, the most popular girl in the sophomore class. One day I found myself backed into a corner of the hallway near the gymnasium—no other students around, but the four girls confronting me.  Kendall stood, blonde, big blue-eyed and powdery-faced, in front of me, wearing a white dress, frilly around the shoulders, looking like a Disney princess. She said hello—those being the first words she had ever spoken to me, even though she had known exactly who I was. We had had four classes together since freshman year, to include P.E., where I had accidently drilled her square in the face, two weeks prior, with a winning shot in a dodge ball game, leaving her nose three times it's normal size. I wondered if me being there that moment had anything to do with the incident, and if I was going to get jumped by four super slender girls and beaten down with Gucci bags

Surprising me, Kendall said she thought I was cool, asked if I'd be interested in joining her girl clique. I couldn't believe it. I felt a joy bubbling up in me, and hoped there wasn't some catch attached to the invitation.

She said there was no catch, but an initiation task, then said she heard that I was going to homecoming with Greg. I told her I was. He had asked me to the dance three days before, bashfully, rustling his chubby hands together, his eyes averted, voice crackling between pre and post pubescence. I knew it took every ounce of courage he had, so I told him yes, even though I wanted to go with Markham Jennings; I was smart enough to know, *he'd* never ask *me*.

Kendall smiled, told me if I did one simple thing for her, I'd be allowed into her cool girl group. Even though, that moment, I could not stop smiling, something told me to turn and run away. But this seemed the opportunity I was waiting for. I felt I had to take advantage of it.

Now, walking across the mall food court toward her, I realized I disliked Kendall more now than I did then.

"Shea Kennedy," Kendall said, stepping over, eyeing me up and down. "Nice dress. Goes perfectly with the motorcycle boots. So sheik," she laughed, turning to Beth for a response. On cue, my friend chuckled, but stopped abruptly when I narrowed my eyes at her.

"Sorry I wasn't home earlier. April said you came by looking for me," Beth said.

"Yeah, and she told me you left her there all night? You can't just leave her by herself and not—"

"C'mon, Shea. Don't tell me how to treat my little sister," Beth snapped. "She can take care of herself."

"Still, you can't just disappear—"

"You know what," Beth said, raising a palm in front of my face. "We're done with this. If you want to hang and talk about something else, fine. But you're not gonna boss me around."

"Fine. You packed and ready for the trip, right?"

Beth turned, glanced at Kendall, as if for the answer.

"Not sure if I'm still going," Beth said.

"What do you mean? For the past week you said—"

Kendall moved Beth aside, stepped up to take her place in front of me. "You're like, leading the trip, right?"

"My sister is, but I'm helping her. Why?" I asked.

"Well," Kendall said, rolling her eyes. "Everyone knows what happened to your father and...I wish there was a respectful way to put this, but we don't trust you to take care of us, if you can't protect your own father. I know you said Sloane is in charge, but Beth is really thinking that if you," Kendall said, waving a finger at me, "have anything to do with the trip, it could mean sure death for all of us."

I looked past Kendall to Beth. "Is this Kendall talking, or is this how you really feel, Beth?"

"I...I..." Beth stammered.

"Don't be afraid of her, Beth," Kendall said. "That badge she parades around with makes her no more special than you or me."

"Close your mouth, Kendall!" I said, pushing around her to confront Beth. "You can't stay here. Do you get that? It's not safe. Not for you, not for April. Not for anyone!" I spun, looking at the kids around me still dancing, laughing, drinking as though everything was freaking awesome, when many of them wouldn't survive another month.

I didn't have the patience for this. Whatever they weren't getting, I had limited time to make it clear. I marched across the food court to the band, right up to Susie, who was holding the microphone, swaying to the music. "May I? Please," I ordered more than asked, wrapping my hand around it. Looking at me as though I had lost my mind, she stopped singing and let me take the mic.

"Everyone," I said, my voice coming out the two large floor speakers to my left and right. Kids continued talking, laughing and dancing, even though the music had stopped. I covered the microphone with my palm, causing deafening feedback to scream out the speakers, catching everyone's attention.

"For those of you who might not know me, I'm Shea Kennedy, Legacy Sheriff." Everyone stopped what they were doing, their faces turned toward me. "The President has asked us all to come to the capital months ago, but we're still here for whatever reason. Whatever they may be, forget them. I've been telling you guys this for weeks; my sister and I are leaving for D.C. in two days. Everyone here, please come with us, or make plans to leave on your own. I don't care how you leave, just leave!"

A drunken voice came from somewhere in the crowd. "Why? This is home for us. My house is here. I'm not going anywhere!"

Cheering and applause came from the kids on the makeshift dance floor, a chant of "Let's stay home! Let's stay home!" started building. Louder and louder it grew until it became too much for me to take. I screamed into the microphone. "Shut up! Listen to me!"

The crowd reluctantly quieted once more. My chest heaving, I looked over them, saw that there was suddenly real concern in their eyes. "All of you are grown. But some won't grow much older before the air takes you. I can't make you go. But know, just like there's no electricity, internet and little gas, food is going to run out, people are going to keep dying, and don't act as though you don't see the fires. Those will be here soon, too." No one said a word. "Tomorrow, my sister is holding a meeting in front of our house to tell you anything you need to know about the trip. You all know where I live. Come, ask your questions, please. Then day after tomorrow, first thing in the morning, we're leaving. You'll see, D.C. is better."

I gave Susie back her mic, and stepped away to go to the refreshments table. I ladled a cup half full of whatever red juice was in the bowl—the stench of alcohol wafting up to my nostrils—and carried it to a corner of the food court. Beth came over a sec later to apologize.

"I didn't' mean to be so...you know, rude. It's just that..." Beth said, looking away, brushing her home-cut, ear-lobe-length, died blonde hair behind her ear. "...losing Mom and Dad have really been tough for me. Leaving here would feel like, I don't know, abandoning them, or you know, the memory of them."

"All of our parents dying have been tough for all of us, Beth," I said, trying to sound as sympathetic as possible. "But whatever has you thinking of staying, I'd forget it. You and April need to come with us. Okay?"

Beth glanced over her shoulder. I saw Kendall standing by the punch table between two other girls, also dressed in glitzy gowns, giving Beth the death stare.

"Give me time to think about it," Beth said, turning back to me. "Okay."

"Fine, but you have less than two days."

# 6

After the dance, I left my motorcycle and walked back with a group of ten kids, feeling like it was my responsibility to keep them safe. Parts of our city could be dangerous during the day; at night, standing outside anywhere in the pitch black could make you a target, especially if hammered like these kids were. I was armed; my gun was strapped to my thigh, underneath my dress.

Houses burned far off in the distance. The winds carried the smell of smoke, and miles and miles away, we could see the glow of flames down the hills and over the treetops.

"Burners really going crazy tonight," a boy wearing a suit jacket vest buttoned up over a white t-shirt said.

I had heard mention of the Burners: religious crazies, faces painted, setting fire to everything, believing the act would somehow purify the air, cleanse the earth, stop us from dying, or save the world from complete destruction. At least that's what I'd heard. I'd never seen a Burner. But then again, I wouldn't have known it if I had.

"The world is coming to an end!" someone else joked.

"God says scorch the earth to cleanse it!" another laughed.

"How far away you think the fire is?" a girl questioned.

"Far," was the carefree answer. "Really, really far."

Still drinking from Styrofoam cups they took from the party, they walked down the wooded street, stumbling drunken and loud behind me, not seeming to care about anything, laughing, reveling in the joy that no adult would stick a head out a window and tell them to quiet down.

One of the kids cried out profanities, more kids joined in, screaming at the tops of their lungs, their voices carrying up high into the night sky.

Sometimes I wondered what planet these kids lived on; did they know the terrible state our world was in? If so, why weren't they taking things more seriously?

Weeks after the first deaths were documented, eyewitness videos started showing up on YouTube. Footage of the middle-aged man, or twenty-something woman, clutching their throats, stumbling across the pavement, choking, eyes wide, head whipping about, looking for someone or something that could save their life. They'd fall to the ground, writhing, kicking, back of their heads banging against the pavement in the attempt to fight of death. I would stand in the dining room, or sit on the floor of my room, Tornado's head in my lap, eyes glued to the screen of my cell phone, watching countless blurred videos of people taking their final breaths, their bodies deflating, lying flat, like the skin of a balloon when the last bit of air left it. Often crying could be heard in the background: voices of loved ones, maybe even strangers, distraught and tired of seeing people die that dreadful death.

"Shut up! Shut up!" I said to the drunken kids on the wooded streets behind me.

I pulled my weapon, stared into the trees around us and down the street, crouched, holding my gun, believing that I had heard something in the tree line to our left. After a moment of hearing nothing, I brought down my weapon.

"What's wrong with her?" someone behind me said with a chuckle.

"Her dad was the sheriff," a girl's voice answered. "Now, because she's

Legacy, she thinks she's Police Girl—Protector of the World."

I turned slowly to face the group, stared in the eyes of the girl who had made the comment. She was one of Kendall's friends. She stood in the dirt, barefoot, the straps of her high heels dangling from two of her fingers. Beth and Kendall on either side of her, the girl stared back at me, raised an eyebrow as though daring me to say something.

I didn't take the bait, turned away from her and said to the group: "If you guys wanna make it home before sunup, you should probably pick up the pace."

When I walked in the house, I stopped in front of my sister who was sitting at the dining room table, working at a small space cleared free of boxes, writing by candlelight, on a small notepad.

"How was the dance?" she asked.

"Sucked fuzzy coconuts," I said.

She laughed. "Well, you look pretty in that dress." She leaned back from her notes. "You convince anyone to come with us?"

"Did all I could. Some of them are still deciding."

"All you can do, is all you can do," Sloane said, getting up to give me a hug.

I lay my head on her shoulder, let her hold me a minute like Mom used to.

"Yeah, whatever," I said. "I'm going upstairs to change so I can take Fur ball out."

Outside, I snatched my bandana up over my nose. It didn't matter; I could still smell the burning trees. I couldn't see the flicker of fire over the rooftops of the houses on my street, but I knew the flames weren't as one boy said, "Really, really far away."

They were heading in our direction, and soon enough, they'd burn down this entire town.

"C'mon, boy. Potty so we can go inside," I said, leading Tornado to his favorite spot, when I felt the sensation I was being watched.

Across the street, I saw Greg standing on his porch, staring at me.

I had never found out where Greg had gone two years ago. He was just out of here, like he had never existed. Days went by, but still most mornings I'd expect my doorbell to ring, Greg to be standing on the porch, his head down, still embarrassed by what happened that night at the dance, but demanding an apology—that never happened. Months went by and I'd find myself at my window, holding the curtains aside, staring down at his house for any sign of him. Nights, I'd sit at my computer, Googling his name, finding no information. Facebook: his page was taken down. Twitter: he no longer had an address. It was like he had never been born, like he had only lived in my imagination.

After two months of life without my best friend, I needed to do something to ease the guilt of driving him away. Unable to sleep one night, I climbed out of bed, sat down at my desk, pulled out a sheet of paper and started to write.

Now, from my porch, I glared across the street at him. He stared right back, like he intended to do it all night if I hadn't said anything.

"What?" I yelled at the top of my lungs, aggravated, my voice echoing up and down the street. "What do you want from me? You want me to admit that I was wrong? I was wrong, Greg. It was horribly wrong for me to do what I did to you."

Stoic, statue-like, he remained perfectly still as I continued to spill my guts.

"You want me to apologize? I do. I'm sorry! I am truly, freaking sorry," I said, stepping down onto the walk from the last stair. "There!" I paused, waited for a response. Nothing came from him but that hard, unblinking stare he had been giving me.

"That's it?" I yelled, my voice cracking with emotion. "You can't even bring yourself to talk to me? We were best friends!" I said, walking into the street.

He took a step forward, freezing me before I got to the sidewalk. He appeared as though he was going to say something.

"What, Greg?" I said then lowered my voice to a plea. "Just talk to me. Please."

He stepped back, pulled his front door open, and went inside.

# 7

The next day, coughing pulled me out of my sleep. I sat up in bed, the taste of smoke in my lungs. My watch read a little after 1 PM, which meant, being out so late, made me miss patrol. I grabbed my jeans from the foot of the bed, slipped them on, when I heard voices outside.

At the window I kneeled, spying through boards that I helped Dad nail to it from the outside, like all the other windows of the house. On the street, I saw four young men walking, wearing hooded parkas. A girl with long blonde hair hanging from under a ratty wool skullcap followed behind them. Backpacks hung from all of their shoulders. Masks covered all but one of the boy's and the girl's face.

Two boys gazed up at my house. One of them pointed, drawing the attention of the others. They nodded in agreement; more words were spoken, then one of the boy's looked back as though they knew they were being watched.

They were making the trip to D.C., I was sure, like all the others before them, following the order the president made four months ago.

I remember when it all started to fall apart, the morning, I woke up to the text message notification light flashing on my phone.

SHEA, MY DAD IS DEAD

I lay in bed, staring down at my phone, unable to respond, unable to move; I could barley breath. What was I supposed to do with the knowledge that the President of the United States was now dead? As I wrestled with that, I received another text.

PLEASE DON'T TELL ANYONE

I replied.

I'M SO VERY SORRY. I WON'T.

I crawled out of bed, padded around my room on bare feet, feeling helpless. My phone chimed with yet another incoming text from Jenna.

I WASN'T SUPPOSED TO, BUT I HAD TO TELL SOMEOBODY.

The day I had learned of President John Sawyer's death, I had known his daughter, Jenna for three years.

Mom's job often required her to fly to D.C. to meet with the president or his board members, have discussions about climate change, air pollution and what environmental factors might kill us all off in the next ten or twenty or hundred years.

My first time in Washington, three years ago, President Sawyer allowed us to spend the night in the White House. Mom slept in the Lincoln Bedroom, and I was given the Queen's Bedroom, where Queens Elizabeth of England, Sonja of Norway and Sophia of Spain, were once guests.

I had met Jenna the next day. Ironically, it was President's day, so we were off from school.

Jenna and I spent the entire day together, ate in Adam's Morgan, watched people play chess in DuPont Circle, checked out beautiful, hundred year-old art museums, and of course, shopped in Georgetown. We had a fantastic time, and after that visit, every time Mom flew to D.C.—on the occasions she'd let me—I went with her.

As before, Jenna and I would hang out, and whether watching movies in the White House family movie theater, or chilling just over the river in Virginia, shopping at the Crystal City Mall, we discovered more things we had in common, and how much we enjoyed the other's company.

When I wasn't in D.C., Jenna and I texted a lot, were friends on Facebook, followed each other on Twitter, and shot each other pics on Instagram.

Despite the two hundred miles that separated us, we became very good friends, which I honestly had a hard time understanding. So much so, that one evening, after knowing Jenna a year, while sitting on the stairs of the Lincoln Memorial, I asked, "Why me?"

Jenna looked over at me, surprised. "What do you mean?"

"You're like the most powerful teenager in the world," I joked. "You're the first daughter. You can be friends with anyone in the world, and here you are hanging around with me?"

"You're funny," Jenna said, leaning back against a stair on her elbows. "You don't give yourself enough credit, Shea. You have a mom who's a super scientist, a dad who's a badass sheriff, and taught you everything he knows. You're the coolest chic I know. I like having you as a friend." She smiled, looked out at the small man-made body of water before the monument, the ducks paddling about on the pool's surface. "And maybe when I'm the first woman President of the United States, you can be the head of my secret service." She turned to me, smiling wider. "That'd be badass, wouldn't it?"

I couldn't help but laugh. "That'd be super badass!"

I left my bedroom wanting to get a better look at the group outside my house, see if they posed a threat of any kind. Taking the stairs down, I saw Sloane at the open front door, peering out onto the street.

"Sloane," I whispered.

She held up a finger.

I walked up behind her, stared over her shoulder. The group of boys and the girl hadn't moved, still stood in front of our house for some reason.

Sloane stared at them another moment, then closed and bolted the door.

"Think they might be something to worry about?" I asked.

"Nah," Sloane said, going to the wall where the roadmap hung. "Kids making the trip everyone else made before them: the same trip we're going to make tomorrow."

"It's late," I said. "You let me oversleep. I missed patrol."

"Help me take the map down. I don't want to tear it."

"You hear what I said? Why didn't you wake me?" I said, walking over and carefully peeling two of the corners from the wall.

"You needed your sleep."

"But missed—"

"I know, Shea," Sloane said, as we gently pulled the map down and folded it. "You missed patrol. But even if you had made it, more people still would've died from the air, still would've been robbed, and some still would've been killed."

"You saying I'm not making a difference?"

"I'm not saying that."

"I'm doing what Dad did, what I promised him I would do. I gave him my word that I'd—"

"Shhh, shhh, shhh," Sloane said, hurrying to me, taking me by the shoulders, sensing I was getting upset. "That's over now. Just like this part of our lives is over. So what happened with Dad, you can finally forgive yourself for that."

"Have you? Have you forgiven me?" I asked, afraid of the answer.

"I never blamed you. A job like that, it was always a possibility. Keeping that with you, that's no way to live," Sloane said, her grip tightening on my shoulders. "Tell me you can drop it."

Never, I thought, but to my sister, I said, forcing a smile. "Sure."

# 8

Two hours later, Sloane and I stood on the stairs of our house, looking over the very small group of people that showed for the meeting I had told the kids at homecoming about last night. The sky was gray and overcast with the smoke that burned from the fires miles away.

I thought there would be more who responded to the flyers we stapled and taped to trees, streetlight poles and signs, announcing this meeting.

Six kids from homecoming stood sleepy-eyed on my front lawn, wearing apathetic expressions. Of those faces, I didn't see my friend, Toni, when she had promised me she'd come. I would go over there after this and make sure she was okay. Greg wasn't there either. It was not as though I expected him to show, especially after the cold shoulder I received from him last night, but he did live just across the street. I would've figured he would've been curious about what was going on in my front yard.

"You all know what this is," Sloane spoke loudly from our porch stairs. "Mostly everyone has made the trip already. Its time we go too. There's nothing for us here anymore. The fires are getting closer, the violence is getting worse: the break-ins, the deaths...it's time.

"Go there for what?" A boy a few years younger than me called out. "We'll have no place to live. We'll have nothing once we get there."

"That's not true," Sloane said. "My sister and the Legacy president are friends. President Jenna Sawyer personally invited her there to be a part of the secret service. I'm sure the president wouldn't allow anyone we bring to be homeless."

What Sloane said about Jenna's request was true, but I felt it did no good putting that news out there.

After Jenna's father died, Mom traveled to D.C. for the funeral, taking me with her; Sloane decided to stay back with Dad at home.

Things were crazy in D.C.: tanks parked on the White House lawn, soldiers and Marines in full battle dress: helmets, night vision goggles, toting automatic rifles, posted at every entrance and exit. It felt as though we were on the verge of war.

Blackhawk and Apache helicopters flew low over the Capital. Surrounded by six secret service agents, I could hear the choppers overhead as I followed Jenna down one of the White House hallways toward the situation room. At the door, Jenna lay her hand on a sensor of some kind and a second later I heard locks in the door disengage. The eight of us walked in.

"Can you step out, please," Jenna said to the agents, before sitting down.

"But Miss Sawyer..." the most senior agent said. He had broad shoulders, and sported a fresh haircut.

"Wait outside, please. I need to speak to my friend alone," Jenna said.

The agents left. The door of the room closed heavily, like the door of some ancient tomb. Inside, the walls were covered with huge monitors, displaying real-time satellite surveillance from street corners in Washington, D.C., to deserts in Afghanistan.

Jenna pulled one of the many seats from under the huge conference table, sat, and gestured for me to do the same.

"Now that Dad's dead, they're talking of making me president," Jenna said, leaning over, one elbow on the table, her hand dug into the hair that hung messy over her shoulders. She looked exhausted.

"President? How?" I asked.

Through strands falling in her eyes, she said, "Some act they're trying to pass. It's the stupidest idea I've ever heard. I'm seventeen years old; I have no business with that much power, but the few cabinet members left alive are forcing it to happen before they die." Jenna stood, walked over, pulled the seat right next to mine and sat down. "What we talked about three years ago—you being part of my secret service..."

"We were just joking, right?" I said, leaning away from her.

"I wasn't. Your dad's been training you for almost ten years to do a job like this. I pretty trust the people they assigned to me, but I don't *know* them like I know you, Shea. If you're here, you'll help protect me."

"Protect you? From what?"

"Seriously?" Jenna said, smiling sadly at my ignorance. "This is, or at least was, the most powerful government in the world. You know how many radical groups, foreign and domestic, have wanted to take control of it. And soon there'll be a seventeen year-old kid in charge. What better time than now?"

"Jenna, I don't think—"

She grabbed my hand; I could feel hers trembling on top of mine. "Tell me that you'll come. You're my best friend. Just tell me that when I ask, you'll come."

I lowered my eyes, felt her hand tighten around mine more in anticipation of my answer.

"Okay," I said. "I'll do it."

On the front porch of our house, I felt everyone's eyes on me.

"It's true," I said. "I'm sure President Sawyer will do whatever she can for the people who make the trip. And I'll do my best to help protect you if you come with us."

"It's bad here, but it could be worse on the road," a young man with dark hair in a ponytail, said. He carried a mop handle like a weapon. "People have died out there."

"How do you know that?" Sloane asked. "Have you been out there?"

"No." His eyes darted back and fourth. "But I'm sure people have died, been killed out there."

"But you aren't sure," Sloane corrected. "You think that's happening, and you might be right. But we know for sure people have been stolen from, beaten and killed here. We know our homes are burning. So—"

"But what if we get to D.C. and there's nothing there? If it's burning just like here?" a frightened girl's voice asked.

All power, cell phone connectivity and internet has been down for over a month. I haven't heard word from Jenna since before then; I had no idea of what could've been happening in the capital, so the girl's question was a valid one.

"I have a friend who made the trip right after the president asked. He came back, said everything was fine there. He said the government was still in place; the Legacy system was working perfectly there. There was food, operating stores, hospitals, and Legacy doctors."

There was whispered conversation among the small group, as if they were debating whether or not they could trust what Sloane said.

"Where is your friend? We want to hear it from him?" someone said.

"The air took him two weeks after he came back," Sloane said, glancing impatiently down at her watch. "Look, you'll just have to trust us. I've told you all there is to tell. Now it's up to you. Bus leaves at 5 A.M. tomorrow morning. If you aren't here, I'll assume you've decided not to go."

After the meeting and the crowd dispersed, I walked in the house to find Sloane, her back to me, finishing up with the packing.

I pulled the security door closed, leaving the inside door open.

"Was it true what you said about D.C.? About them being up and running and all that?"

"Yeah," Sloane said, not turning to face me.

"What friend were you talking about?"

"You didn't know him."

"Why didn't you ever tell me about what he told you?"

Sloane walked over to me, looked at me as though trying to read my mind before she responded. "That was three months. He said D.C. was fine then, but things could've changed. I didn't want to have your hopes too high if things have changed out there. Okay?" She smiled, slapping me on the shoulder.

"Okay." I smiled back.

“I didn’t see Toni out there,” Sloane said. “Thought you said she was going with us.”

“I know. I’m going there now to find out what’s up.”

# 9

I grabbed Tornado for company, the dog jumping on his hind legs, his tail wagging, always excited about taking a ride. When I pulled up to Toni's house to check on her, I saw a boy standing on the porch.

I had known Toni since eighth grade. She had a tough time getting out of grammar school, and in high school, the work became even tougher. I tutored her when she allowed, but she ultimately dropped out after her sophomore year. No longer a student, and resisting every attempt I made to get her back in class, she started waiting tables at a nearby Denny's. That was where she got involved with a boy named Potter. 5'10", muscular with broad shoulders, his face often covered with three or four days of hair growth, Potter had a bad reputation for being trouble. He knew my Dad, but not the way one would want to know him; he was intimately familiar with the cell at the police station, being brought in and jailed on everything from shoplifting to public drunkenness to assault and battery. He also had a problem with his hands, putting them on people he shouldn't have, namely Toni.

I slowed my motorcycle, and turned into the drive, realizing it wasn't Potter on the porch with Toni, but a boy easily three or four inches shorter, his body shaped like a barrel, his t-shirt clinging tight to his belly. The boy on the porch wore wire-framed glasses, had a face as smooth as a nine year olds and appeared very upset about something.

I cut the engine on my bike, choosing not to get off, but waited to see what happened. "Who is that guy?" I asked, whispering to Tornado, rubbing his furry head. "Any clue?"

Toni and the boy, whoever he was, gestured dramatically, their hands flying all over the place, whispering loudly like they had something to hide.

I threw my leg from over the seat of my bike, taking more interest in whatever their conversation. "Sit tight," I told my dog.

"I don't have anything else to say about it, okay. It's not going to happen," I heard Toni say.

The boy was silent, shook his head, looked like there was more he wanted to talk about, more he wanted to do, but was helpless. He walked down the stairs and came toward me, a frown on his chubby face, his dimpled fists bawled at his sides.

"Hey," I said.

"Hello," he mumbled, continuing past me.

"Who are you?"

His back to me, he turned around.

"Ask her." He nodded toward the house where Toni stood. I turned. Toni stared sadly at me from between the crack of the metal door, pushed it open and waved me inside.

I stood in her living room as she walked two bottles of water from the kitchen, handing one to me, then walking to one of the living room chairs, and carefully lowered herself into it. She brushed her bobbed, brown hair out of her eyes, blew an exaggerated breath and smiled at me.

I sat down across the coffee table from her.

"This is much harder than I thought it would be," Toni said.

"Never heard of a woman in history who said being pregnant was easy."

She was four months along with Potter's baby.

"How's the little one doing in there?" I asked, glancing at her belly, which appeared to grow rounder everyday.

"All right, I guess. Never done this before." She smoothed a loving hand over her stomach. "Can't wait till its over and little guy is out, running around. How are you, Shea?"

"Surviving." I smiled uncomfortably. "You packed for the trip tomorrow?"

"I...I'm not going," she said, apologetically.

"But you told me you were. Said it'd be a clean start, and—"

"Potter doesn't want to, so..." she trailed off.

"So leave him here!"

"I'm just not going, Shea."

"Got anything to do with the guy at your door?"

"What guy?" Toni said, playing dumb.

"The guy with the glasses. They guy you were arguing with."

"We weren't arguing."

"Fine. Talking. Who was he?"

"Someone I know."

"Someone Potter knows?"

"No," Toni said.

"Someone Potter knows you know?"

Toni shook her head. "He doesn't know I know him." She lowered her head, shamefully.

I got up, moved, sat on the coffee table right in front of her, the caps of our knees almost touching. I took one of her hands in mine. "What do you think Potter will do when he finds out?"

She looked up at me, pushing her bangs off her forehead. "There's nothing to find out. Nothing."

She was lying. I put a hand on her shoulder and rubbed the side of her arm. "I worry about you. There's still time. You need to leave. Let me talk to Potter."

"No! You know he doesn't like you."

"Yeah, I know. But I don't like him much either," I said. "Tomorrow morning at five, do whatever it takes to be there. But know if I don't see you, I'm coming back here."

## 10

Riding down a desolate, double lane road, squinting through my goggles, the brown/green blur of tree trunks and leaves whizzing past on both sides of me, I knew I couldn't let Toni stay here. Not alone, and not with Potter. If it was the last thing I did, I'd make sure she'd leave with us tomorrow.

I sped the bike up, then immediately applied the brake, slowing, when I saw some distance up ahead, two figures: boys—one laying out across the pavement, not moving—the other, kneeling over him.

I sped up again, Tornado temporarily knocked off balance in the sidecar. As we raced closer, the kneeling figure lifted his head startled, as though only then hearing the motor of my bike. It appeared like a harmless situation, something that has sadly become routine: a friend or loved one mourning over a body that had only just died from the air. But I realized there was always the possibility of there being more than what it appeared. I was taught that from the day I was given this job; a day I could never forget.

Dad used to take Sloane and I on patrol with him. Rolling slowly along the streets, seeing windows of stores boarded up or shattered, we'd look for activity, hoping not to find any. Dad's wrist draped over the steering wheel, an elbow hanging out of his window, he told us, "These people aren't bad." He turned into a parking lot littered with broken glass, smashed electronics lying on the pavement, in front of the Best Buy. "But a few are. That's why we're out here patrolling. People need to know they still have someone to turn to for protection. But regardless how safe a situation looks, will always be danger. You understand?"

From the back seat of the police car, my eyes met Dad's in the rearview mirror. I felt that message was especially meant for me.

I heard Sloane answer. "I know."

I nodded my head.

After patrol, Dad stopped in front of our house, pulled the key from the ignition, but didn't move from his seat. Sloane got out, but I sensed something was going on with Dad he wasn't telling us about. I grabbed the back of his seat, looked over his shoulder.

"You okay?" I asked.

"I'm fine, Shea." He patted my hand, turned and smiled at me. "You girls go inside. I'll be there in a minute."

Ten minutes later, after pulling cans of food out of the kitchen cabinet for dinner, I turned to Sloane. "What do you think is wrong with him?"

"What do you mean?" Sloane asked, grabbing three bottles of water from one of the lower cabinets.

"He's like, depressed. What do you think it could be?"

"With Mom and all his friends being dead...you know, Shea, I have no idea what it could be," Sloane said, sarcastically.

"Jerk!" I said. I went to the living room, looked out the front window, but didn't see Dad in his car. "He's not out there," I called back to Sloane.

"What do you mean he's not out there?" Sloane asked, sounding concerned, stepping into the living room. I hurried past her, and headed toward the back of the house.

Looking out the porch windows, we saw Dad standing in the yard, his back to us, his head tilted up toward the line of towering trees bordering our backyard.

I started toward the door, wanting to open it. Sloane caught me by the arm.

"Maybe he just wants to be left alone," she said.

I knocked on the glass anyway, getting his attention.

"Shea!" Sloane said.

Dad turned around, saw us in the window. His expression brightened. He waved us out to join him. Tornado followed behind and outside, heeled at Dad's left leg.

The night had cooled; it was quiet. No prattle of automatic gunfire off in the distant as there had been some nights in the past, just the chant of crickets and cicadas. Dad's eyes were not on us, but up in the branches of the trees again, Sloane and I waiting patiently for him to give us some indication that all was fine with him.

"I could've been taken some time ago, probably should've been," Dad said, finally turning to us, his voice low. "But I feel I've been spared this long to continue to prepare the two of you."

He dug in the pocket of his uniform trousers, pulled out his fist, turned it over, and in his palm were two deputy sheriff badges. "These belonged to Davies and Moreland." They were Dad's deputy sheriffs, were both in their early thirties and had been with Dad for more than five years. They were good people and were always nice to me when I visited the station. Sadly, they had fallen to the air, both of them dying not two months ago.

Staring down at Sloane and me, Dad looked sadder and more uncertain than I'd ever seen him. "I won't be here much longer."

"Don't say that, Dad!" I said. "You don't know—"

He smiled as though he thought my denial was cute.

"Sloane," Dad said, turning his eyes on her, unlocking the clasp that held the point of the straight pin on the back of the metal badge. "I had no idea when I taught you guys to shoot and defend yourselves, that it'd be for this."

I steadied myself, wondering if what I thought was about to happen was actually going to.

When the air turned, more than half the world's adult population had been taken. Doctors, engineers, electrical technicians, sanitation workers, farmers, computer programmers, police officers: those who managed services vital to our every day existence, all died, and with them went the knowledge and experience that kept the lights on, the electricity flowing, the internet and cell phone towers operating, the public healthy and law abiding.

In the event, as scientist were predicting all over TV and the internet, that everyone over the age of twenty would die, an attempt at a stopgap for all the potentially lost expertise was made. This possible solution was based on the theory that many of the men and women working in those vital professions might have taught their children about those vocations. Wanting to give their children a head start, those professionals might've allowed themselves to be shadowed at work, or given their children jobs during the summer, so in the future, after college, technical school, grad or medical school, those children might chose to take their parent's places.

With the population being drastically reduced every day, there was no longer the luxury of waiting till the youth turned eighteen and went to college for formal training. Those of us who might have had knowledge of an indispensable skill were needed to fill those positions vacated by those taken by the air. That training, regardless of how little or how extensive, made the children of certain professionals indispensible—candidates the government hoped who would be able to continue performing those much needed duties. They were called Legacy Appointments.

Dad took a step toward Sloane, ready to pin the badge to her chest, and yes, do as I thought. He was preparing to deputize her.

But Sloane took a step back.

"I'm sorry, but I don't want it, Dad."

I gasped, angry with her for turning down, what I felt had to have been the greatest honor that could've ever been given to either of us.

"I'm really sorry, but I hope that's okay," Sloane apologized again. "I know the job has to be done, but I shouldn't be the one you trust to continue your work. With what I've learned in school, I'd be more valuable helping those needing medical care. Besides, you know I'd probably just shoot myself in the foot."

Dad chuckled, sadly. "You'd be better than that, but I've always known you wanted to be a doctor like your mother."

Sloane glanced knowingly at me.

"I'll always be here to help Shea in any way she needs, but she'd be better for the role than me. We both know it."

I turned to Dad, stared at him admiringly. I've dreamt of this day happening sometime after I finished college. But to take Dad's place before he was gone felt too much like giving up hope that he might not somehow live. Despite how much I wanted that badge—to be Dad's deputy, his backup—I would've happily declined it for a guarantee he'd survive.

"We don't have to do this right now, do we?" I said. "There might still be a chance that—"

"You know better than that, Shea," Dad said. "I'll be gone soon enough, but the law will always need to be upheld, and you and your sister are the best candidates. I respect Sloane's decision not to take the job, but you...I think for sometime you've been—"

Realizing there would be no talking him out of this, I interrupted and said, "Yes, I'd be honored, Dad." Excited and humbled, I stepped forward, my arms at my sides, chest inflated, preparing myself for all the responsibility he would entrust me with.

He smiled, and appeared proud enough to cry.

"Please raise your right hand and repeat after me."

I did as I was told, and glanced at Sloane. She smiled and I could not help but smile back before turning to Dad to recite the oath.

It was a list of sentences I would often stare at as a young child, the words carved onto a plaque, hanging on the police station wall. I had memorized them long ago, and more times than I can remember, stood in my bedroom mirror, right hand raised, reciting those words, as I had been about to do.

"I, state your name," Dad said.

"I, Shea Kenni Kennedy..." I said, but instead of pausing for Dad to instruct me on what next to say, I spoke the words with him. "...do swear, that I..."

Dad paused, smiled, realizing that, although under the most horrible circumstances, this was the moment I had been preparing most of my life. He continued with me.

"...will truly serve our sovereign state and city as a law enforcement officer without favor or affection, malice or ill will, that I will see and ensure our community's peace be kept and preserved, prevent offenses against that peace, while discharging all duties thereof, unselfishly, faithfully and bravely, according to the law. So help me God."

"So help me God," I said, my words trailing softly behind his. I lowered my hand, felt Dad pinning the badge on my shirt, my heart pounding underneath, a tear spilling from my eye and racing down my cheek.

Dad stepped back, snapped his right hand up to his brow, in a crisp military salute. "By the power invested in me, you, Shea Kenni Kennedy, are now a deputy sheriff of the sovereign state of Virginia. Always be careful out there, baby," he said, lowering his salute, and giving me a big hug.

I remembered that warning as I skidded to a halt in front of the boys on the side of the road.

"Is he okay?" I asked, climbing off my bike. "You need any help?" I hurried toward the two then tripped and faltered to a stop, astonished, after getting a good look at the living boy. My eyes had to have been playing tricks, because in front of me stood Markham Jennings. Not the one from my high school: the clean cut, beautiful, well-dressed, team captain I had a crush on, but a post-poisoned-air, Markham Jennings, who wore a filthy white t-shirt, the sleeves hacked off, his veiny, muscular arms exposed, and jeans, fraying and ripped, two sizes too big, drawn tight at his narrow waist.

"Markham," I said softly, hesitating to speak any louder, thinking if he hadn't heard me, hadn't responded when I called, it might not have been him.

Markham didn't answer, just stared at me with those hazel eyes—no longer seductive, but scary, like those of the mangy, stray cat that would hang around my house when I was a child, screeching all hours into the night. He wore no mask, but on his face was smeared a crude cross of what looked like charcoal or black shoe shine, the lines intersecting at the bridge of his nose and the level of his brow.

Tornado was going crazy behind me, his barks high-pitched, as he pulled against his tether, attempting to free himself; he was frightened, or frightened for me, I couldn't tell which, but in that second, as Dad warned could happen, I felt I was in real danger.

"Markham, what are you doing here?" When he didn't answer, I said, moving cautiously toward the body on the ground. "Who is that? Did the air take him?"

Still Markham didn't respond, just stared at me, his chest heaving as though catching his breath from a struggle.

"Is he alive? I can help him," I said.

Tornado still going crazy, his barks coming faster and louder, I stepped closer to the boy on the ground. "I'm just going to take a look at him," I said, kneeling over him, quickly examining the boy. I shook him by the shoulder. The back of his head rolled back and forth, lifeless, against the pavement. I pressed my fingers into the flesh of his neck, searching for his pulse, but felt nothing. About to stand, something caught my eye. I pulled back the boy's collar and saw ligature marks—like the boy had been strangled—red and irritated, around the neck. I spun on one knee, drawing my gun, pointing in the direction Markham had been only a second ago, to find him gone.

I hurried back to my bike, falling on it, reached over to the sidecar, released Tornado, and ordered him to, "Go, boy! Get!"

Tornado hurdled the windshield, landing on his forepaws, digging into the dirt and tore off, as I followed behind, running as fast as my body allowed.

Ahead, I saw a figure turn into the line of trees. Tornado ripped through a low wall of twigs and leaves after him. Feeling as though it was choking me, I tore my mask from my face, and broke through the thatch of branches, bushes and leaves—a narrow trail of hard-packed dirt beneath me—followed it, the gun still held out before me. The trail ended in a clearing. I turned a circle, complete silence around me, my heart banging in my chest, anxiety gripping it like a vice.

"Tornado!"

Thrashing noises twenty feet ahead, Tornado cried out.

A scream caught in my throat. I darted in the direction of my dog's cry, hurdling roots that reached from beneath, clawing at my feet, while needlelike branch tips split my skin, drawing narrow lines of blood across my cheeks.

My heels skidding on wet leaves, arms wind-milling, I stopped as though about to fall off a cliff, when I caught sight of Tornado wrestling in the dirt with Markham. They rolled over each other, Tornado's long, white teeth bared, chomping at the boy's neck, only catching air, as Markham's hands, dug wrist deep into the fur of Tornado's neck, desperately held my dog off.

I stepped forward, my gun up, the site following the white of the Markham's t-shirt, hoping to find a shot, when I saw, from out of a sheath in the small of Markham's back, a long hunting knife emerge. Markham held it over Tornado's back, as though to drive it into his spine.

"Tornado, heel! Come now!" I screamed, terrified.

Tornado twisted out of the knot he and the boy were entangled in then ran to my side. I stared Markham down, still feeling like I was in a nightmare, that this could no way be true, the gun in my fists, aimed at the space between his eyes.

"Raise your hands!" I yelled. Markham did what I told him.

"What happened to you?"

No answer.

"The boy back there," I jerked my head in the direction we came from, my arms still outstretched, my aim stone steady. "The air kill him or did you?"

Still Markham said nothing.

"Answer me, or I'll shoot!" I yelled. Tornado barked twice, backing my threat. Markham seemed to doubt me, and as though he knew I would not, could not pull the trigger because he might've heard about how I'd failed Dad, the corners of his mouth turned up, as he lifted a foot, taking a step back. Sweat coating the insides of my leather gloves I yelled, "Don't!"

He took another step, ignoring me.

I steadied my aim on him, prepared to squeeze the trigger, but uncertain of Markham's role in the boy's death, not knowing if he was the killer or had stumbled upon the body like I had, I hesitated. Ceasing the opportunity, Markham turned and ran into the woods. I watched him, shaking my head, still questioning if what just happened was real. "It's okay," I said, kneeling beside Tornado, rubbing his fur, calming his trembling body, as he quieted his barking. "He's gone now."

I looked back at the boy lying on the side of the road. I walked back, kneeled and more carefully examined him. I saw no additional injuries: bruises, bullet or knife wounds, other than the marks around his neck. Those could've been self-inflicted. I've seen attempts at survival many people dying from the air have made: clawing, gripping, scratching violently at their own throats, desperately trying to open an airway so they could breath the very air that was killing them.

I stood at the sound of a crack—a twig breaking underfoot—in the woods to my left. I looked over my shoulder, but saw nothing.

Grabbing Tornado's leash, I roped the end of it around my fist and held tight to him, making sure he didn't run off. "Keep an eye out, boy," I told him, then with my other hand, searched the boy on the ground. I found a wallet in his back pocket, set it on his torso, flipped it open, and pulled the ID from inside. His name was Tommy Hardon. He lived a few miles from where we were. He just had an 18th birthday. The air didn't kill him, I told myself; he was too young.

I slipped the ID into my pocket and went to retrieve my shovel from out of Tornado's sidecar. I didn't want to just leave him out here; there were wolves, and lots of stray dogs, even the occasional bear in this part of the country. I didn't know him, but it would be wrong to leave him here exspoed.

I dragged the body just off the road where there was soft dirt. I broke ground with my shovel, heard another crack deep in the trees, and looked up to see and smell fire.

Across the two-lane street, flames peaked out from behind wide, dark trunks, the fire blossoming quickly, running up the sides of trees, singeing the grass boarding the road's pavement, seemingly wanting to find a way to cross, come over here and roast Tornado, Tommy and me.

I wanted to keep digging, carve a space just deep enough to slide Tommy into and cover him up, but I knew there would not be enough time for that.

The wind was whipping up pretty good, stirring the flames: I watched them double in size, in height and width; I could feel the heat from clear across the road; the entire area would be enveloped within a few more minutes.

"Sorry, Tommy. I tried," I said, ordering Tornado back into the sidecar. I threw the shovel in with him, hopped on the bike, kick-started the engine then raced off.

Walls of flames lit up both sides of the two-lane road, the trees crackled like torches: heavy limbs, on fire, breaking off and plummeting to the ground.

Hunched over the handlebars, my fists aching around the grips, the small engine screaming beneath me, I pushed it to its limit, while trying to keep the thing on the road.

The sky was darker with thick smoke, making it almost impossible to see through my mask lenses. I needed to get off the road, get home; a terrible feeling was growing inside of me.

I twisted around on the bike, stealing a peak over my shoulder to see a bright orange glow from over the horizon. Stealing a glance at my dog, Tornado looked worried.

"We're almost there!" I yelled over the wind and the engine's scream. "We're almost home!"

I gave the bike more gas. We sped up a little then began to slow. I pulled harder on the throttle; the bike choked, bucked, traveled another quarter of a mile then stopped.

Dropping the stand, I climbed off, checked the tank, and saw that it was empty. I kicked the tire, paced away, shaking my head.

Tornado whined.

"Sorry, boy. We're walking the last two miles home."

The entire trip I had my weapon drawn and a tight hold on Tornado's leash, fighting the terrible suspicion that we were being watched.

Reaching my block, I was thankful to see my house come into view.

Finally home, we walked the pathway up the stairs and onto the porch, where I turned quickly, spooked, as if expecting someone to step out from behind cover and attack me. I shook the thought, pulled the cord with my key on it out the collar of my shirt, slid it into the security door, opened it then unlocked the inner door.

Just as I was going to push it open, I felt Tornado yank hard on his leash, spinning me around to see, darkened by the night, running across the front lawn: five figures, masks raised over their faces like bandits, knives strapped to their thighs, hammers holstered in their belt loops.

Tornado whirled around, bared his teeth, barked twice, but the robbers were already on us. Tornado was blanketed by a large tarp, flipped over, wrapped up, no longer able to protect me. I was taken from behind, grabbed around the neck and by the arms. But before they could breach the house, I screamed out, "Sloane, run! They're coming in!"

Then I was clubbed over the head.

## 11

I felt my senses returning. My head throbbed, and although I tried, I couldn't open my eyes. I was locked inside my mind, some dark place, forcing me to remember how I had failed to do this job yet again—to take care of those most important to me.

In the first month after the air turned, people who had yet to die, rioted and looted in reaction to the deaths and the lack of answers to explain them. A curfew was set in response. No one but law enforcement was to be out after 11 PM.

The green fluorescent numbers on Dad's police cruiser dash read 10:07 PM when he pulled into the gas station convenience store.

I went for my seatbelt.

"You can stay here. Just going in for a sec," Dad said.

"I can go with you." I didn't like him going anywhere alone this late at night. I had already been deputized, was authorized to carry a gun, but sometimes it felt like he still saw me as his little girl.

"I'll be fine," he said. "Want a candy bar or something? A soda?"

"A Snickers. And be careful."

He climbed out, smiled at me as he walked around the front of the car. I watched him pull open the gas station door, step in, then disappear behind the large paper posters that hung in the store's windows, advertising everything from Bud Light to cell phone service for just $9.99 per month.

I slumped in the leather seat. The police scanner was silent. With no power and everyone but Dad passing on the small police force now dead, the way we were informed of crimes was to run up on them while they were being committed.

Restless, I sat up in the cruiser and looked out the window. I didn't see Dad. He told me to stay put, but I was his backup; he wouldn't have told any of his old deputies to sit in the car.

I climbed out the car, walked across the lot and pulled open the convenience store door. On the floor, ten feet in, just beside the checkout counter lay who I figured was the cashier on duty. He wore a red, short-sleeved zip up jacket, a patch reading GO-GAS! on the breast pocket. His eyes and mouth open wide, he stared at me. I stared back, thinking, what he was doing down there twisted up, one arm folded behind his back, a leg bent into a V, appearing as though kicking himself in the butt? Then I saw the blood, shiny and red, same color as his jacket, oozing out from under him. I heard struggle behind me, whirled around, snatching the gun from my holster, the site landing on two bodies writhing, punching, heels dragging, leaving black scuffs on the tile.

It was Dad. He was on top of another, bigger man—their hands around each other's throats. A gun lay a foot away from them.

"Dad!" I screamed.

"Shea!" Dad yelled back breathless, still fighting.

I saw the man's angry face, watched him take the split second to look over my father's knee for where my voice came. He saw me, started to struggle harder, going after the gun that was on Dad's hip.

"Shea," Dad called again, panting, fear in his voice. I think it was the first time I had ever heard that. "Get out of here! Go!"

"No! No!" I steadied my gun. It was shaking like crazy as I tried to aim the site on the man's skull. There was too much movement: the man and my dad, rolling and flipping on the floor. I wasn't aiming at bottles like Dad had taught me; if I missed, the bullet wouldn't go sailing into the trunk of a tree a hundred yards away.

I chased the man's exposed body parts with the site of my gun, not confident enough to pull the trigger. The criminal toppled Dad off of him, at the same time reaching again for Dad's gun, this time stealing it from his holster.

For a split second, the man was fully exposed. He stared suprised at me, as if expecting to have been shot dead that moment, which he should've been. It was my window—I didn't take it. Instead I watched him reach out, slither behind Dad, snake an arm around his neck and press the barrel of the gun to Dad's temple.

Huffing, getting to his feet, dragging Dad up with him, the man said, "Drop the gun or he's dead!"

"Kill him!" Dad shouted to me. Blood oozed from his nostrils into his mustache, spilled from his mouth into his beard. One of his eyes was starting to swell shut. "Shoot him dead, Shea!"

A corner of the man's shoulder, an inch of his hip, his right shin and foot, the side of his face, the outer corner of an eye: those were the targets available to me, my gun jumping from one to the next, then back again, me wondering which gave me the highest percentage of a hit. They were all no larger than the width of a beer bottle's neck. That was the target Dad had sometimes assigned for me as a 10 year-old kid during my shooting practice, where he taught me to just concentrate, focus, breath, set my aim, let the air out of my lungs then squeeze the trigger.

"Put the gun down!" the man yelled again. "Put it down and he lives!"

"You can do it, Shea. You know you can," Dad said, no longer yelling, but encouraging me, almost calmly, like he was ready to accept whatever outcome there was: him dying or the man, as long as it involved me taking the shot and me walking out alive. "We've done this. Kill him," Dad said, closing his eyes, as though waiting to hear the shot from my gun at any moment.

"Shea. Shea!" Sloane's voice and Tornado's frenzied barks echoed in my head as I looked around and blinked the blurry surroundings of our living room into focus. Everything was turned on its side. My wrists were bound behind me. I was on the floor, tied up, helpless. Sloane looked down at me from her chair. Her arms were also tied behind her back; they hadn't gagged either of us.

"You okay?" she asked me.

"Head hurts a little, but I'm fine." I squirmed, trying to get to my knees. One of the boys watched Sloane and me—apathy on his face—from a chair across the room. A gun hung from his hand like he wanted no part of the thing—like he had been forced to hold it. He had dark hair, big eyes, a boyish face; his body was slim, narrow around the shoulders and hips, like a girl's. I had seen him somewhere before. Today, in the small group passing outside our house.

"What do they want?" I whispered, already having an idea.

More than a few times, I had walked into supposedly vacant houses, doors hanging open, to find the places ransacked, walls riddled with bullet holes, everything of value taken and bodies of who I figured were the owners, lying dead, blood drying on their injuries.

"I don't know. Steal our stuff, maybe take the house," Sloane whispered.

"You got a plan?" I managed to sit up on my butt, pressing my back against the sofa.

"No, but—"

"Shut the hell up!" a boy said, walking into the living room. His commanding tone said he was in charge. An inch or two taller than me, he had dirty blonde hair that hung at uneven lengths around his ears. Squat and broad-shouldered, he had the body of a high school wrestler. He walked over, grabbed me by the arm and hoisted me up on the sofa beside Sloane.

"What do you want?" I said, my tone harsh as his.

Two boys stood on either side of him wearing clothes that were torn and caked with dirt. Their hair buzzed down to stubble, bandanas hanging beneath their chins, their cheeks sunken; they looked as though they were starving. Another boy stood in a corner, eating one of our cans of food, greedily spooning beans into his mouth.

"We want whatever you have?" High School Wrestler said in answer to my question. "Anybody else live here?"

"It's none of your damn business!" I said. "You need to get out of our house."

The squat boy chuckled, shaking his head. He reached out, grabbed me by the cheeks so hard I grunted in pain.

"Tough girl, you two live here alone, or are we going to have to tie someone else up when they come through the door?"

"Screw you!" Sloane spat in the boy's face. He wound up, threw a backhand across her jaw, pitching her sideways into my lap. Tornado struggled harder from the corner of the room, barked louder under the tarp, as if he could see through it and wanted desperately to make the boy pay for beating his owner.

Wrestler grabbed Sloane by the arm, set her back up. "Shut that dog up!"

"He's a dog. Dogs bark!" Sloane said, spitting blood onto the floor.

"Fine," the boy said, raising his shotgun, aiming it in Tornado's direction. "Let's see if dogs bark with buckshot in them." He cocked the gun.

"No!" I screamed, attempting to stand from the sofa, jump in the way of the bullet before it struck my dog.

The dark-haired boy I recognized this morning from the street, stood, his arm outstretched. "Don't! Shotgun will be too messy. I got it!" He hurried to Tornado, pulling a gun from the small of his back as my poor dog floundered and wrestled under the heavy tarp.

I got to my feet, struggled with my wrist straps, but unable to break free, I screamed at the boy, ran at him, but was too late. He fired two silenced shots into the tarp, causing Tornado to cry out.

I collapsed, as I watched my dog's body dropped to the floor. I moaned, falling on my side again, not three feet from Tornado, now silent and still.

"Tornado!" Sloane screamed somewhere behind me. I got to my knees again, crawling across the floor, crying, begging for my dog to get up, to show me a sign that he was alive.

Tornado's killer stepped in front of me, his boots blocking my view. He bent down, scooped Tornado up in his arms.

"I'm gonna throw him out back, Pete," the boy said to Wrestler.

Pete nodded. "And Jonny," he said. "Don't take all day."

Jonny looked back at Pete, nodded obediently, then carried Tornado's dead body toward the back porch.

After Jonny disappeared, Pete turned the shotgun back on us, where we sat, slumped over, tears rolling down our cheeks.

"I'm gonna try this again. Anyone else live here?"

Sloane sniffled, stared infuriated up at Pete. "No!"

The back door slammed closed. Jonny walked back into the living room avoiding the vengeful stare I set on him.

"All these supplies in the dinning room," Pete said, nodding into the neighboring room. "You taking a trip?" He paced in front of us, the shotgun held over his shoulder like a baseball bat. "You heading to D.C. like all the other pipe dreamers, thinking what's going on here ain't happening there? Think there's a dome over it, like in that TV show, and the air's not killing people there, too?"

"We're leaving tomorrow," Sloane said. "Let us take our stuff. We'll go right now. You can keep the house."

"Sloane!" I said. "You can't just—"

"Maybe that's a good idea," Jonny said.

Pete turned, eyed Jonny as if he had overstepped some boundary.

"What makes you think you have an opinion? We hardly know you." He shoved Jonny like a pestering little brother then faced us again, raising the shotgun like he planned to gun us down as Jonny had my dog.

"Get up," Pete told us.

I stood, wondering if they were going to execute us. "What are you going to do?" I said.

Ignoring me, Pete reached out, grabbed Jonny by the shoulder. "Take them to a room somewhere and..." he covered his mouth with a hand, making the rest impossible to hear.

"What are you gonna do to us?" I said again, more demanding this time.

"Something really bad if you don't move," Jonny said, walking behind me, shoving me in the small of my back.

## 12

Jonny had taken us to Mom's study. Sloane and I leaned forward in the two chairs that faced Mom's desk, our hands still tied behind our backs. I couldn't tell what time it was, but I knew, easily, two hours had passed since we were taken from the living room.

Jonny sat high up on Mom's desk chair, his feet planted on the seat, his butt balanced on the chair's spine, the gun dangling awkwardly from his hand as though it was a plastic toy and not a deadly weapon. I glared, breathing heavily, as I considered—armed or not—making a go at him. He pretended he didn't notice my death stare, looking everywhere in the room but at me. Finally, he gave me his attention, asking: "Why are you looking at me like that?"

"I'm going to kill you for doing that to my dog."

"Shea," Sloane said, elbowing me in my ribs.

"I'm sorry, but—" Jonny started.

"Doesn't matter your excuse," I said. "First chance I get, I'm gonna gut you like a fish."

"Shea!" Sloane said, her voice louder.

"What?" I said back.

"That's enough!" Sloane said. "Apologize to him."

"What?"

"Apologize. He didn't mean to do it. You saw it wasn't his idea."

"He jumped at the chance."

"I didn't want to," Jonny said. "It was just...I said I was sorry."

"Good enough," Sloane said, narrowing her eyes at me, tilting her head like there was some message I was supposed to be receiving from her. "She accepts your apology, don't you Shea?"

I clenched my jaws, trying not to remember Tornado as a puppy, trying to blot out the memory of him sleeping on my pillow beside me the first night in our house.

"Yeah," I said, turning away, no longer able to look up at my dog's killer. "I accept."

The boys in the living room clearly didn't think much of Jonny—didn't consider him one of the group; it appeared he was as much a prisoner as we were. They hadn't come to check on him, relieve him, or ask he if he wanted a can of food or stick of beef jerky.

"Why are you with them?" Sloane asked.

Jonny looked up from a year-old science magazine Mom used to read.

"What?" he asked, timidly.

"I heard the other boy, Pete, say he barely knew you. You're not like them. Why you with them?"

This couldn't have been Sloane's master plan—pleasant conversation?

Jonny gave the question a moment before saying, "I just am. That's all you need to know. You shouldn't be talking."

"You won't let them hurt us, will you?" Sloane asked.

"Of course he will," I said. "He killed Tornado. What's to stop him from letting them kill us?"

Jonny looked disturbed by what I had said, but didn't correct me.

"You need to let us go," I said. "You need to come over here, untie us right now, give us your gun, and—"

"Shea!"

"No, Sloane," I said, refusing to be quieted again. "I'm the sheriff. You came into the wrong house. Let us go now and I'll make sure you make out better than the rest of them."

Jonny looked like he was seriously considering my offer when the door flew open and Pete ordered him to move us back in.

## 13

It had gotten dark in the time we were locked away. Our captors had lit the candles in the living and dining room, and when we were marched back in, the shadows of them holding weapons were cast, long and thin, across the walls.

I caught sight of the clock: 8:02 P.M. I couldn't stop myself from thinking that if I hadn't been so careless as to let these boys sneak up on me, invade our home, I would've been out walking my dog as I did every night at this time.

I was grabbed by my wrist ties and told to stop. I looked toward the living room's front window, glancing out of it, my heart aching, expecting to see Tornado on the front lawn, rolling around playfully on his back. I wasn't shocked he wasn't there, but to my surprise, I saw Greg standing in the middle of the street. No expression on his face, he stared directly at me, his rifle slung over his shoulder. I didn't know if he could see what was going on, but I had to suppress the desperate urge to run screaming toward the front door, waving my arms. I remained calm and kept my eyes on him. He nodded, pointed at me then held up a clenched fist. I returned the nod, assuming he was gesturing for me to stay put, that he would come up with a plan to rescue Sloane and I.  I lowered my chin the slightest bit, hoping my movement wasn't detected. I watched Greg point himself in the chest with two fingers, then to the right side of the house. I carefully nodded again, believing he was telling me that he would try to get in through there somehow.

"Hey!" one of the boys said, hurrying toward me. "What are you looking at?"

"Nothing," I said, averting my eyes.

He didn't believe me, grabbed me by the arm, and followed the direction my eyes had been looking. Thankfully, Greg had gone.

"I have to use the bathroom!" I said.

Pete looked at me as though it made no sense that people, every now and then, had to relieve themselves. "What?"

"Can I go, or should I use it in my pants?"

"Take her," Pete said, waving a hand at Jonny.

Jonny grabbed me by the arm, allowing me to lead the way down the narrow corridor.

"You know when this is over, I'm gonna kill you for what you did to my dog."

"I told you, I had no choice."

"Doesn't matter. Enjoy what time you have left. It's coming to an end real soon."

Jonny whirled me around, yanked me to him, our faces so close I could see the fine hairs above his lip he passed off as a mustache.

"I said I was sorry, but that was the last time," he said, trying to sound hardened like the others. He failed. "If you were smart, you wouldn't say anything else to me. Get it?"

"Yeah, okay. Got it."

He turned me back around, trailing me to the bathroom door, then tried following me in. "Excuse me. A little privacy?" I said.

"I can't let you go in there alone. What if you try to—"

"There are bars on all the windows," I said, nodding at the ones in the bathroom.

He looked at the bars through the sheer curtain.

"Now untie me so I can do this, or would you prefer to help me go?"

Inside the bathroom, I locked the door, stood in the mirror staring at myself, breathing heavily, hoping whatever Greg told me, I read correctly. Reaching into the collar of my t-shirt, I pulled out my key that unlocked a door inside the window's security gate, just in case of fire. I glanced back over at the bathroom door, flushed the toilet, masking noise to mask me reaching between the bars and hoisting up the window halfway. I unlocked the gate, opened it just enough so that Greg could see that it was unsecured. Afterward, I pulled the sheer curtain back over the window.

I ran the faucet water, and rinsed my fingers. When I opened the door, Jonny stood in front of me, eyeing me suspiciously and looking over my shoulder.

"You taking me back, or do you need to go potty too?"

He re-tied my hands, walked me back down the hall and shoved me, sending me tripping over my feet, into the living room.

Pressing me down with a firm hand on my shoulder, Jonny sat me in a chair beside Sloane, our backs to the living room windows. I wanted to tell her about my communication with Greg, and what I had done, but there was no opportunity. Instead, I sat, watching the other two boys stand guard on opposite ends of the room, as Pete paced in front of us, rubbing his chin, the shotgun still thrown casually over his shoulder.

"It took us a while, but we came to a decision on what to do," he said. "Food will last longer with two less mouths to feed. So..." Pete raised the shotgun, setting the tip against Sloane's forehead. "I'm going to have to say goodbye to both of you."

"No! No," I screamed, watching Sloane shut her eyes, brace herself for the shot. "Don't do it! We'll give you whatever you want. Please!"

Jonny ran up behind Pete, grabbed him by the arm. "Maybe you should think about what she's saying."

Pete shook Jonny off, slapped him across the face, sending Jonny stumbling back and falling to a knee.

"You really want to kill them?" Jonny asked, looking up, rubbing his face. "Look at 'em. They're hot, right?" He stood, walked slowly over to me and ran a hand over my hair, caressing my cheek, looking to the other boys to see if they agreed. "Lets use 'em for a while, then we can do whatever. What do you say, Pete? How long has it been since you had some?"

Pete glanced at the boys behind him. They nodded, smiled, one of the boy's grabbing the crotch of his jeans.

"No. No!" I struggled against my wrist ties, rocking in my chair, not caring if they noticed, when from the corner of my eye, I saw something move down the hall: it was no one…nothing, just my mind hoping. But before I turned away, Greg peered out from behind a wall. The backs of all the boys were to him as he pointed in the direction of the front door, wrapping his hand around an imaginary doorknob, and pulling it open.

I turned to Sloane, aware that she had seen what I had.

She whispered to me, "When I move…" she titled her head toward the door, "…you go."

As though Greg heard what Sloane had said, he popped out from cover, stood in the middle of the hallway. "Hey!" he yelled drawing the boy's attention. Two went running after him. Wrists still tied, I leapt from my chair, started as fast as my legs would carry me toward the front door.

The boy standing closest took off after me. But before he could reach me, Sloane threw herself head first, colliding with him, knocking him to his knees.

At the door, huffing, my legs trembling so badly I thought they'd give out, I turned my back to the locks, blindly unfastening them. Undoing the last one and pulling open the inner door—two of the boys steps from me—I unlocked the security door. From outside, Daniel yanked open the gate, stepped in aiming his rifle at the advancing boys.

"Another step, you're dead. Like, really," Daniel said, stopping them.

"How about we see who shoots first," Pete said, standing behind the sofa, pointing his gun at Daniel.

"How about it?" Greg said, stepping out of the hallway, his rifle pointed at the back of Pete's skull.

Our wrists untied, Daniel and Greg holding their rifles on three of the boys that invaded our home: the two that followed Greg down the hall were bleeding from non-fatal bullet wounds to the shoulders and thighs where Greg had shot them.

I marched over to Pete, picked my weapon off the floor, where he was forced to drop it.

Sloane shoved me out the way, reared back and caught Pete on the chin with a punch that buckled his knees, nearly laying him out him. Staggered on his feet, he angrily spat out a glob of blood, saliva and a tooth.

"So what do we do with them?" I asked, holding my gun on the invaders.

"We take their weapons and whatever they have: their packs, supplies then we let them go," Sloane said.

"But they killed Tornado!"

"I know, Shea. And I hate it as much as you do. But do you suggest? Kill them? Is that what you all want to do?" She looked to Daniel, then to Greg for their opinion, after turning from me.

"No," Greg said. "But if they come for us again..."

"If they come again," Sloane said, staring at Pete. "It'll be for the last time."

"Fine," I said. I raised my gun, gesturing for them to move toward the door when I noticed someone missing. "Where is the other boy?"

"Somebody's missing?" Daniel said.

"There were four of them," Sloane said.

I ran down the hall, looked in the bathroom, searched Mom's office, the rest of the first floor and every room upstairs. Coming back down, winded from my search, Sloane asked me, "Did you find him?"

"No. He had to have ran."

"Which one was he?" Greg asked.

"Jonny," I told him. "The one that killed my dog."

After taking their gear and weapons, and forcing Pete and the other two boys out of our house, we kept our guns pointed to their backs as we watched them run off into the darkness.

So caught up in fighting for our home, only then did we see the glimmer of the fire that brightened the night sky. The flames were just over the roof and behind our house. We ran back there and stood, mouths open, astonished at the height and the fury with which the fire burned.

"Burners," I heard Daniel gasp.

"What?" I asked, seeing Markham's charcoal smeared face, and wondered had he done this? I questioned if I had managed to stop him then, if I had gunned him down, would this fire be threatening my home?

Sloane pulled my arm. "Fire is moving this way. We have to go now!"

I started behind Sloane, but caught sight of the tarp that covered my poor dog and froze, ashamed that I had all but forgotten about him. One of his paws hung out from under the canvas.

"Shea, come on!" I heard Sloane calling. I yelled something back, not caring how high or hot or close the flames came. Tears coming to my eyes, approaching the tarp, I saw something puncturing the cover—something resembling darts. I dropped to my knees, saw that they were actually tranquilizers Tornado had been shot with. I pulled them out, snatched my knife from my belt, cut the rope that tied that tarp closed, whipping it off my dog.

He still appeared dead, but I pressed my ear to the side of his furry chest, listened for a heartbeat, and although shallow, I heard one. Tornado was alive!

# 14

Standing in front of our house, watching the fire grow behind it, the flames licking the dark sky, smoke forcing coughs out of us, we knew we could no longer wait till morning to leave.

Greg held Tornado in his arms. As I rubbed his head, he started to wake up and lick my hands.

"You were standing there in the middle of the street, looking into our window," I said to Greg. "How did you know we were in trouble?"

The fire lighting the frown on his face, he said without turning to me, "You take Tornado out every four hours, just like you've always done. When I didn't see you, I knew something was wrong."

I wanted to tell him how much I appreciated him. That if he hadn't been there, hadn't cared enough to wonder, things might've ended much worse for us.

"Thank you," I said, unable to look at him. And as though I hadn't said a thing, Greg walked around me and stood beside Sloane.

"We gonna toast marshmallows, or are we leaving?" he asked her.

"You packed?" Sloane said.

"You know we are."

"Then we're out of here in a half an hour, an hour at the most. No point staying to watch our house burn down."

I thought of Beth, April and Toni, the people I had been trying to convince to go with us. "We can't go yet. My friends: I have to tell them we're leaving."

"You said they didn't want to go, that they made up their minds already. We don't have time," Sloane said.

"I'll take her in the bus," Greg said to Sloane. "Give Shea a chance just to let them know we're leaving. If they wanna come, we'll bring them back. If not, I have no problem leaving them."

"Sloane, does that work for you?" I asked.

"You have thirty minutes. Or me and Daniel are leaving without both of you."

Kendall, Beth and April were standing outside on Beth's front lawn, their faces aglow, looking upward, as though at a fireworks display. I was shocked that Beth and Kendall said they would leave with us to D.C. and that they even had bags ready. It must've finally dawned on them just how dangerous staying here would be. But speeding our way to Toni's house, it was April who smiled and whispered to me that it took nearly two hours of convincing, but she was the reason her sister and Kendall changed their minds.

Not ten minutes later, Greg stopped abruptly in front of Toni's house. I stood at the front of the bus, waiting for him to lever the door open.

"They going to be ready?" he asked, looking like he only wanted to hear one answer.

Considering just hours ago, Toni had no intention of going, I knew there was no way she'd be ready. I figured it'd take me two of the five minutes just to convince her to come with us, leaving her three to throw on suitable traveling gear, and chuck some stuff she could not live without into a backpack.

"If she's not, it'll take five minutes," I said.

"Five minutes," Greg repeated. "That's all she's got." He yanked on the handle, opening the door. I started down the steps. "Come back in six, I'll be gone," he said.

I ran off the bus, up the stairs, and banged on Toni's door.

"What are you doing here?" she asked, answering the door, appearing shocked to see me.

"I told you I was coming for you." I pushed passed her into the house, moving toward her bedroom. "Any kind of bag you can strap to your back, grab it, put some food, clothes, and some toiletries in it. Now!"

"Shea, what are you talking about?" Toni said, following behind me, an arm wrapped around her belly.

In front of me, Potter stepped out of the bathroom, zipping up his pants; he blocked my path. "What are you doing here, Shea?"

I stared him in the eyes. "Toni's coming with us to D.C. I came to get her. Now if you'd get out of my way so I can help her get ready."

Potter stepped around me, snatched Toni by the arm, and stood nose to nose with her. "You trying to leave, take my baby without me knowing?"

"No, Potter! I don't know what she's talking about. I told her we aren't going."

When Potter turned around to deal with me, he stared into the barrel of my gun.

"Potter, I've never killed before. I don't want you to be my first." Keeping my eyes locked on him, I spoke to Toni. "Get a bag, fill it to the top, because we needed to have been gone like three minutes ago."

"Toni, you ain't going nowhere without me!"

"I'm not going nowhere period. I told Shea that!" Toni said.

Annoyed, I hurried to the front window, glanced out, saw that the bus was still idling outside, but didn't know for how much longer. "Toni, you don't see it now, but there is fire not far from here and it's coming this way. When this house burns down, where will you go? Where will you and your baby live?" I turned to Potter, hoping I could guilt him into leaving. "If you don't want you and your family to die, we need to leave!"

Potter looked conflicted, and surprised. "You mean, I can come, too?"

"Of course. Just make it now!"

Greg brought the bus to a stop back in front of my house. Things were as I had feared; the house was silhouetted by a wall of fifty-foot high flames.

Sloane waited by the curb with our bags and the weapons we'd take in order to ensure our safe travel to the capital. Tornado sat by her side, looking concussed, like he had no idea of where he was, but was happy to be alive.

"You get everybody?" Sloane asked.

"Yeah, and Potter too. Hope you don't mind."

She glanced at Potter, reactionless, then said, "It's fine. We just need to get out of here."

Me, Daniel and Sloane loaded all of our stuff onto the back of the bus, packing everything in tight; there was just enough space. I slammed the door shut. With Beth, April, Kendall, Toni, Potter inside, Greg at the wheel and Daniel sitting in the seat behind him, we were all set to go.

"You sure this is everything?" I asked Sloane, before heading to the front of the bus.

"It's all we'll need. More important, it's all we can carry," Sloane said.

I turned the corner of the bus to make my way toward the door, when I was surprised by someone standing in front of me, a pack strapped to his back, his hands on the bars of a mountain bike. I didn't know his name, but remembered him from earlier, walking away from Toni's house after arguing with her.

"What are you doing here?" I asked, guarded.

"Everything's on fire. I saw you come get Toni."

"You spying on her?" I said, more worried about this guy than before.

"You're going to D.C., right? You can't leave me here."

Feeling eyes on me, I looked up into a window of the bus, saw Toni staring down at the boy. She quickly looked away.

"What's your name?" I asked.

"Oliver," he said. "I need to go with you. You have to take me with you."

Something told me his desperation was about more than just the fire. But he was right, I couldn't just leave him here. "Get on the bus, Oliver."

I climbed on after our newest passenger, and with the fire behind the house continuing to rage, Sloane started up the stairs onto the bus. "Let's do it, Greg! Get this thing going!" she ordered.

Greg turned the key. The bus cranked, but wouldn't turn over.

Leaning over his shoulder, looking through the windshield at the growing fire, Sloane urged, "Come on, Greg, get us out of here!"

"I got it!" He shut off the engine, stomped the gas pedal several times then turned the key again. The engine groaned. Greg pumped faster, then the engine roared to life.

He shifted the bus in gear, started to roll off when Sloane yelled, slapping a palm against the bus door, trying to push it open. "Stop! Wait! Open the door!"

"What?" Greg said.

"Sloane, what are you doing?" I said, standing from my front seat.

Sloane grabbed me by the sleeve, pulled me to her. "Mom's notes!" Her voice was hushed so no one else could hear. "They're still upstairs in the closet. It'll only take a sec for me to get them."

Worried, I glanced out one of the windows. Fire had clung bright and furious to one side of our house, and was creeping up onto the roof.

"I'll go," I offered.

"No, Shea. I know exactly where they are."

"But you're..." I said, glancing down at her belly, thinking of the life growing inside of it, needing to say nothing more.

Sloane smiled then chuckled. "Nice try," she said. Then to Greg, shouted: "Come on! Let's go!"

Greg hesitated, but opened the door to let Sloane out.

I climbed out with her, watched her hurry across the lawn and disappear into the front door. Fifteen seconds...thirty seconds, I waited, staring at our home, trying not to be overwhelmed by the wonderful life we had here, and the fact that after tonight, it would all be lost.

"C'mon, Sloane. Hurry it up," I said, feeling anxious.

After what felt like an eternity, she stepped out the front door, carrying the leather satchel, containing what might have possibly been the future for all of us. She ran down the stairs, and that moment, despite the fact the world we knew here was going up in flames, that our parents had died, and in no time, we'd most likely follow, Sloane was smiling. She was maybe thinking, notwithstanding our many losses and the rough times we still had to face, we had each other, and there was slightest chance that we might still make a difference. At least that was how I felt. Having her still here meant everything to me—nothing was more important. And as Sloane ran toward me, crossing the front lawn—twenty feet away—I held out my arms to take Mom's notes from her. But Sloane tripped. The satchel jumped from her arms, and she fell to the grass on her knees.

I hurried toward her expecting Sloane to get right back up, laugh off the fall, as she brushed dirt from her jeans. She didn't do that, and I was horrified to see her reaching for her throat, wrapping both her hands around her neck.

"Sloane?" I said, running toward her, throwing myself to the ground, kneeling in front of her so that I could look into her eyes. I was horrified to see that they were bulging, that she was gagging, gasping and choking. Her hands frantically reached out to me, clawing, clutching, like a drowning victim trying not to go under.

"No! No! No!" I cried, taking her hands, holding them, while looking over my shoulder toward the bus, screaming for help. This couldn't be happening. It couldn't be! I grabbed Sloane by the shoulders, then wrapped my arms fully around her, pulling her close to me, praying this wasn't what I feared. "Somebody help me!" I screamed again, hysterically.

Her mouth open, I felt her body convulsing against mine as she desperately tried to suck in air. She couldn't. She was choking! I screamed in my head. I was losing my sister; she was dying in front of me. I wanted to grab her face, stare in her eyes, demand she be strong, not let this thing take her, not leave me alone, but I knew she had no choice in the matter. Begging her to stay would be selfish. I had to comfort her, let her know this was not her fault, that she was not failing us—failing me. She grabbed tighter to my arms, her fingers digging deep into my biceps—her attempt to hold on to life as it was being ripped from her. Tears spilled from both our eyes, and I heard some of the girls from the bus sobbing as they stood around me. Sloane's face was turning a light shade of blue, and I knew this was the time to ease her into death. I pulled her to me again, felt her cheek pressed to mine, her heart thumping, her body trembling, jerking.

"It's okay, Sloane It's okay," I said, blinding by the tears that poured from my eyes.

I felt the other's arms around us, embracing us, my friends speaking to Sloane, reassuring her as I did. "We love you, Sloane," they cried. "We'll be fine. We love you."

"Don't fight it, Sloane," I wailed. "I'm here for you. Just go. I'll always love you!" I said, feeling her body shudder harder, her muscles lock, her grip tightening on me more, the sound of her gagging so loud in my ears it was deafening. The spasms ripped through her several more times, and then finally, nothing.

I froze, my arms locked around her, my chin over her shoulder, my eyes shut, feeling no more struggle, Sloane's body limp against mine. I eased away. Her chin fell against her chest and I knew she was gone.

The flames had engulfed the entire back half of our house as I stood on the ledge of Sloane's grave, watching Greg, Daniel and Oliver pitch dirt onto my sister.

After Sloane died, I buried my face into her chest, screaming. I remained there, thankful for the respect the others gave me by backing off and letting me have that moment. As quickly as I could, I composed myself, stood, tried to lift Sloane from the ground, carry her in my arms to where I knew she wanted to be.

"What are you doing?" Greg said, behind me.

"We need to burry her. Her grave is already dug in the back."

"We need to go!" Potter said.

"We don't go anywhere till my sister is buried!" I yelled at anyone who might've disagreed.

"You're crazy!" Potter yelled over me, the fire at his back. "You're sister is already dead. You wanna die, too?"

I wanted to claw his eyes out for even suggesting we leave Sloane this way.

"We bury Sloane, then we go," Greg told Potter after stepping in front of me. "You want to go now? You can start walking."

We carried Sloane to her grave and gently lowered her in.

Standing on the ledge, the fire so high and so close I could feel its heat nearly scorching my skin, I was not in control enough of my grief to speak the words describing how wonderful a sister, a friend, and human being Sloane was.

"I love you. I'll always miss you. You are my hero, Sloane," was all I could say. I grabbed my shovel, sunk it into the soft mound beside the ditch, but when I moved to lift it, I broke down again in tears.

"I got it."

I looked up to see Greg over my shoulder, taking the shovel from me.

"I'll do it, Shea," he said, easing the shovel from my hand.

I watched him as he hurriedly, but respectfully covered my sister with dirt. When he was finished, I kneeled on the mound, crying harder, feeling responsible for the horrible way Sloane spent the last hours of her life, terrified by those intruders. I allowed them in, let them beat my sister, threaten her life, and I was supposed to be the sheriff.

Shaking my head, on the very spot in my backyard where my father had pinned it to my chest, I pulled the sheriff's badge from my shirt. "I'm sorry I failed you, Sloane," I said, setting the star on top of her grave. I stood, looked behind me to see Greg, compassion in his eyes. "C'mon," I said, wiping tears from my face with the back of a hand. "Before we all die back here."

## 15

Not only had I lost my sister who was my best friend, but my unborn niece as well. It was almost too much for me to take. But there were things that needed to be accomplished—things that Sloane intended to dedicate the rest of her life to.

After we lay her to rest, we walked back toward the bus. Sitting on the front lawn where my sister died, was the satchel that contained Mom's notes. I picked it up, lugged it up on the bus, set it on the front seat, where it sat beside me now.

The bus running, Greg left the driver's seat, walked over and stared down at me. From under the hand that I held to my forehead, I saw his Converse sneakers, his jeans—a little too long—hanging over them.

"I don't want to bother you," he said. "But I need the directions to D.C."

I wiped more tears from my cheeks. "Sure." I reached under the seat, dug into Sloane's rucksack and pulled out a handwritten page of exit-by-exit directions. I held it out to him. "Just 200 miles or so to D.C. Interstate 495, then 95. Got it?" I asked, trying my best to stop my voice from quivering.

"Yeah," Greg said, taking the page. He stood there another moment. "Sorry about Sloane. I wish I could—"

"It's okay," I said, cutting him off. I didn't want his pity. He nodded, took his seat back behind the wheel, shifted the bus in gear and moved us out.

Tornado lay pressed very close to me, whining softly every now and again. I knew he was missing Sloane. I stroked his fur, comforted him best I could, my forehead pressed against the window, as I stared out as the neighborhood I loved and knew for all my life, enveloped in wild torrents of flame, disappeared behind us.

A second later, I felt a weight on my seat and turned to see April, her face bawled up, pink and sad. I reached out, grabbed her as though she was the one needing to be consoled.

"I'm so sorry," she said, holding me. "I don't know what I'd if I lost Beth."

You'll have to know, I thought, but would never say that to her. Beth was just a year younger than Sloane. Sadly, she wasn't going to be around much longer either.

"Shhh, shhh, shhh," I said, kissing the top of April's head. "I'll be okay. I'll be just fine." I hugged her again and told her she should go back to her sister and keep her company.

April stood, smiled sadly, and I watched as she made her way back, grabbing onto the seats on either side of her, wobbling down the aisle of the bus as we sped toward the interstate. Beth stared back at me. I forced a smile and she did her best to bring one to her face.

Looking away, I gazed over the occupants of the small bus: some of them leaning back, attempting to sleep, some wide-eyed, looking fearful and doubtful: all of them holding tight to the bags that carried their most valuable stuff and probably not enough food to take them all the way to D.C. If Sloane was here, she would've seen what I was seeing, and knowing the importance of keeping everyone's spirits high, she would've gotten up, stood at the front of the bus and called for everyone's attention. She would've raised her voice over the engine and said words that rallied us, words that not only drove our fear away, but gave us hope, had us looking forward to the good that awaited us.

I turned away from Beth and April and saw Kendall, her designer jacket bunched up behind her head as she dozed against her window. Across from her, Potter snored like a large animal, his mouth open, leaning against Toni, who, fighting sleep, held him close, her arms around him as though fearing he would leave if she were to nod. She stared drowsy-eyed toward the front of the bus, but not at me. Her sightline led me to the boy, Oliver, who miraculously appeared at our bus just before we left.

Staring at the back of his head, something told me he was looking right back at Toni. I wondered what was going on with them, what their connection was. But there were so many more things banging around in my head, I hadn't the time to be concerned about the mystery of them.

I scooted down in my seat, pushed my fingers into my pocket, fished out the ID of the boy I had found dead earlier this evening: Tommy Hardon: eighteen—just a year older than me, and yes he was destined to die in two years, maybe a bit later, but no one had the right to steal the time he had left.

Markham's face flashed across my mind again along with so many questions. Was Markham truly a Burner? How did that happen? Did he kill Tommy, and if so, why?

I pushed the ID back into my pocket, looked up from my thoughts, unintentionally locking eyes with Daniel, Greg's friend, who sat across the aisle, directly behind the driver's seat. We held each other's stare for a moment, then he spoke, his words totally drowned out by the loud engine roar.

"What?" I said, leaning toward him, cupping a hand to my ear.

He scooted to the outer edge of his seat. I did the same, both of us leaning toward the aisle.

"I said it's not fair," he said, raising his voice.

"What's not fair?"

"That all of our parents died for just breathing, you know, and that those who survived resort to breaking into houses, robbing and killing people, acting like we've forgotten what life was like just four months ago. It's not fair."

"Who said life was fair?" My question came out harsher than I intended.

Daniel stared, giving my response a moment of thought, then turned back to me. "I used to think that it should be, but I guess I don't anymore. My parents were doctors. I was their only kid. We had everything I wanted: huge house in California, and for my 17$^{th}$ birthday, they bought me this brand new, black BMW." Daniel smiled looking off into his thoughts. "I had a girlfriend I was going to propose to after I graduated college. I know it was stupid," he smiled. "Too young right? But I loved her.  Then the air turned," he said, frowning. "After my mom and dad died, my girlfriend was all I had left. Then she up and dumped me. Said how badly I dealt with the death of my parents was too much for her. I was devastated. I allowed myself to be too in love with her. I should've known better." Daniel clenched his jaws, staring angrily at me as though I had been the one who had kicked him to the curb.

"You can't lose hope," I said, not knowing exactly how he'd pull that off, feeling I was ready to give up myself.

"What's the point of it all anymore? It used to be money. That's worthless now. Love? I'll never find that again, and why even bother. I'll be 19 soon. That gives me..." his eyes rolled upward, checking the math in his head. "...a year? Year and a half max, if what they say is true."

"The world might surprise you. Stay positive, and good things will happen," I said, still trying to cram happy thoughts down Daniel's throat.

He stared blank-faced at me, then suddenly laughed out loud, showing his bright smile. "You don't believe a word of that crap you're saying, do you?"

"Nope," I said, smiling then laughed with him. It felt good. "I really don't."

"Okay," Daniel said, reaching out his hand to me.

I took it and we shook as though meeting for the first time.

"Get some sleep, Shea," he said. "And sorry about your sister. The short time I knew her, she seemed like a cool girl."

I nodded, appreciatively. "She was the coolest."

I pushed back in my seat, but wanted to check for the last time on the people I inherited responsibility of—make sure everything was okay—when I heard someone say, "You got a problem looking back here?"

The question came from Toni's boyfriend, Potter, who was no longer sleeping, but wide-awake and pissed off. He hadn't been talking to me as I had thought at first, but to the boy sitting behind me—the boy I found at Toni's house.

Oliver whirled around, faced forward, as if hoping that would calm Potter down. It hadn't. Potter scooted around Toni's legs, rejected her pleas for him to just sit back down and ignore Oliver's stares. Potter pushed up the aisle, swaying back and forth with the rhythm of the bus, stopping in front of Oliver's seat, his shoulders bunched up around his ears, ready to fight.

Trembling, Oliver shut his eyes and ignored Potter.

"Why the hell you looking back there at my girl? Or was it me you were checking? Huh? You like me?" Potter questioned.

No response from Oliver, which had Potter reaching down, grabbing a fistful of Oliver's t-shirt to lift him from his seat.

"Let him go, Potter!" I said, standing.

"This got nothing to do with you, Shea. It's not your business."

"Let him go!" I grabbed Potter by the arm. He released Oliver, grabbing me, and reared back, about to throw a punch.

The bus screeched to a halt, jolting all of us forward. A moment later, Greg stood at the front of the bus, his attention focused on Potter.

Greg said to Potter, "What's your name again?"

"It's okay, Greg. I got this," I said, not really certain of that, as I stared up at the fist Potter still had cocked over his head.

"I never said," Potter grunted to Greg. "What's yours?"

"You just heard her call me, Greg. Whether you're deaf, stupid or both, doesn't matter to me. But I need you to go back to your seat."

Potter lowered his fist and released me. "Whose gonna make me?"

Daniel stood from his seat, shoulder to shoulder, beside Greg.

"Like that, huh?" Potter nodded. "Two against one. Fine," he said, turning around, feigning a punch at Oliver, who cowered awkwardly to the far side of his seat, almost banging his head against the window.

"Greg," I said. "You didn't have to—"

"Sit down, Shea," he said, not even looking in my direction.

He sat back behind the wheel, turned the key on the ignition, and as it had before, the motor struggled to turn over. Greg shut it off, pumped the gas several times then tried again. Nothing.

"Let me give it a try," Daniel said.

They switched places, Daniel repeating the same steps as though there would be a different outcome. Everyone on the bus, Beth, April, Kendall, Potter, Toni, Oliver, me and Greg, stood, tensely, worry on our faces, hoping that by some miracle the bus would start. After a couple more tries, Daniel looked up at Greg, shook his head then levered the bus door open. "We gotta check under the hood."

On a stretch of road without any kind of streetlight—the sky above crowded with low-lying clouds—we were in almost complete darkness.

The hood was up and everyone was off the bus, standing anxiously in a semicircle, watching as Greg and Daniel worked with a flashlight, trying to diagnose our problem. Worried they knew only as much as I did about engines, I kept my eyes on Potter, hoping to guilt him into action.

"We don't know what it is," Greg said, stepping out from under the raised hood, wiping his hands on the front of his jeans. "We just know it won't start."

"Potter's a Legacy mechanic," I said, calling him out.

"You wanna strong arm me, threaten to gang up on me, but now you want my help? No, way!" Potter said, waving all of us off. "You guys know it all. Figure this one out yourselves."

Greg looked as though he had a response, but I spoke up before him.

"We're all here together, Potter. We're stuck here means you're stuck here, too. So I say you get under that hood and see if you can help us out."

Potter stared angrily at me, then at Greg and Daniel, finally kicking up dirt with the toe of his boot and stomped to the front of the bus.

"Get out the way," he barked at Daniel, snatching the flashlight out of his hand.

Potter climbed up on the bumper, leaning all the way over the engine, appearing as though he would fall in. Seconds later, he climbed out.

"Good news is," Potter said, "the alternator is busted, but I can fix it with my eyes closed."

I heard a combined sigh of relief among us.

"What's the bad news?" Daniel asked.

"Unless there's a Auto Zone down the street where we can get the part, which I know there isn't, we need to start thinking about walking."

# 16

"We're not walking," I said.

"Then we ain't going nowhere, because this bus ain't moving," Potter said, intentionally brushing my shoulder as he walked passed me.

"Are you sure?"

That was Greg. Potter faced him, both boys standing on the soft dirt shoulder of the road. Looking as though he wanted to hit him, Potter spoke sarcastically saying, "Naw, I'm not sure. I'd rather stay out here in the dark than get to where we're going. But like I said, that ain't happening. Not before we get an alternator." He turned away shaking his head, then as an afterthought, changed direction, started toward me, pointing a finger in my face. With the other hand, he drew my attention to Toni, standing a few feet away, her arms crossed over her chest, hands clamped to opposite shoulders, fighting the night chill.

"See that girl over there?" Potter said, stopping just in front of me, the tip of his finger an inch from my nose. "Before you came banging on our door, we were fine. We were safe. We were warm, and we were fine. You tell us we have no choice but to come with you, then you put us on a bus that breaks down." He stepped closer to me, nearly bumping me, then quickly turned to Greg, his palm outstretched. Greg had already started over. "You need to stay right there," Potter told him. "I'm not gonna touch her, but this is between me and Shea."

Greg looked as though he found what Potter said reasonable then leaned back on his heals. Potter turned back to finish dealing with me.

"I don't deserve this. I had gotten my life together, was working over at the garage, I was Legacy owner, doing everything I was supposed to. I found a good woman," Potter said, glancing over at Toni. "Yeah, I messed up here and there along the way, made a couple of mistakes, but I haven't been arrested for nothing in like six months," he said, turning to the group as though important that they believed him. "You can even ask Shea."

"Yeah," I nodded. Dad hadn't had to drag Potter, cuffed and kicking, into the jail in a while. "That's right," I co-signed.

"Then the air turns. It's just not fair. I don't deserve this."

"None of us do," Greg said.

Potter spun, shot a hateful stare at him. "I'm not talking about any of you. I'm talking about me. I'm gonna be a father soon, and I'm out here in the dirt and pitch black, and Toni's there carrying my baby."

"Guess God doesn't like you," someone said.

Like a dog trying to follow the path of a ball that hadn't actually been thrown, Potter spun, trying to catch from where the remark came. Unable to see that it had come from Oliver as I had, Potter turned back to me.

"With all this crap going down, my son is my future. He's all I've got, all I care about." Potter leaned closer to me, placed his lips near my ear and whispered. "If something happens to that baby because you can't get us to D.C. like you said, you'll be very sorry, Shea. That's my promise to you."

"Understood," I said, staring into his eyes, knowing he was right. Responsibility for them was on me now. "Ideas?" I asked, as everyone stood around, pulling the collars of their jackets up to their ears, blowing warm breath into the cups of their freezing palms, hopping about in place to keep warm against the night chill.

"How long were we driving?" Daniel asked.

"Half an hour or so," Greg said. "We might have gone twenty five, maybe thirty miles."

"Twenty five miles of a two hundred mile trip. That's not bad," I said, trying to stay positive.

"Not bad for who?" Kendall said, taking short, quick steps toward me, wearing a mini skirt, tights and heals. "You could never do anything right in high school. I don't know how you got elected to take us to the capital."

"I didn't get elected," I said. "Sloane planned this trip. But since she's dead now," I said, hating the reality of those words, "I'm doing what I can to pull this off."

"You're doing a horrible job. The bus breaking—was that one of Sloane's plans?" Kendall said.

"The bus is on me," I heard Greg say from somewhere. "It's my bus. It should've been better serviced."

Kendall's stare landed on Greg and immediately softened as if pleased by what she saw. "Greg. Greg Gary, right? I remember you," she smiled, wagging a finger at him. "You went to homecoming with Shea two years ago. She did that awful thing to you and—"

"Yeah, that was me. What do you need, Kendall?" Greg asked, his tone all business.

Kendall walked across the gravel over to him, only stumbling once in her heels then looked him at him with a smile and a nod as though considering him for a date.

"You've changed a lot since I've seen you last." She tapped a finger to her chin. "I don't blame you for the bus. The way Shea rushed all of us out, it gave no one enough time to properly prepare. So you're okay with me," Kendall said. She reached out and patted Greg twice on the shoulder before very carefully, walking back to stand in front of Beth.

"Now that that's over," I said. "I was asking if anyone had any—"

I couldn't finish my sentence for Greg grabbed me tight by the arm and held out a hand, gesturing for everyone to remain quiet. His eyes narrowed, his stare focusing over my shoulder into the tree line behind me. He nodded to Daniel, and Daniel, quiet and careful, walked up beside Greg, staring in the same direction, toward the dense wall of trees.

"What?" I whispered.

Greg raised a finger to his lips. "There's someone out there." Then to Daniel: "You hear?"

A twig broke in the dark spaces between the trees.

"I hear." Daniel nodded. "Check it out? On three?"

His hand still around my arm, Greg nodded then turned to Potter. "You in on three?"

Potter stepped in front of Toni, extended an arm over her belly, as if to protect his child from whatever might come out of the woods. He nodded, whispered, "Yeah."

"One…" Daniel said.

Greg released me.

"Two…" Greg said, taking a step to my right as Daniel and Potter lowered their shoulders like sprinters about to explode from their starting blocks.

"Three!" Daniel said, and the boys darted away.

I spun, watched them run toward the trees, saw as the darkness reached out and gobbled them up. As if from behind a dark curtain, we heard the boys thrashing through leaves, blindly calling to one another: sounds of a skirmish, snap of branches breaking underfoot, then a high-pitched scream from an unfamiliar voice, and Potter crying out in pain.

"Potter!" Toni shrieked, attempting to run for the trees. Oliver was behind her. He grabbed her by the wrist and held her there. We all stood frozen.

A moment later, by the little bit of moonlight that reached us, we saw a stranger emerge from the trees.

Beth gasped as I reached for my gun. Then from behind the boy, we saw that Greg and Daniel held him by either of his arms. Potter limped, slowed by what looked like a sprained ankle, behind the three of them, wincing in pain.

The boy, whoever he was—it was too dark to get a good look at him—struggled and fought weakly in between Daniel and Greg. He was thin from what I could make of him, his clothes and face filthy, like he had crawled through the dirt to the place where he was just found.

"Let me go! I wasn't doing anything!" he protested, the sound of his voice striking a familiar chord. Had I head it before? No, it couldn't have been, I told myself. But something compelled me to move toward them, squinting, trying to see through the dark, confirm what my gut was questioning.

"He was spying on us," Greg said, pushing the boy stumbling forward. "We don't know who he is, but—"

But I did, recognizing him that moment. It was him!

My vision tunneled as I marched quickly toward the stranger, pulling my gun, and with just a few feet separating us, I aimed the weapon at his forehead.

Seeing me coming, the boy shut his eyes, screamed, and dropped to his knees, crumpling to the dirt, his arms elevated over his head, as he was still held by Greg and Daniel.

They ordered me to stand down, but I remained where I was, my fists wrapped around my weapon, the pistol shaking in my hand.

"What the hell, Shea?" Greg yelled.

"It's him! It's Jonny!" I cried. "He was with the boys that broke into my house! He was the one that ran."

Greg and Daniel shook the boy loose, letting him fall on his back into the dirt.

"You shot my dog! You shot, Tornado!" I yelled, stepping over him, holding the gun on him. Jonny held his hands over his face as though they were bulletproof.

"But he's alive. Your dog's alive, right?" he squealed.

Tornado was on the bus, in my seat, his nose pressed to one of the windows, smearing slobber marks all over it, barking bloody murder, probably having recognized the boy as I had.

"They wanted to kill him. But I did what I did so they wouldn't," Jonny whimpered from behind his splayed fingers. "Please! The dog's only alive because of me."

"You broke into my house!" I shouted over his cries.

"I had no choice. They forced me!"

"I don't believe you," I said, jabbing the point of my gun down at him. "I said I would kill you! Now I will."

"Shea! Don't do it!" Greg yelled. He and Daniel crouched in front of me, looking like they'd jump *me* if I continued to threaten the boy.

"Please!" Jonny screamed, his voice so high pitched I wanted to cover my ears. "When they wanted to kill you and your sister, who was it that stopped them?"

The horrifying moment flashed through my brain, Sloane lowering her head, closing her eyes, as if to accept her death.

"By suggesting they *use* us." I said.

"But it worked," Jonny cried. "It made time for you to be rescued. If not for me, you'd be dead."

Still staring at him over the sight of my gun, I tried to disprove his story, but he was right. "You're with them," I said, still not wanting to believe him.

"I ran just like you said," Jonny said. "If I was with them, why would I have left?"

Shaking my head, I didn't see the boy in front of me, lying helpless, cowering on the ground, but the boy who held a gun to my back, that barked orders at me and my sister, and threatened us. I dropped a knee down onto his shoulder, smashing it into the ground, causing him to cry. My hands still trembling around the gun, I did everything possible not to trust what he was saying. Everything he had said was true, and as much as I wanted to make him pay for braking into my home, what he had done was instrumental in saving us. I holstered my gun. "Get up," I said. "But make the wrong move and I don't have to tell you what'll happen."

On the bus, Jonny asked about food, said he was starving, and I recalled while the other boys gorged on the little that Sloane and I had left, Jonny was given nothing.

"Anyone want to share with him?" I asked.

No one offered, so I dug out a short can of mixed fruit in heavy syrup with a pull top lid and tossed it to him. He took it to the back of the bus, sat down in the very last seat, ripped off the top, turned the can up to his lips like a man dying from thirst, allowing the food and thick juice to slide into his open mouth.

In the front of the bus, Greg stood over my shoulder, watched as I kept my eyes locked on the boy, while everyone else tried to make themselves comfortable, preparing for the night we'd spend in the bus.

"You don't trust him?" Greg asked.

"Why should I?"

"What he said; he did those things, right?"

"So?"

"Then that's why you trust him."

Licking fruit syrup from his fingers, Jonny peered over his seat at me.

"Sorry, but that's just not enough," I said to Greg, starting down the aisle.

"Where are you going?"

"To talk to him," I said, not looking back at Greg. I stopped beside Jonny's seat, told him to scoot over.

Cradling the empty can of fruit cocktail in both hands, looking as though he thought I might hurt him, Jonny slid across the seat, stopping when his shoulder hit the window. "You got anymore of this?" he asked after I sat. "I'm still hungry."

"Not my problem. You said you weren't a part of that group that broke into my house, why were you with them?"

Jonny set the empty fruit can between his knees as though he might need it for something later. "Been trying to get D.C. for weeks, but didn't want to go alone. I heard what happens to people on the road: robbed, beaten, left for dead, sometimes worse. I thought those last boys were decent people. They weren't."

I stared suspiciously at him. "We drove almost thirty miles. How did you find us if you weren't following?"

"I found a bike. I started back on the path to the capital, and after riding for almost two hours, I saw the bus. I didn't know you were on it. I hid in the trees, hoping that maybe whoever you guys were, you'd be friendly, give me some food, maybe let me ride with you." Jonny stared at me as though wondering if I believed his story. "You are going to the capital, right? Take me with you? Please."

"Bus is busted," I said, standing up, sliding out of the seat. "But even if it was working, no way I'd let you go. Grab your trash. This is where you get off." I walked to the front, pulled the lever to open the door, stood and watched as Jonny took his time, trudging toward me, his head shamefully lowered.

"Hurry up! You got your food, so you're better off than you were."

Stopping halfway up the aisle, he said, "You can't just..." he bent over some, fearfully looked out one of the bus windows at the cold and dark awaiting him. "You can't leave me out there alone. I won't make it. Please!"

I hurried down the aisle after Jonny. He ran back toward his seat, shrunk in his seat, wrapping himself up in a ball. No one spoke, but I felt the members of my group glaring at me from me over their seats, seemingly questioning how I could be so mean as to kick this kid out into the night.

"Shea," Greg said, walking to the bus door. "A word?" He stepped off the bus.

I glanced over at Daniel. From his seat, he hunched his shoulders like he had no idea of what Greg wanted to talk about either.

Outside, I walked past Greg, not interested in anything he had to say.

"Getting rid of him does what?" Greg asked, following me onto the shoulder of the road.

"Makes us safer. I don't know who he is."

Greg glanced back toward the bus, pushed a hand over the tiny curls in his closely cut hair. "When you didn't walk Tornado, when I didn't see you outside, like I said, I knew something was wrong. And when I saw those boys inside your house, there was no question in my mind that Daniel and I were going in there, even though I knew how things would most likely end up." Greg stepped closer to me, lowering his voice. "I was prepared to do whatever it took, even give my life to save yours. But I didn't have to do that, because that boy," Greg pointed back at the bus, "that boy who looks frightened of his own shadow, bought me enough time to get you out of there. For that, I think you owe him."

"Owe him?" I said, astonished.

"You heard me," Greg said, staring seriously at me. "He did right by you. Not turning on someone in their time of need is how you reward them when they've done right by you."

I sensed this conversation was no longer just about Jonny, but how Greg thought I had treated him two years ago.

"So what would you have me do?" I asked.

"Let him go with us. It's the right thing to do. The more we are, the better, the stronger it makes us. Isn't that what Sloane said?"

Looking back at the bus, I saw Jonny in one of the windows, staring out at me with round, uncertain eyes.

"He's dangerous, I'm telling you." I said. "I don't trust him."

"I know," Greg said. "And I'll be the first one to throw him out a window if he tries anything, but he's earned this. Even you should be able to see that."

Another stab at me for being such an awful friend. Was this how it was going to be between me and Greg from now on? Trying to avoid that at all cost, I said, "About what happened—"

Greg closed the short distance between us so fast I thought he wouldn't stop, just run over me. His voice hushed, he said, "Some foolish boy thinks he's in love gets screwed over by a girl who obviously didn't give a damn about him. What does that matter now? Really, Shea? What does it matter?"

"It matters."

"Not to me," he said. "Our parents are dead, everything is burning, and we're all dying, so why should I care about what you think?" In his voice I could hear that he was still hurting.

I swallowed hard, choking back the lump in my throat, suppressing the tears I was ashamed to let him see fall. I said, lowering my eyes, "I guess you shouldn't."

# 17

I awakened, my body aching from the contortions I had to perform to sleep on the bus seat. Bright morning sun hit me in the face, and already started to warm the interior of the bus. I felt a twinge of anxiety about the time we had lost. I raised my wrist over my head, checked my watch as Tornado squirmed underneath me, his body warm like some giant grizzly bear pelt.

It was just after seven in the morning.

I stood, looked down the aisle, saw no heads, just feet dangling over the edge of seats, blankets draped over them.

"Hey," I said. "Everybody, we have to go."

No one responded.

That came as no surprise. We were up until a little past three in the morning.

After my conversation with Greg about Jonny, I climbed back on the bus and walked into a discussion about what went on moments before we sped away from our homes.

"The fire," Beth was saying, her hands resting on the back of her seat, peering over it as if for protection against an oncoming threat. "I thought we weren't going to make it. I thought it was going to catch us as we drove away."

"You think it was the Burners?" Toni whispered.

"No such thing," Potter said. "Just nonsense somebody made up."

"Then how are the fires getting started?" April asked, not sounding very concerned, leaning against her sister, her head resting on Beth's shoulder.

"It's that time of year," Potter guessed. "Like the fires in California. There's a season where they just start and burn all the trees down."

"So, no Burners?" April said, sounding as though she didn't fully buy Potter's explanation.

"Nah," he said, confidently.

"Dude, you're wrong," Daniel said, standing, one knee on his seat. "They're out there."

"How do you know?" Potter asked.

"I had a friend," Daniel said. "He told me one of them tried to recruit him."

"Recruit?" I gasped, the word slipping out without me wanting it to.

"Some guy at our school," Daniel said, glancing at me. "Asked my friend if he wanted to come to a meeting with him and some friends to read scriptures. He gave him literature, stuff about the end of the world, about the apocalypse...I don't know, fire cleansing the earth stuff. Like what was here has to be destroyed in order for us to start over."

I glanced at Greg. He looked back, not letting me in on what he was thinking.

"So, they recruit?" I asked. "Like they're actively looking for members?"

"Yeah. But the guy didn't say why."

"So there can be more of them to burn everything down faster," Kendall said to me with a dramatic wave of her hand. "Don't you know anything?"

"So you're saying these Burner people are for real?" Toni said. "People like you and me?"

Daniel nodded.

Everyone was in quiet contemplation about what was just said. Feeling as though I was being watched, I turned to see Jonny staring at me then quickly turn away.

I pushed aside the thoughts from last night, narrowed my eyes against the morning sunlight, walked to the front of the stalled bus, and honked the horn three long times. Greg was first to pop up from the seat he had taken near the back of the bus, then Beth and April, Potter and Toni.

Eyes squinting, yawning mouths opened wide, fists stretched high over shoulders, the group started to rouse, Kendall yelling, “What the hell, Shea?”

“Everybody get up!” I said. “It’s time we get on our way.”

## 18

With the addition of Jonny, who I never let completely out of my sight, there were ten of us. I didn't believe it was yet as hot as it would get today, but some of us were already taking off our jackets, dabbing sweat from our necks and faces. We had been dragging along for hours, shoulders slumped, hands on our hips, desperately needing a break, and I felt responsible for putting us out among the elements. We'd be walking until we were able to find the next vehicle, so we no longer had the luxury of cargo space. We had to separate what was most valuable to each of us, leaving the rest behind.

Before starting out this morning, we spread the road map on the ground, and April did the calculation on how long it would take us to make it to the capital if we weren't lucky enough to find another working vehicle.

"A hundred and seventy five miles, walking at three miles an hour, for ten hours a day, will take us six days—more or less—to get there," April said, dropping the stick she used to do her calculations in the dirt. She clapped the mess from her palms, as everyone stood silent, our eyes darting back and forth, each of us seemingly waiting for the other to say what we all were thinking.

"We need to find more transportation," Potter said.

"I don't think any of us has enough food for six days, do we?" Beth whispered, as if not wanting to startle anyone.

"We'll find another car or truck or something, right?" Oliver said, pushing his glasses up on his nose. "I mean we have to. There's no way that everyone here can make that kind of walk."

I saw his eyes land on Toni.

"We'll find more transportation," Greg said. "We will."

"What if we don't?" Toni said.

"Then we'll walk the entire hundred and seventy five miles," I said. "And we'll be forced to make the food we have last."

Continuing on our slow path to D.C., I had trouble blocking out what Daniel said on the bus about the Burners. I had been watching him, walking in the front of our group with Greg most of the way. When he fell behind, away from Greg, I hurried up to him.

"How you making it?" I asked, bumping his elbow with mine.

"Shea," he smiled, as though we were old friends who hadn't seen each other in years. "Keeping an eye out for any and everything, not thinking about how many miles we have."

"Tell me about it," I said. Even though I had only known Daniel for a short time, I'd grown to like him. Whether or not Greg choosing him as a best friend had anything to do with my acceptance of him, I wasn't sure. "About the Burners..." I said looking over my shoulders, making sure no one was in earshot of what I was about to say. "You ever hear of them killing?"

Daniel looked surprised. "No. Why do you ask?"

"No reason," I said, thinking it best not to tell him. We were already spooked out enough without thinking that these Burner people might be out here killing kids.

We walked two more hours along the hot pavement of Interstate 95, past scores of deserted vehicles, some of them smashed into trees, some into the highway guardrails, most appeared to have just stopped in the middle of the road. The fuel doors were open on nearly every one of them, gas caps missing, or sitting on the ground beside the car—indicators that the vehicles had already been siphoned for what gas was in the tanks.

"Shea!" April whispered, yanking on my arm.

I ignored her, keeping my eyes on the road counting off in my head, the next ten minutes until we'd break again.

"Shea!" April said again, tugging at me more forcefully.

"What, April!" I said stopping, as everyone else dragged on.

"There!" She pointed toward a grassy knoll sloping away from the interstate shoulder. I took a step in the direction she pointed, looked up into the thatch of trees and saw movement. Another step, and I thought I saw a girl about my age, bent over a shovel, stomping the spade into the ground, hoisting up dirt and tossing it over her shoulder.

"C'mon," I said softly to April, letting the others march ahead, not wanting to stop the progress of the entire group.

As April and I approached, the girl hadn't noticed us. She was making a lot of noise, grunting and sobbing, hoisting dirt out of a huge hole, a dead body laying a foot away from her. The girl wore hiking boots, big-pocketed cargo pants, leather gloves, and a parka around her waist, the sleeves knotted in front of her. Dirty light brown hair hung over the suntanned skin of her face, a grimy pink bandanna tied at the back of her neck, hung below her chin as she breathed heavily. Two backpacks were thrown off to the side.

"What do we do?" April whispered.

"We talk to her," I said, stepping out from behind the cover of a tree. "Hello?" I called to the girl, knowing nothing else to say.

Without acknowledging us, the girl quickly tossed the shovel aside, snatched a double-barreled shotgun from the ground, cocked it and pointed it at us.

"Take another step and I'll rip you in half!" she warned.

April raised her hands, as I did.

Behind us, I was startled by the sound of rifles readying.

"Don't do it!" Greg called out.

I spun to see our entire group standing behind us, staring at the girl and the grave she had only half finished digging. Greg and Daniel stared down the sights of their rifles, their fingers tensed on the triggers.

"Put down the shotgun!" Greg said. "Or we'll—"

"Or you'll what?" the girl said, sounding as though she had already lost everything, and didn't care if her life was next.

"No!" I ran toward Greg, forced the barrel of his weapon down, then begged Daniel to lower his. When I turned back to the girl, she still had her gun pointed at me.

"Put that down. No one's trying to hurt you," I pleaded.

"I don't know that, and I don't know you." She shifted her aim from me to Greg, then to Daniel.

"No, no! Keep it on me," I told her, not wanting her to spook the boys. "You need any help?" I glanced down at the body at her feet. It was a boy, maybe her boyfriend, or possibly a relative. He looked not much older than Sloane, but bore a resemblance to the girl: same smooth tanned skin and dark hair.

"Don't look at him!" the girl shouted.

"I'm sorry, I'm sorry," I said, feeling I knew the pain she was going through. "We have shovels. Let us help."

"She said she doesn't want us here. Let's just leave," Potter said.

"We're not leaving!" I said over my shoulder. I turned back to the girl. She lifted the barrel of the shotgun higher, like she planned to shoot me in the face. I felt the tension in the boys growing behind me, knew they were moments from doing what I'm sure they thought had to be done. I turned to the group. "Leave. All of you!"

"What are you doing, Shea?" Toni asked.

"Please, all of you—leave. I want to talk to her alone."

Greg stared at me, shook his head as though what I was doing was foolish, then asked that everyone move back toward the interstate.

"You too, April," I told her, when it appeared that she wasn't going anywhere. "Don't worry. I'll be fine."

"You sure? Because..." she reached for the gun in her ankle holster. "I can cover you."

"Put that back. I'm sure, April." I gave her a reassuring look. "But thank you."

I watched April follow the others down the grassy slope and out to the interstate, then turned back to the girl. It appeared she had relaxed a bit. I pulled my ruck sack off, set it on the ground, grabbed my collapsible shovel from my pack, starting to erect it as I walked toward her.

"What are you doing?" the girl said.

"I'm gonna help you with this." I climbed down into the ditch she was digging, purposely not making eye contact, figuring she wouldn't gun me down without looking me in the eye first. I jabbed my shovel into the dirt, then looked up at her. "If you're going to shoot me, get on with it," I said. "But you'll have to dig another hole, because I'm going to be lying in this one." I tried a smile. It was lost on her.

The girl looked over her shoulder, saw that my group was no longer in sight, then set down her gun and picked up her shovel. "Why are you doing this?"

"My name is Shea." I held up my hand to her. "What's yours?"

Skeptical, she looked down at my hand, then stared me in the eyes, scrutinizing me for what seemed a lifetime. Finally she took my hand, and shook. "I'm Angie."

"And who was he?" I nodded to the body of the boy. "If you don't mind me asking."

Angie glanced down then quickly looked away, seemingly devastated by the loss. "My brother."

"The air?"

"Yeah."

"I'm sorry."

"You're helping me. Why?"

"Because I know what you're going through. I buried my sister last night."

While we worked, Angie told me that she and her brother were on their way to D.C. as we were.

"We lost our parents to the air a while ago, and we thought we could just stay hold. When gangs started breaking into the houses in our neighborhood, we decided it was better to take our chances on the road."

After Angie and I finished digging, we gently dragged her brother Kenneth over—me taking his feet, Angie carefully taking his head—and lay him in the grave.

We stood on opposite sides of the ditch, staring down at him, his arms crossed over his chest, his eyes closed. He was a handsome young man. He had just turned 20 three weeks ago, Angie said.

"Would you like me to get the others to acknowledge his passing while you say—"

"No. They didn't know him. Them being here, I don't know, wouldn't feel right."

"Do you want me to leave?"

"No." She looked at me, gratefully. "You're helping me. You didn't have to. I think you should stay. If you want to."

The words Angie spoke to her brother before we covered him, I could not hear; I had taken a number of respectful steps backward, lowering my head. On her knees, she shed tears, cried aloud, a piece of cloth—his bandana or something—clutched in her fist and pressed to her lips.

It had taken Angie and me a little over an hour to bury him. It was time my group couldn't afford to lose. As we walked back toward my people, they were all sitting under the shade of some trees. By the looks on their faces, that they weren't happy.

"Her name is Angie Mathews and she's coming with us. Is that okay with everyone?" I asked.

"Seems like you already made up your mind. Is that how this goes now?" Potter said, standing. "You make all the decisions for us."

"I'm sorry you feel that way, but that's not what this is. You have a problem with her coming with us, Potter?" I said, taking a step closer to him. We glared across a six foot gap.

"Whatever," he said, walking away.

"Does anyone else have a problem with Angie coming with us?" I looked over the group. Most of them went about their business hoisting their packs back onto their shoulders, including Greg. Daniel on the other hand, seemed interested in our new companion; he couldn't seem to keep his eyes off of her.

"Daniel," I said, startling him out of his trance. "Would you like to meet Angie?"

She turned to see whom I was speaking to.

"We're about to move out," Daniel stammered, stuffing something into his bag and zipping it up. "Busy now. Maybe another time."

“Yeah, okay,” I said.

## 19

The evening sun going down, a cool breeze passing over us, we had stopped before walking our last two hours of the day.

We hadn't had any luck finding a vehicle, although again, we stood among more cars: doors hanging open, windows down, and inside, glove boxes open, the contents spilled out over the passenger seats and floor matts. We checked them anyway, found that none of them worked or contained nothing of value.

I stood just off the side of the interstate pavement, watching the others.

Daniel whispered something. Greg nodding and avoided eye contact with me, even though I figured he knew I was staring right at him.

Toni sat on the highway guardrail, looking particularly durable for a girl four months pregnant, her parka draped over her shoulders, the hood pulled halfway up over her blonde hair, as she sipped from a bottle of water that passed between her and Potter.

Beth stood holding a compact mirror steady in front of Kendall as she applied lipstick, a little blush to her cheeks, and fluffed her hair with a pink, plastic comb. I felt the overwhelming urge to walk over there, snatch the mirror from Beth, throw it to the ground and stomp it into glass dust, then smack the cosmetics from Kendall's hand. I'd tell Kendall that how cute she was, what brand of clothes she wore, or how many Twitter followers she had, didn't matter anymore. Afterward, I'd turn to Beth, tell her that Kendall was no better, or no more important than she was, and that Kendall should feel as fortunate to have her as a friend as the other way around. But I knew that would change nothing: Beth secretly had always wanted to be accepted by Kendall and the popular girls. I couldn't blame her; two years ago, I felt the same way. But when I went to her after being confronted in the hallway by Kendall and her fashion model wannabe girlfriends, told Beth they were interested in me joining them, Beth said: "Why would you wanna do that?"

"Because they're like the coolest, most popular, in-the-know chicks at our school," I said, still high and excited for being asked.

"No, Shea. They are the lamest, shallowest, most superficial girls in our town, and they only go through the trouble of getting all glamour-girled up to distract people from the fact they have zero brains."

"Okay," I admitted. "You're probably right. But still, isn't it cool?" I said, wanting my friend to be as excited about my invitation as I was. "Once I'm in, I'll put a good word in for you. You'll be part of the clique in no time."

Beth looked me up and down, scrunched her nose as if a foul odor was coming off me, and shook her head. "No thanks, Shea. I thought you knew who you were and had more confidence than to have to run with lames like Kendall. I guess not," she said, turning her back and walking off.

Everything she said to me that day was right. Turns out Beth didn't mean a single word of it, was just angry with Kendall because the opportunity hadn't been presented to her instead of me.

But when all of Kendall's followers died or left for D.C., and Kendall was looking for replacements, Beth jumped at the chance, feeling honored to play Kendall's personal assistant.

I focused my attention again on Jonny, where it had been most of the day, walking the interstate, staring at the back of his head as it bobbed on his skinny neck, his filthy t-shirt draped over his narrow shoulders. Something wasn't right about him or his actions: constantly looking over his shoulder, looking frightfully in every direction, as though someone was after him.

He sat under a tree, stripping the bark from a small branch with dirty fingernails, longer what should've been on any boy's hand. I strolled toward him, and seeing me coming, he straightened up.

"Thanks for letting me go with you guys," he said before I could speak. "You didn't have to—"

"Wasn't my decision. I wanted to leave you where we found you."

"Well, thanks to whoever then."

"You seem jumpy." I said after he took a few furtive glances up the interstate. "Everything okay?"

"What?" he said, his eyes back on me.

"Unsettled...you seem spooked, like you're worried about something happening. Everything cool?"

"Just hungry. Everyone else has food, but I—"

"I'll see what I can find you." I stepped closer, bent at the waist, hands on my knees and spoke softly to him. "Other than that? There's nothing I should know? Nothing you have to tell me. Because if there is, I think it'd be in your best interest—"

"No," Jonny said, seemingly hoping to erase any doubt in my mind, his long, straight hair flittering across his forehead. "There's nothing."

I held his stare for a moment, trying to get a better feel for the boy, then did my best to smile. "Okay, I'll see about that food for you."

## 20

As we started our tenth and final hour of walking, rumbling came from above, and wind whipped through the trees. We walked in a loose formation, but no one more than a few steps from the other. April held Tornado by his leash, the dog walking slowly and obediently at her right side.

I trotted up the ten paces Greg and Daniel kept in front of the group.

"We're going to have to find somewhere to pitch camp for the night. Okay?" I said, walking between them.

"We were just saying the same thing," Daniel said, looking at me, then further back to Angie. Catching the knowing smile on my face, he shook his head, smiled a little and said, "I know what you're thinking, Shea, but one broken heart is enough for me."

"A girl can dream, right?" I said.

"Yeah, whatever," he smiled. "We'll keep an eye out for a decent spot."

"It should be soon," I said, starting to worry about the toll the miles we had covered would take on our group. I was about to take my place back between Beth and April when I saw a small gathering of people sitting on a highway guardrail, several yards ahead.

"Greg!" I whispered, nudging him.

"I see them. No big deal," he said, calmly, still walking. "They don't bother us. We won't bother them." He turned to Daniel, told him to fall back and tell everyone to ignore the people we were about to encounter.

Our eyes forward, we kept moving, but as we walked passed them, I couldn't help but sum them up: four boys, stuffing their faces with whatever they spooned up out of the cans they held. Beside them, sitting further down, were three girls. I guessed they ranged in age from 10 to 16 years old: eyes lowered, long, tangled hair hanging over their faces. They wore thin t-shirts: no way enough to protect them against the evening chill.

I stared at them. Not one looked up.

"Keep moving," Greg urged, his voice low.

"This doesn't look right," I whispered.

"It's none of our business. Keep moving!" he whispered harshly, grabbing firmly to my arm.

"I can't," I said, pulling away and taking steps toward the boys. "Where you guys headed?" I asked, looking them over: all pretty thin, road dirty, one boy wearing a Mickey Mouse t-shirt, another must've been missing an eye; there was a patch where I assumed it once was. They wore no masks and two of them had handguns stuffed into the waists of their jeans.

"Nowhere," what appeared the oldest boy said. He was maybe eighteen, his hair shiny black and slicked back on his head. "We're just walking to wherever the road take us."

"That's right," the boy next to him said, smiling. He was tall, better than 6'4" and extremely thin. "You guys headed to D.C?"

"Yeah," I said.

"You probably should be going then," the older boy said, looking up at the low, dark clouds. "It's gonna rain like hell."

"You all aren't hungry?" I said, taking a few steps over to the girls.

"They aren't," another of their group answered.

I didn't look back to see which one, but said, my eyes still on the girls, "I didn't ask you. I asked them."

"Shea," Greg said, hurrying over, grabbing me by the shoulder, then to the boys, said: "You all take care, and don't get stuck in the rain."

The slick-haired boy nodded and watched closely as Greg forced me away. All the while, I watched the girls over my shoulder.

Half an hour later, we stood on a plot of grassy land behind an interstate welcome center. It was where we'd sleep for the night.

I walked over to Greg and Daniel, watched them as they set up their tent. Greg glanced at me then back down to the work he was doing, as though not wanting to be bothered.

"It's not right for us to leave them like that," I said.

Annoyed, Greg set down the brick he was about to whack one of the tent stakes with.

"Them?" he stood. "You're concerned with them when we have almost a dozen people here needing to travel a hundred and seventy five miles, and you're worried about some girls you don't even know."

"We should go back and get them," I said.

"Yeah, okay. Go back and then do what, exactly?"

"Tell them to release the girls."

"I didn't see any cuffs, no ropes. They could've been there because they wanted to be."

"Really? Is that what you think? Fine! You don't have to come." I turned and started away from him. Greg was quickly behind me, grabbing me by the arm again.

"You are not going there!" he said turning me.

"Who's stopping me?" I said loud enough to draw attention. Beth, April, and Kendall starting toward us, questions on their faces. The others followed behind.

"Lover's quarrel?" Potter sniped.

"Shut up!" I said.

"The people we saw a while back," Greg said to the group surrounding us.

"The girls?" April said.

"Yeah," Greg said. "Shea has it in her head the girls were being held against their will, that they might be in some kind of trouble."

"That's what I think, too," April said.

"It looked that way to me too," Oliver said.

"Anyone else think that?" Greg asked.

Toni and Beth slowly raised their hands.

"See!" I said. "We have to do something."

“Agreeing with you on what you believe is happening back there, and agreeing to do something are two different things,” Greg said.

“Then take a vote,” I said. “Whatever is decided, that’s what we’ll do.”

“Fine,” Greg said. “It’s a stupid idea, but those who feel we should actually stick our noses in business that has nothing to do with us, raise your hands.”

I watched as April’s and Oliver’s hands rose, Beth’s, then no one else’s. I shot Toni a look, demanding she vote with me.

“There’s too much to lose,” she said, everyone hearing her, Greg nodding his head, as he looked righteously at me.

I turned to Daniel, needing his vote. He looked away, and I knew he was not on my side.

“Four votes to six. It’s the right decision,” Greg said. “Lets pitch our tents, get a good night’s sleep, and hopefully we can find a working vehicle in the morning.”

# 21

For two hours, I stared from my sleeping bag at the low ceiling of my tent, listening to noises of the approaching storm, while I thought about the girls we encountered on the road. Despite how much I tried, I couldn't live with leaving them there.

I unzipped my sleeping bag, threw back the fold, grabbed my handguns and holstered them—one in my belt, the other in my shoulder harness.

After opening the tent flap, I heard the crackle of the campfire going. I climbed out, zipped the tent closed, and walked over. Oliver sat on a bench, stoking the fire in the visitor center trashcan with a long branch.

"How's watch?" I asked.

The flames lighting his face and reflecting off his glasses, he said, "Good. Where you going?"

"Gotta tinkle," I said, feeling stupid, after saying that.

His eyes on my guns, I saw doubt pop into his head.

"I shouldn't be long."

"Okay."

I walked away, keeping a close eye on Greg's tent, hoping he didn't climb out of it.

"Think you might need help?" I heard Oliver ask.

I turned, wondering what kind of perverted question that was.

"Dangerous trying to go rescue those girls alone, don't' you think?" he said, tossing a chunk of wood into the fire. "That is where you're going, right?"

"Just wanna make sure I was wrong about what I thought," I assured him, keeping my voice low as not to awaken others.

"What if you're right?"

"That's a bridge I'll have to cross, you know."

"Take Greg's friend with you," Oliver said, seeming to show concern for my wellbeing. I was surprised, considering how I treated him the first time we met.

"Daniel?"

"He looked like he was on your side, just didn't want to go against his friend."

"You might be right, but I can't do that. Don't wanna risk him telling Greg."

"If I insisted?" Oliver said, pulling his stick from the fire and setting it down to stand, walk over to me, as if to physically detain me. "I know you think what you're doing for those girls is right, but you go in there, get hurt or worse, where does that leave us, if you're the leader? You are the leader, right?"

I had no idea. But that had nothing to do with the girls. "I won't do anything crazy," I said. "I'll just go get confirmation, and if I'm right, I'll come back here for help."

"Promise?" Oliver said.

"Promise."

The clouds were thick; it was almost pitch black. Although I couldn't see them, I heard the conversation between a girl and a couple of boys as they neared me on the interstate. The girl said she thought it was unsafe to be out that late. As they passed me, their forms barely visible in the darkness, one of the boys made brief eye contact, raised his chin acknowledging me, as the other boy overconfidently told the girl she had nothing to worry about. That boy was wrong; they shouldn't have been out so late, and neither should I have been. Like Greg had said, the girls I believed were being held had nothing to do with us, so they shouldn't have mattered. But what I didn't tell Greg was that this wasn't just about saving those girls, but saving myself from the guilt of failing my father. Rescuing them would fix what I had messed up months ago in that gas station convenience store, while that man held my father around the neck, and Dad begged for me to "Take the shot!"

I remembered having my gun trained on the man. I steadied myself then, settled on the exposed side of the criminal's face. I'd sneak a shot into that corner of his eye. I took a deep breath in.

"I said put it down!" the man cried again, tightening his grip around Dad's throat.

I set my aim. I let the air out.

"Drop the gun and he lives! Or else, I swear I'll blow his brains out! I swear!" Spittle flew from the man's lips, his voice shrill, he was seemingly determined to do what he had promised.

I squeezed the trigger to the point just before discharging the weapon, realizing only then I preferred the guarantee of my father living than rolling the dice of me possibly killing him with a misaimed bullet. I released the trigger, slowly removed one of my hands from it then lowered the gun to my side.

Both Dad's and the man's eyes widened.

"Shea, don't—" Dad cried.

But before Dad could finish, the man smiled at me then discharged his weapon.

The sound of that shot, the explosion of blood and bone, the last look on Dad's face: disappointment, sadness, fear of what might become of me, aware he would die a second later is something I'll never forget.

After the man killed Dad, he threw him aside, turned the gun on me and started shooting. I had spun, already in horrified retreat, head down, blindly firing off shots behind me, busting out of the gas station, the glass in the door shattering as bullets whizzed past my head. I ran to the car, shots pelting and piercing the metal skin of the cruiser as I threw open the door, screaming, arm shielding my head, scrambling across the seat, turning the ignition key and bringing the car's big engine to life. More bullets: the passenger window shattered. I yanked on the column shifter, stomped on the gas, raced the car away, the wheels squealing, spitting up smoke, the back end swerving, broadsiding, and toppling over a barrel of trash as I sped off.

Running into the house, breathing heavy, Sloane was sweeping the area rug in the living room. She looked up, knew immediately something was gravely wrong.

"What is it?"

Silently shaking, I was frozen, unable to speak.

"Shea!" Sloane said, dropping the broom. She ran to me, took me by the shoulders. "Where's Dad?"

"A man..." I said, feeling like a fool. I had believed him. He promised me that if I put down my gun he would let Dad live. It was the only reason I didn't take the shot, the only reason I disobeyed Dad, and did what the man said. "...at the gas station shot Dad in the head. I think...no," I corrected, knowing it would be wrong to give my sister false hope. "I know it. Dad is dead."

Sloane grabbed one of the shotguns that stood against the dining room wall, gave me another, snatched me by the arm, and forced me out to the car.

"There. That one," I pointed to the store when the gas station came into view. I didn't want to be there. I didn't want to see the place where I failed Dad and caused his death—didn't want to see the place where Dad lay dead.

Sloane cut the wheel and broke hard, the car skidding to a halt, back end hiking up in front of the store. She threw open her door, turning to me before she exited.

"Come on!" she said, trying to hide the blame I knew she felt for me.

I came out of my thoughts, reassuring myself I was doing the right thing.

I looked around, saw that I was at the exact place we stood hours ago when I asked the girls if they were okay. Thankfully, wind blew many of the clouds away to reveal a full moon that provided just enough light to see where I was going.

I stepped over the guardrail onto the grass and climbed a small embankment that led into a wall of trees. I came out on the other side and saw through the darkness, what looked like a domed, two-man tent. I dropped to my knees behind a fallen tree trunk, hoping I hadn't been seen. There was no campfire, which meant little chance someone was standing guard.

I looked out over the log, catching sight of what appeared to be a pallet of light colored blankets spread across the dirt, three bodies sleeping there. The girls, I told myself.

I ducked, turned, sat on my butt, pressing my back against the log, my pulse racing, my heart pounding. I pulled one of my guns. What to do, Shea? What to do? Scenarios filled my head, some of them I died in. I focused on the ones that had me running behind the girls as we distanced ourselves from this camp unharmed.

I crouched, having not decided on a course of action, but determined to bring the girls back. I breathed deeply, preparing to make my move when I heard quickly approaching footsteps behind me.

I flipped backward, gun held out, about to blanket the space before me with bullets.

"Don't! It's us!" Greg whispered, harshly.

I lowered my weapon, shaking because I had almost shot him and Daniel, who stood beside him.

"We took a vote, and you do this anyway?" Greg said, angrily. "You're coming back with us." He reached out to grab me. I swatted his hand.

"Those girls are down there. See!" I pointed in the direction of the pallet. As they looked, I whispered the plan I just decided on. "No guard. The girls are outside. The guys are in the tent. I go down, wake them, tell the girls to come with me, while you guys cover. In and out—simple."

Silent, Greg turned to Daniel.

"Whatever you think, man, I'm game," Daniel said.

"Can't risk it," Greg said to me. "We need to go."

“See you two back at the camp. I’m going.” I stood, prepared to stomp away like a child throwing a tantrum. Snatching me by my hand, Greg yanked me back down behind the cover of the log.

“Fine!” he conceded.

Not sixty seconds later, after running down to the camp, I stood, gun pulled, over the makeshift bed, the imprints of three bodies huddled under the blankets. I glanced over my shoulder, gave a thumbs up to Greg and Daniel who crouched behind trees, covering me through the scopes on their rifles.

I peeled back the blanket of the body lying nearest me to reveal the sleeping face of the oldest girl. I shook her by the shoulder.

She snored softly, rolling away from me.

“Wake up. Wake up!” I whispered, keeping an eye on the tent thirty feet away. “Wake up!” I said, shaking the girl again. Her lids slowly parted, then seeing me, they rounded with panic. Her mouth sprung open with an impeding scream. I quickly covered her face with my hand.

“Shhh! I’m here to take you guys away from here,” I whispered. “Wake the others,” I said, reaching to pull the blanket down from the girl sleeping next to her.

She forced my hand from over her mouth, begging me not to do it. It was too late. I pulled back the blanket to uncover, not another girl, but one of the boys holding them captive. His eyes blinked; he was only half awake, but when he saw me, he yelled, “Tommy!” then hit me in the chest with the butt of his palm. Knocked off balance, I fell to the ground, my gun jumping from my hand.

One of the girls screamed, and as I lay groping in the darkness to find my weapon, I heard the boy grunting to fight his way out of the tangle of blankets and get to his feet. Further away, I heard rustling in the tent: the other boys waking.

Rolling on my stomach, dirt in my mouth, dust in my eyes, my hand found it’s way around the grip of my gun seconds too late. I was grabbed from behind, flipped onto my back. The boy I had woken stood over me, his gun pointed in my face. Here I was again, about to die because of the stupid decisions I had made. I shut my eyes, crossed my arms over my face, braced for the shot that would kill me. There were two of them then I felt the weight of the boy's dead body.

"Get up, Shea!" I heard Daniel calling. I whipped around, saw Greg and Daniel running toward me, their riffles held in firing position.

"You okay?" Daniel asked, having to raise his voice over that of the girl still screaming. The other girl, who had slept beside the now deceased boy, was awake, crawling on all fours away from the blankets.

"I'm okay," I told Daniel as he hoisted the dead boy up, allowing me to crawl out from under him.

"Get these two," he said, referring to the girls, his rifle pointed at the tent. "Take them back. We'll hold the guys off and grab the other girl."

"Where's Greg?" I asked, still holding tight to the arm of the screaming girl.

"Don't worry about him," Daniel said, as a gunshot whizzed past us from the direction of the tent. "Now go!"

I ran holding onto both girls, more gunfire erupting behind us, as I fought the thought of never seeing Greg or Daniel again.

## 22

I paced in front of the campfire Oliver had going brighter and hotter than before. I stared, pissed off at him, now knowing he had told Greg and Daniel that I had left.

After getting back to camp, I had rushed him, grabbing him by his shirt, stood inches from his face, screaming. "You told them?"

"Yeah, so?" he said, his glasses knocked crooked on his nose. "Your still alive, because I did."

"But are Greg and Daniel?" I said, pushing him away.

It was the question that haunted me as I paced, the girls sitting silent after eating a meal of crackers and a bottle of water.

"I'm going back for them," I said to everyone, no longer able to take the waiting.

"I'll go with you," April said, standing, tiny fists balled at her sides.

"You're not going anywhere," Beth told her, then said the same thing to me. "They're fine, and on their way back with the other girl. You have to believe that," Beth said.

I looked around trying to read the faces of our group. They all turned away,

except Kendall.

"What if they don't come back, Shea? Where does that leave us?" she said, hand on her hip.

"I'm sorry." There was nothing else for me to say.

"You might've sacrificed the two most important members of this group for a few girls you don't even know. Chicks that do us way more harm than good." Kendall turned to look at them by the fire. Shivering and fragile, they stared sheepishly up from under mops of dirty hair, seemingly knowing they were being spoken badly about. "And why? Because Shea wanted to. Because Shea thought it was best." Kendall walked over, poked a finger in my face, her voice rising in pitch. "If those boys are dead, we won't be too far behind, because Potter over there..." Kendall said, pointing him out, seeming not to care that he stared hatefully back at her, "...is nothing but a bully, and will only confront those three sizes smaller than he is. And that guy...wherever he is," she turned to Oliver. "I think I could probably whoop him in a fight. If Daniel and Greg don't come back, their deaths are on you."

Kendall stomped away, and sat in front of the fire, beside Oliver.

Determined to repair the damage, I started off to find Greg and Daniel, but saw Angie hurrying beside me, her shotgun slung over her back.

"I'm going with you," she said.

"No, Angie. It's best you—"

"Not up for debate, Shea. You helped me. I'm helping you."

"Suite yourself," I said, thankful she offered. We were about to move when we heard rustling in the trees in front of us. I pulled my gun, and saw that Angie already had her shotgun leveled in the direction from where the noise came.

Greg and Daniel stepped out from behind the trees.

Suppressing my urge to run over and throw my arms around Greg, I asked, "What happened?"

His face hardened; he walked right by me. I asked Daniel the same question. "Where's the other girl?"

"Two of the guys are dead, the other two took off," he said.

"And the other girl?" Angie asked.

"Dead, too," Daniel said, his eyes on me, thankfully not filled with the blame

I saw in Greg's.

"Sorry, Shea," Daniel said, setting a hand on my shoulder. He glanced at Angie then trotted off in the direction Greg had gone.

I followed, trying to give Greg an apology he would not accept.

"Those the girls?" he asked, looking across the camp at them.

They stared at us, questions in their eyes—the most pressing, I imagined—what happened to their friend?

"Yeah, that's them," I said.

Greg marched over. I followed, both of us halting in front of the girls.

"You two okay?" he asked.

They nodded.

"Did you know those boys? Were you with them because you wanted to be?"

"No," the older, thinner girl said. Her name was Tracy. She told him what she had told me on the way back here: the boys caught the three of them on their way to D.C. Their packs and food were taken, then they did whatever they wanted with the girls, stuff that Greg frowned at when he heard it. I glanced at him as he listened, nodding, hoping he would now see things my way.

"Who was the other girl?" he asked.

"My sister," Sarah, the shorter girl, Amy, said. "Where is she?"

"Dead," Greg said, without emotion and very little compassion. "The boy's killed her." He turned to me, his eyes all but accusing me of murdering the Sarah with my own hands. "Happy?" he asked me so softly only I could here. He walked off.

"What was I supposed to do?" I yelled at Greg's back, getting everyone's attention. He stopped in the dirt, ten feet away, turned, came back, his voice raised. "Left it alone like everyone agreed you should've!"

"I tried to save—"

"No! We all agreed!" He yelled, angrier than I thought he should've been. "You don't do whatever the hell you want, just because you think it's right. Rules have to be set right now, or Daniel and I are out!"

"I said I am sorry."

"Sorry doesn't help the girl they killed, the people Daniel and I killed." I could tell by the look on his face, those deaths weighed heavy on him. He paced away from me, shaking his head. "If we're to stand any chance of making it to D.C., everyone's opinion has to matter. No one person can just chose for all of us. You understand?"

"I do," I said.

"Take a vote to see who's in charge. Cause it sure shouldn't be Shea," Potter yelled.

There were cries supporting the vote to replace me, oust me from an office I hadn't even known I held. But I also heard others disagreeing with the idea. The entire time, Greg never took his off me.

"Fine," I said. Greg raised an eyebrow as if surprised I would so easily give up what he must've believed I held so dearly. "Take a vote. But first," I said to Potter. "Who's going to replace me?"

"Greg, I guess," Potter said.

"Any problem with that?" I asked Greg.

He shook his head.

Potter hurried to the center of our group, stood between me and Greg. "All of you who still want Shea to call the shots, raise your hands."

Of the twelve of us, hands were raised, and those of who I expected would vote for me, did: Angie, Oliver, April, Beth and Toni. Angie nudged me, whispering in my ear: "You gotta vote for yourself, if you want a chance at winning."

I wasn't sure if I wanted that chance. Greg was better suited for this thing. He had just proven that, so I kept my hand down, deciding I'd rather take orders than suffer the consequences of giving the wrong one again.

"Anymore votes for Shea? Last call," Potter said.

Greg shot a glance at me, then looked away.

Potter counted hands. "Five votes for Shea."

It would be over in a second, I thought. Already, I started to feel less burdened. I glanced over at Greg. He whispered something to Daniel, as Potter said, "Okay, all those who want Greg to be leader."

The hands of those who hadn't voted already rose, to include mine. Greg looked at me as though he had no clue of what I was thinking, nor did he care.

Again, with a finger, Potter counted the hands, smiled and said, "Five votes for Shea. Seven for Greg. Greg is the new—"

"I changed my mind," someone said. "My vote is for Shea."

I looked up, astonished to see that it was Daniel who had spoken.

"You can't do that," Potter said. "We've already—"

"It's my vote," Daniel said. "And I'm giving it to Shea."

Potter shook his head. "Then that means we have a six to six split, so we have to vote again, or—"

"I changed my mind too," Greg said, staring angrily at me again. "My vote goes to Shea."

## 23

The next day we had been on the road for five hours, our formation the same. We walked down a narrow, two-lane service road, wide stretches of overgrown land on both sides of us, the temperature thankfully neither too hot or cold.

Angie walked beside me, as I stared at Greg's back. He marched in the right front of our group, his rifle cradled in the bend of his arms, Daniel on the left, carrying his weapon in the same fashion.

"I'm glad you won," Angie said, smiling. "Girl's rule the world, right? The president, now you."

"I don't' think I wanted it," I said, picking up my pace, and leaving Angie's side. I hurried up beside Greg. "Why'd you do that?" I said, after a full day, finally finding the courage to ask.

He didn't look at me when he said, "Doesn't matter. It's done."

"You're the one that called me out like that. You're the reason a vote was even taken," I said, walking backward in front of him, so that I could face him. "All that just to vote for me, have me officially as leader. Why?"

Greg didn't respond, but kept walking.

"Nothing has changed!" I said, stopping in front of him, forcing him to recognize me.

"Something has changed. You were held responsible for going against the decision of the group."

"That's no punishment. I'm still in charge. Why?"

Greg looked over his shoulders as though to make sure no one overheard him. "It was the right choice. Yeah, one of the girls died, but it could've been all three of them. I voted for you because when I wanted to keep moving, you realized those girls needed help, even if that meant risking our own lives. No one can survive alone out here. You realized that. I didn't. That's why you're leader," he said, then stepped around me and walked off.

We stopped at a vacant BP gas station, just off the interstate. Potter, Jonny and Oliver ran to the gas stands under a high canopy, yanked the pumps from their docks, squeezing the triggers, finding all of them dry. It's what we had encountered everywhere we went—every gas station, every gas tank in every car, already siphoned dry.

As I finished searching the trunk of an old Toyota Corolla, Angie called me from around the side of the station. I walked over, Daniel following me, to see Angie holding her bandana up over her nose and mouth, standing over a body dressed in jeans and striped t-shirt.

"How old do you think she was?" I asked, believing the body belonged to a girl because of her small feet—one of her shoes was missing—and the bra strap that peeked out from the neck of her shirt. She was otherwise unrecognizable; her face and most of her hair had been chewed away, as had much of the skin from her arms and hands.

"I don't know," Angie said, sounding as though she was about to vomit. "Not much left to go on—early twenties?"

"What got to her?" Daniel asked. "Dogs, fox, bear maybe?"

"Any or all of the above," I said, calling Greg and Oliver over. They stopped as soon as they caught sight of the girl, appearing as disgusted as we had been.

"We should burry her," April said, sympathetically.

"No time," I said. "But we can put her in a car and shut the doors. At least no more animals will feed on her."

"You heard her," Greg said to those willing to help.

After five of us carefully transferred the girl's body to a white Chevy Impala and locked the doors, April, Beth and I stepped inside the attached convenience store to find that the place had already been ransacked: cash register turned over on the floor, empty drawer ripped from it's housing, nude magazines, crushed boxes of candy bars, cookies and drained bottles of soda and water, all scattered about the floor.

"Any luck?" I called out to the girls.

"Nothing," April called back.

"No food here, either," Beth said, lifting the door of a floor model ice cream freezer.

I pushed inside of the woman's restroom, taking careful steps, the doors of the four stalls were all open. It was eerily quiet as I walked past them, checking for rolls of toilet tissue. There were none; someone had beaten me to them.

I tried the spigots at the sinks, and was surprised to find that one of them worked. Water pouring freely from it, I yanked my canteen from my belt, opened it, filling it under the tap. I would tell the others to come in and do the same when I stepped out.

Turning the faucet off, I glanced up and was shocked by my reflection: face smeared with dirt, some of it in my hair. My eyes were sunken, tired looking, like I hadn't slept for days, and although that wasn't true, it felt that way. I ran the water again, wetting my hands and smearing the dirt from my cheeks, forehead and chin. The water dripping from my skin, I looked myself again in the mirror, shutting my eyes, hoping that when I opened them, I'd be back in my bed—that all of this would've been a nightmare.

I jumped, startled when I opened my eyes; Kendall was standing beside me. She smiled at my reflection then stuck her fingers in hair, fluffing, patting and styling it.

"I still can't believe you did that to Greg," Kendall said, like the incident had occurred just yesterday. "He was, like, your best friend. Loyal as a dog, and you do that to him because you actually thought Markham Jennings would've gone out with you."

I did believe that. That belief was based on the time, two yeas ago, when I waited in the slow-moving lunch line to pay for my food. Students talking loudly and laughing, running around in the cafeteria, I looked up to see Markham in the other line. I couldn't help but stare at him. When he spotted me, I quickly averted my eyes, but felt him approaching.

"Mind if I cut? That line is dragging," he smiled, his straight white teeth, and kissable lips causing me to stammer.

"Uh...sure, yeah." I took a step back, letting him get in front of me.

"What's your name again?" he said, setting his tray of food on the rail.

"Shea...Shea Kennedy," I said, bashfully, unable to believe Markham Jennings was actually talking to me. I looked around excited, hoping other kids witnessed it.

"That's right," Markham said, nodding. "You dad's the sheriff, right? He raided a party I threw, caught me and my friends with liquor and marijuana. He told my dad, got me in a boat load of trouble. Not cool."

"I'm so sorry," I said, pushing my try closer to the register, foolishly apologizing for Dad doing his job.

"No biggie," Markham said, sliding his tray up to the cashier.

"Five, twenty three," the large woman in the white paper hat and hair net said after tallying up what was on Markham's tray.

"You mind paying for this?" he asked me. "I don't feel like checking my wallet for cash."

Honored, I said, "Sure!" I went into my purse, fumbled out some singles, about to pay for both our meals.

"Thanks. Maybe I'll talk to you later," Markham said, taking his food and walking off.

That was the best day of my life. I was worthless the rest of the school day, my head filled with thoughts of where Markham and I would go on our first day, how envied I'd be walking hand in hand with him on campus, and what it would be like to kiss him. Overly thrilled, I told my best friend Greg about the encounter on the way home from school.

"I mean can you believe it? *He* spoke to *me*?" I said skipping beside Greg, gesturing, arms whirling overdramatically. "I know it's just a matter of time before he asks me out."

Silently, Greg walked beside me, a new outbreak of fresh pimples spotting the left side of his forehead. He said without looking at me, "If that makes you happy, I hope it happens too."

"Seriously, you're a really rotten person for what you did to Greg," Kendall said, snatching me back into the gas station rest room from my thoughts, which felt strangely like our high school girl's bathroom—Kendall's turf—where she was superior to all of us. There was nothing I could say in my defense. Greg was my best friend, so Kendall was right; it was an absolutely rotten thing to do. I stood there, staring back at Kendall's reflection, my eyes narrowed.

"I tell you," Kendall continued. "You wouldn't believe it, but first I asked if *he'd* play a prank on *you*. I'm not a fan of yours, Shea. I'm sure that comes as no surprise."

I shook my head, grunted, "No, it doesn't."

"But Greg was like there was no way he'd ever do anything to humiliate his best friend, Shea Kennedy," Kendall said. "You should've seen his chubby little, pimple-ridden face," Kendall chuckled, rolling her eyes. "He was really pissed, ready to defend your honor with his life. But that meant nothing to you. Throw a good looking guy like Markham in for bait, and backstabbing Shea Kennedy does to Greg what he swore he could never do to you. You couldn't even see it, but he was so in love with you. But now, I think he can't stand the sight of you, and I totally get it. From the first day I saw you, you thought you were better than everyone else. Father was the sheriff, mother was the big-time Washington scientist, and you were the BFF of the President's daughter. You walked around thinking you pooped potpourri."

"I never thought that, Kendall," I said to her reflection.

She faced me, looked me up and down. "You sure acted like it. But look at you now. Your mom and dad are gone, and Sloane just choked out on your front lawn. Now it's just you, the wanna-be sheriff, who can't even do that right," Kendall shook her head. "You let your own father die, and can't hold onto a boy who used to love the ground you walked on. You're nothing Shea. Nothing."

"Is that right?"

Kendall turned back to the mirror, traced a finger around her mouth to sharpen the line of her lipstick. She fluffed her hair again, flashed me a Miss America contestant smile, and said, "You damn right, that's right."

Outside, Potter stood by one of the pumps, happily smoking a cigarette.

"Found them in the john," he told Daniel. "Must've fell out of someone's pocket." He shook the pack. One poked from a small whole torn in the top. "Want one?" he asked, squinting an eye against smoke spiraling up beside his face.

Daniel shook his head, and walked away.

Standing there, I felt antsy, exposed, and vulnerable. I needed for us to be on our way.

## 24

The group had all been asleep for easily an hour. Angie and I took watch. We sat in the dirt, legs folded, warming ourselves by the small campfire we used to boil water and make instant coffee. The sky dark and lit with stars, we stared off into our thoughts, mine uncertain and frightening and full of self-doubt. I focused on Angie, thinking if her thoughts were as negative as mine, I figured I'd be doing her favor by saving her from them.

"How's your coffee?"

Angie blinked then trained her eyes on me. She took a sip from her plastic mug and frowned. "Tastes like a bum's bathwater. Maybe a little worse." She smiled. "Yours?"

"Would be perfect with two tablespoons of Coffeemate, Dutch apple pie coffee creamer. Can you run to 7-11 and grab some, pretty please?"

"I think they're closed," Angie kidded.

"7-11s never close," I smiled.

"Well, they are now. Forever."

I didn't know if Angie realized the gravity of what she said until the words were out. It hit us at the same time, draining the levity from the air, the smiles from our faces, and forcing us back into our contemplative stares.

Angie stared into the space just over my shoulder. "My father used to always drink coffee in the morning," Angie said, her eyes still far off. "I was like eight or nine, and I'd watch him stir in sugar and cream, bring the mug up to his lips, taste it, add a little more stuff if it wasn't perfect, or smile to himself if it was. I told him I thought it looked and smelled nasty. He laughed and said I would drink it one day and I would love it." Her eyes open wide, like she saw her father actually standing right behind me, a content smile appeared on her face as she continued her story. "'Why do you drink coffee, Daddy?' I asked him. He said because it helped him focus on what was most important in life. I asked him what that was, and he said, 'You, your brother and your mother. Our family. The people I love.'"

Angie looked down at her coffee, then looked up at me. "Shea, we have the coffee to help us focus, but what good is it if we no longer have what's most important to us—if we no longer have a family?"

I stared sadly at her, unable to answer the question, at least not the way she probably wanted me to. "Stay right here. I have to go get something."

"Sure," Angie said.

Inside my tent, I kneeled over the satchel that held Mom's notes, determining how stupid it would be to show these to someone—Sloane's voice was in my head, warning me never to show or tell anyone about them. She said they were valuable, that someone might try to steal them and sell them. We were well aware of the power and control and the bad the notes could be used for if they fell into the wrong hands. We promised to show them to no one but Jenna. But Sloane wasn't here, and wasn't faced with the despair and the nagging desire to just give up; I felt it almost all the time. I couldn't even imagine how lost and directionless everyone else might have felt.

I grabbed the strap of the bag and left my tent, hoping Sloane would understand.

I set the bag down beside Angie, kneeled over it, unzipped it, and pulled a couple of hundred pages out, setting them in Angie's lap.

"What's this?" Angie asked.

"That's what's most important to us now. That's why we drink the crappy coffee. So we can focus on what you have in your lap."

"A bunch of paper?" Angie stared at me as though I had lost it.

"Look at them," I said. "Go ahead."

Angie sifted through the pages, held them closer to the firelight so that she could see better what was on them.

"It's equations," Angie frowned. "Looks like chemistry, a lot of words I can't pronounce, written in Greek or Mandarin or Martian, I'm not sure which." Frustrated, she set the pages back on the stack on her knees. "What is it?"

"My mom was a scientist. She worked for the World Health Organization trying to find a cure for..." I swirled my hands above my head. "...whatever this is."

"I'm guessing she didn't find one, considering people are still dying. So why are you showing me these?"

"Because there's a cure," I said, standing, taking the pages from Angie. "At least my mother thought she was close to finding one, and it's somewhere in these. I know it is," I said, placing them carefully back in my bag, zipping it closed. "That's why it's so important we get these to somebody in D.C. who'll be able to decipher what's on those, and may—"

"Maybe find a cure?" Angie said, quickly standing, overcome by the excitement we now shared of Mom's notes saving all of us.

"Yes!" I said, equally excited.

Angie threw her arms around me, actually lifted me off the ground just a little and spun me once around. She held me tight for another second, then backed away, appearing concerned.

"You can't show those to anyone, or tell anyone about them. They might try to steal them."

Nodding, I said, "I know. Sloane said the same thing."

"You probably shouldn't have even told me. But no one else after this, all right." Angie picked the bag up from the ground, shoved it in my arms. "Put these back wherever you're hiding them, and not another word about them until we're handing them off to the president," Angie smiled.

"Not another word," I smiled back. "And Angie..."

"Yeah?" she said, about to settle back down in front of the fire.

"About what you said about not having a family..."

Shaking her head, Angie said, "C'mon, you're not about to say some corny stuff like—"

"That's right," I laughed. "We your family. Everyone in this camp is your family."

"Yeah, right," Angie said, laughing off what I said.

I stared seriously and straight-faced at her. "No, I mean it. You and me are sisters now. Same with the other girls, including Kendall." Angie chuckled, realizing how much it pained me to say that. "And boys are our brothers. They are our family...*our* family. Okay?"

Angie gazed thoughtfully at me as though fully accepting the importance of what I said and the all the responsibility that came with it. "Okay."

# 25

The next day, we were roughly fifty yards into trees off the interstate, carefully stepping over exposed roots, pushing past branches that extended out like arms trying to stop us from getting on our way.

Daniel walked out in front of the group, April a few paces behind him, speaking low to Oliver. Behind them, I walked silently a few paces behind Greg. We hadn't become anymore friendly; he hadn't said anymore to me then necessary, and it felt as though that's what our relationship—if I could even call it that—would be from now on. We'd do just enough, say only enough to safely get to D.C., where then, I supposed, we'd part without as much as even a handshake.

I glanced behind me, took count of the rest of the group. I saw Kendall struggling with the terrain, Beth beside her, holding her by a forearm, looking more concerned for her friend's safety than her own or her little sister's. Potter marched along, stabbing the ground beside him with a long branch he found and was using as a staff, following.

Holding her shotgun in the bend of her arms, Angie walked alongside the rescued girls, Tracy and Amy, laughing at something one of them had said.

I shot her a glance, as if to ask if everything was fine back there.

Angie gave me thumbs up.

We had been walking silently like that for better than half an hour, when Toni said, "Does anyone know exactly how many people died from the air?"

"Last I heard, some news lady said three quarters of the earth's population," Oliver said, walking backwards. "But that was when there was still electricity. Probably more since then."

"That's a lot," Tracy called from the back of the group.

"I can't accept the fact that I'm supposed to die from this," Kendall said.

There was silence in response to her comment except for the sound of us kicking through leaves and pushing through branches, as though we all just realized we'd all most likely face the same end.

"Stop walking...everyone!" Kendall said, halting in the middle of the group of trees. She glared at each of us, frustrated, like she had told her favorite joke and no one got it. "I mean I'm fine. I feel fine!" She took an exaggerated breath in, making sure all of us heard it. She held it for a second then breathed the air out. "There's nothing wrong—"

"Kendall, we need to keep moving," I said.

"No, Shea. There's nothing wrong with my lungs. I'm eighteen years old, and you're telling me in two years I'm not going to be here. That's unacceptable!"

"Kendall, none of us will be here in two years," I said, losing my temper. "Except April." I glanced at her, April lowering her head as though ashamed to be the lucky one. "So keep it moving, or stay here. I really don't care which you choose."

Beth walked up, wrapped an arm around April's shoulder. "Someone's gonna find a cure before then," she told Kendall.

I started back on the path.

"But if they don't, we'll all go extinct," Jonny said.

"You don't know what you're talking about," Potter said, striking a tree with this make-shift staff.

"I don't?" Jonny questioned.

"The human race will never go extinct," Potter said.

"If there's no one living past the age of twenty, how will the world get repopulated? People are gonna die before they have a chance to have children."

"We'll have babies before twenty years old, before the girl's die," Potter said.

"Fine," Jonny said. "We start having babies at sixteen. So the kid is four years old when her parents die. Who raises all the four year-olds with dead parents? Who teaches those babies, feeds them, protects them?"

"Then we have babies at twelve, maybe even ten years old," Oliver said. "Right? That'll give the parents more time to raise their kids. Give Legacies time to train them."

"Girls can't have babies at ten years old, cause they haven't had their period yet, Ding-a-ling," Potter called over to Oliver. "You don't know nothing."

"More than you think," Oliver said, under his breath.

"We're gonna die, and those of us who have kids will be abandoning them, just like our parents did us," Jonny said, sounding unbothered by our fate.

"Orphans," Beth said. "That's what I feel like. Like my parents just left us here."

"What's wrong with you?" April angrily said to Beth. "You act like they just packed their crap and took off in the middle of the night. They're dead, Beth. In case you forgot. Everyone's parents are dead!"

"And they all got what they deserved," Jonny said.

The group slowed to a stop, everyone gazing at Jonny as though he had committed some unforgivable sin.

"What?" Jonny said, returning everyone's stare. "They cared nothing about us."

"Sounds like somebody has mommy issues. Or daddy issues," Angie said.

"Or both," Daniel said.

Jonny continued. "If the adults cared, they wouldn't have let things get this far. All of your parents knew they were polluting the air. They knew they were killing the earth, but they were like 'Who gives a damn? It'll be our kid's problem, not ours.' None of them thought twice about us," Jonny said, emotion quivering his voice.

"You need to shut your mouth right now," Potter said, walking up on Jonny, pointing a finger in his face. "My mother gave a damn about me."

Jonny stared at Potter's finger like he considered biting it off, and spitting it in Potter's face, then said, "Doesn't matter now, does it? She's dead like all the rest of the parents; dead, like we're all gonna be soon enough." He hoisted up his pack by the straps on to his back, and started marching again.

## 26

It was dusk and the sky was darkening. I felt the temperature drop almost immediately after the sun dropped out of sight moments ago.

I walked the perimeter of the campsite we had chosen for the night, deciding to take Tornado, the dog moving quietly beside me, stepping through the tall grasses as I was. He had fared well on this trip, but I had expected nothing different. There were times at night, lying beside me in my tent, when he would whine or toss about while sleeping. I would put a hand on his fur and rub him till he quieted down. I knew he was missing Sloane.

But she would be proud of him, and as I stepped over a huge, fallen tree, I smiled, thinking that Sloane might've been kind of proud of me too. We were well on our way to D.C., and yes, we've already had some struggles along the way, but we would get there. It'd be a huge accomplishment, nothing I thought I was capable of doing just a few long days ago.

"C'mon Tornado," I called, seeing that he was roaming toward a dense wall of vegetation.

He ignored me, continued sniffing about, searching for something.

"Torn! Come boy!"

He froze, looked at me over his shoulder, then turned back, and spotting an opening in the brush, he ducked into it. With a shudder of the bushes around him, he disappeared from my site. I ran after him, throwing myself to the dirt, grass and leaves to see where he had gone.

"Torn!" I whispered loudly. Torso deep into what was a snug tunnel of branches and leaves, I froze, hearing him moving around somewhere in front of me, outside this tunnel, on the other side.

I crawled, ignoring the sharp ends of branches gouging my hands and knees. Coming out the other side, I saw Tornado looking down from an overhang.

I stayed low, whispering to him again. "Whatcha see, boy? Whatcha looking at?"

He glanced at me, whined then turned back.

Grabbing him by the collar, I lay on my belly, forcing Tornado to do the same as not to be seen by the group of people I spotted camping fifty feet below us.

"What do you think they're doing?" I asked Tornado, using a finger to count three older girls, three older boys, a child of maybe eight years old, and another little girl, half that age. They sat in a circle around a low burning fire.

"Are they good people, Torn? Can we trust them?" I asked my partner, wondering if maybe they could be asked to join our group. "Or are they bad?"

Tornado whined, restlessly, shifted a little beside me.

The youngest child toddled away from one of the girls. The group laughed as the girl stumbled about, chasing after the child. Catching the boy, she scooped the toddler from the dirt, carried him over and transferred him to the arms of one of the smiling boys, who bounced him in his arms, and snuggled him about the neck.

I was getting a good feeling about these folks. "I think they might be okay," I said, getting to my knees, when I felt Tornado try to yank away from me. He growled, the hair on his back, standing needle-straight.

I dropped back to my belly. "What is it, boy?"

His body trembling, I felt him pulling from me, wanting to leap down from the cliff.

"What? What's spooking you?"

Then, at the tree line, behind the campers, I saw someone step out. The figure wore soiled white pants, a light colored t-shirt smeared with grime, and I had to squint to see it, but there on his face, was a sloppily drawn cross.

Burners! No. A chill ran over me as I turned on my side, grappling to get my gun with the intention of sniping the Burner if he came to close. But before I could aim, another figure appeared from behind the trees, and another, and another. The campers had no idea—they continued talking and laughing around the fire—they were being surrounded. A dozen of them now, all dressed in filthy clothing, some of their faces painted white with crosses—others smeared only with the cross—they advanced slowly and silently toward the campers.

What was I to do? As much as I wanted to help them, as much as I felt Tornado struggling to free himself so he could attempt to save them, I knew I couldn't allow that to happen.

One of the girls caught sight of the Burners as they closed in.

She screamed, alerting the others, but they were overtaken, the Burners attacking them from behind, grabbing them around their necks. The campers struggled, beat at the arms of their captors, kicked, fought, taking blind swipes over their heads. Nothing worked, and as I lay there, tears running down my face, I saw as the first of the girls became weak, her body going limp, succumbing. Three more of the campers suffocated moments later. Half of the camp lay dead, the other half quickly dying, and all I could do was turn away, sob like a baby, stay hidden, and hold tight to my dog.

When I was brave enough to look back, the dozen burners stood over the eight dead campers. They stepped over the bodies that stood in the way of them all coming together. There they stood in a small circle, held hands and bowed their heads.

I watched, awe struck, wondering exactly what they were doing. As if by magic, a flame appeared in the center of the group, and in less time than it took for them to steal the lives of the innocent campers, they broke apart, holding torches. They each ran to an edge of the camp, setting fire to the base of trees, to the campers tents, even bending down, touching their flames to the clothes of the deceased, setting them afire.

"Come, boy!" I said.

Hurdling whatever was in my way, leaf-heavy limbs swiping at my body and face as I raced past them, Tornado running quickly ahead of me, I had to get back to worn my friends. At home I'd seen the bodies, saw the bruises around the necks of the dead, and assumed they were related to the fatal air. Never had I imagined, those we referred to as Burners, might have been accountable for some of the dead.

Reaching my camp, Tornado jumped around, barking wildly.

"Shea, what's wrong?" Angie said, grabbing me, holding me, after I had almost fallen, throwing myself into her.

"We have to go!" I cried. I tried pulling away from her to warn the others, but she held tight to me.

"What are you talking about? What's wrong?"

I beat her arms away. "Burners! They killed a whole camp of people. I saw it!" I pointed in the direction. "Ten minutes from here. Pack everything now! We have to go!"

Daniel appeared in front of me, then Beth and Toni.

"What? Burners? Are you sure?" one of them asked. I was uncertain of which, because I was too busy pushing past them, running through the camp, trying to lay eyes on each member, so I could tell them personally that we were leaving.

"Shea," someone called from behind me.

I continued moving, grabbing hold of the corner of a tent, shaking it, again crying out to whoever was inside that we had to leave.

"Shea!"

I was called again, but this time I was grabbed and whirled around, my eyes landing on Greg. His fists were clamped tight around my arms, his eyes locked on mine.

"Are you sure that's what you saw?"

My chest heaving, my entire body trembling, Tornado barking with a ferocity that frightened me, I said, voice quivering, "I'm positive. And unless we all want to die right now, we need to grab our things and run!"

## 27

As quickly and quietly as we could, we ran, our packs on our backs, in a single line: me at the head, Greg at the very end, making sure no one was lost or left behind. We raced through the woods, tripping and falling over rocks and roots, having to hoist each other up, quiet each other, for fear of being heard. I chose a path parallel to the interstate, hidden by the trees so as not to be easily spotted, that was if the Burners had even known we were near by.

I couldn't take any chances. I saw how they killed those innocent campers, knew they'd do the same to us if given the chance. Not long after we had made our escape, fire rose up over the trees off in the distance behind us, which made me push the group harder, made me fear that we had not escaped and still might all die tonight.

We stopped, wheezing and gasping for air, when we no longer smelled smoke, and saw the brightness of the fire in the distance faded considerably against the dark sky.

After quietly pitching our tents, we gathered together at the center of the circle the tents formed, uncertainty on our faces.

"Is this far enough?" Potter asked, looking into the sky, as if that would give him a lead on how close the Burners were. "Sure we shouldn't keep on running?"

"I can't go anymore," Kendall said, leaning over, her palms on her knees, Beth standing beside her incase she needed more support.

"No, we should be fine," I said, speaking softly. Where we are, the route I took: no one will find us. I made sure of that." I looked into everyone's eyes: Angie's, Toni's, Jonny's, Oliver's and the rest. I wasn't sure if they believed me, but they had no choice. "This is where we stay tonight," I said. "Everybody try to get some sleep. I'll take the first watch."

"I'll take it with you," Greg said.

We sat on the ground, our backs pushed up against a couple of tree trunks. I stared at him, his rifle pointed up, the butt dug into the dirt, as he looked off to the sky where the glow of burning trees grew a little brighter. Thankfully, I felt an occasional rain drop on my hands and cheeks. It would come and put out the fires that were burning.

"We should be all right," I said. Those were the first words I had spoken to Greg in the hour we had been sitting watch. "I don't think the fires will come this way."

"What you said you saw them do to those campers...do you think they all do that, that they all murder people?"

"I don't know. But I chased one the other day," I said, figuring it was time to finally tell someone.

"What? Where?" Greg said. There was serious concern in his voice.

"While on patrol, before we left. He was kneeling over the body of a boy that could've been killed by the air, but was only eighteen, so I think the Burner did it." I said it like it was no big deal, while making little x's in the dirt with the stick I was holding. "Me and Tornado went after him, and..." I paused.

"And what?"

"I think...no, it was Markham Jennings."

Greg was up on his feet, had marched toward me, stopped, stared angrily at me a sec, then paced away, holding the rifle in one fist, raking the other hand through his hair. He spun back to face me. "You think Markham Jennings is a Burner that you thought just killed some guy and you chase him? What's wrong with you? What were you thinking?"

"I was thinking about doing my job. I was thinking about finding out if Markham killed the kid on the ground."

Greg shook his head, unbelievably, at me. "Well?"

"Tornado caught him, was wrestling with him, then Markham pulled a knife. I had him in my gun site. I could've taken him."

"But you didn't!"

"I wasn't certain he killed the boy."

"Or maybe you aren't certain you're capable of doing the job your father gave you."

Hurt by the comment, as I'm sure Greg intended me to be, I said nothing.

He turned, walked back over to his tree, staring at the spot where he had been sitting. "I'm sorry. I didn't mean that," he said. "You should've told me that had happened." He lowered himself to the ground.

"I was meaning to."

"Don't keep me in the dark about something that important again, Shea."

"I won't."

He shot me a stare. "I mean it. This is not a game. These are our lives we're dealing with."

"I know that."

He still didn't trust me. After the one, very catastrophic mistake I had made, he could no longer believe in me. My best friend in the entire world, the boy that I would build igloos with on frigid snow days when I was nine, the boy that tried to stand up for me against a bully when I was ten, and the boy I shared my first, awkward kiss with when I was eleven.

It was on the afternoon Greg and I had watched the old Spiderman movie at my house—the one with Toby McGuire and Kirsten Dunst—a huge bowl of popcorn between us. We were both intrigued by the upside down kiss shared between Spiderman and Mary Jane, and watched the rest of the movie in silence, after both scooting to opposite ends of the sofa.

But the next day Greg showed up at my house wearing the web slinger's mask, asking if I wanted to reenact the scene.

I knew it had nothing to do with Greg devising a clever way to finally kiss me. He wasn't interested in anything like that, at least not back then. It was just about how cool of a scene we both thought it was.

After rewinding the Spiderman DVD a gazillion times and memorizing our parts, we went out to my backyard, and with the mask pulled back down over Greg's face, he climbed one of the trees and hung by his legs from a low-swinging branch. I stood in front of him trying not to laugh out loud, because even at only eleven years old, I knew how ridiculous and dangerous what we were doing was.

Hanging upside down, he spoke his lines, I acted mine, and afterward I reached up and very carefully rolled down the mask from Greg's neck, only exposing his chin, mouth and nose. I leaned forward, touched my lips to his, and found myself thinking that if I were into kissing, this wouldn't have been that bad.

A second later, Greg's legs gave, and with a high-pitched scream, he fell from the tree, hit the ground and broke his wrist.

Giggling, and barely able to hold the marker straight, I was the first to sign the cast he had to get later that day. I wrote, "You are amazing, SpiderGreg!" and drew a crude picture of the superhero's mask beside it.

"Why are you smiling?" I heard Greg say evilly, yanking me back into the present.

"No reason. It's nothing," I said, lowering my head, as if ashamed of thinking such a wonderful thought in the midst of the hell we were going through. I looked back up at him, and it saddened me to see him staring at me with such hate and resentment. "You ever think you'll be able to trust me again?" I asked.

"Keep watch," he said, not answering my question. "I'm closing my eyes for a second. Wake me up if anything happens. Doesn't matter for what, wake me," he said again, as though talking to a child.

"Okay," I assured, then lowering my voice, I said, "You can trust me."

# 28

I sat with Tornado, my forehead resting against my stacked forearms, a good distance from the group, when I felt my dog suddenly pull away. Startled, I looked up to see Jonny standing above us, his hand out to my dog, Tornado eagerly sniffing it.

"Don't do that!" I reached for my dog, trying to reel him in, but he was intent on snatching whatever was in Jonny's hand.

"What did you give him?" I asked, trying to take from Tornado what he was happily chewing on.

"It was just the last of some jerky I had. I was stuffed," Jonny said, patting his flat stomach and smiling.

"Everyone's running out of food, and you give your last to my dog. Why?"

"I never apologized for shooting him. I see him staring at me sometimes, and I wonder if he dreams of coming into my tent at night and getting even."

I didn't want to, but I couldn't help but let out a laugh, imagining Tornado's butt sticking out the door of Jonny's tent as he attempted to sink his teeth into the boy.

"He has a vengeful heart," I joked, rubbing Tornado's neck. "You're smart to think that way. But I guess he realizes you weren't meaning to hurt him." Tornado licked the hand Jonny continued to hold in front of him. "Looks as though he's accepted your apology."

"I'm glad." Jonny gave me another uncertain smile. "Can I sit with you guys a second?"

I looked toward the rest of the group. They appeared beaten up and in no hurry to move. "I think it's time we really need to be going," I said.

"I see. Okay," Jonny said, disappointed. He started to move on.

"Well, maybe everybody could use a couple more minutes of rest." I nodded to the spot on the other side of Tornado, feeling Jonny had more to say to me. He took a seat, roped his arms around his knees, and stared off.

"You miss your parents?"

"Of course I do," I said. "Don't you miss yours?"

"No parent's. I was in they system since four years old," Jonny said. "Well...there were the foster ones, but they aren't that big on love, you know. They were all crap. But they're in the ground now, where they belong."

"I'm sorry," I said, sincerely.

"Don't be." He smiled again. It wasn't genuine. "Over the years you toughen yourself against the yelling, the insults, and all the tools—planks, belts and baseball bats—they used to beat you into being what they believe is the model child. The bats are the worse, but I'm not really fond of extension chords, either. The whelps those things leave on your back have you looking like a runaway slave." He started at the buttons on his shirt, opened it up, and began to pull it off before I could say, "No, no, don't!" I'm sure to him it sounded as though I was disgusted by the idea, but I was more afraid to see what they had done. "I mean, that's okay."

Jonny smiled, seemingly not taking offense.

But as he was pulling back his shirt over a torso so narrow I could see signs of his ribs underneath his skin, I also saw something on his right up arm.

"What's that?" I said.

He quickly pulled his shirt all the way, fastening the buttons. "Nothing!"

I reached out. "It looked like a burn or—"

"I said it was nothing," Jonny said, cringing away, as if the memory of his beatings were still that fresh in his memory.

"Sorry," I said. "I didn't meant to—"

"It's okay. Really." He smiled, shook his head. "But to think, all those years I was looking forward to turning eighteen so I could be released from foster care, be my own person, find friends, maybe someone that wanted me around not because of the paycheck they knew they'd get for keeping me, but just because they liked me, maybe...I don't know, even loved me. Then right after my eighteenth birthday, the air turns. Guess my life is supposed to be crap from beginning to the end, huh."

"Don't say that. There's still time."

"For what?" Jonny said, standing, clapping the dirt from the back of his jeans. "I'm nineteen. Your group—none of you guys can stand me. Think any of you will care when I choke out under some tree somewhere? Will you, Shea? Will you care that I've died, or remember me after I'm gone?"

I didn't even know this guy, so no, I wouldn't remember him. And even though I knew he wanted me to tell him I would, I wasn't going to lie, so I stood, tried my best to smile and said: "I'm sure everything will work out just fine."

When I walked back toward the other group members, I heard Kendall say, "I told you, I have to go to the rest room. Beth, grab the toilet tissue, and come with me."

I couldn't believe what I had heard. The way Kendall said it made it seem as though she not only wanted Beth to accompany her into the woods while she took a piss, but wanted her to wipe between her legs when she was finished. I looked up, caught the shocked expression on Angie's face, and believed she got the same impression.

"Get it yourself!" April said, throwing down the shovel she was holding.

Beth had already retrieved the roll from Kendall's bag, and looked as though she was preparing to follow Kendall into the woods.

"My sister is not your flunky," April said to Kendall, then turned to her sister. "Put down the stupid toilet paper, Beth."

"I never said she was," Kendall said to April. "And what business is this of yours anyway, little girl?"

"Beth," April said. "Put down the freakin TP!"

"Beth!" Kendall called. "Come on! I don't like holding it."

"You don't have to do that anymore," April said to her sister.

"Beth," Kendall said. "If you don't come right now, then I'll—"

"You'll do what, Kendall?" April questioned. "You're going to tell all your girlfriends that my sister is not cool anymore? There's no more high school, no more fashion clubs, or popularity contests. There's nothing but you, wishing you could live in the past, and my sister, needing to decide if she's going to let you do that, or decide she doesn't need to be your flunky just so people can like her."

"I'm really getting sick of you," Kendall said, starting toward April.

"Don't, Kendall," I said walking toward her.

"Oh, look who it is? Super Shea Kennedy," Kendall mocked. "And what are you going to do, me up? You going to shoot me, because you're mad I'm trying to teach this child not to mouth off, or because you have all of us out here, and I'm the only one that realizes you have no idea of what you're doing, probably don't know where we're going, and there's the chance that none of us will make it to the capital alive!" Kendall said. She was frowning, clenching her fists, and shifting her weight from one foot to the next. "But I can't deal with that now because I really gotta pee, and Beth needs to get her butt over here and bring the toilet tissue, now!"

"Beth—" April started, but appeared to know her sister wasn't paying her any mind, because Beth was already hurrying toward Kendall, the TP tucked in her arm like a football. Everyone watched the two of them go, stepping over large rocks, then disappearing behind a thatch of tall bushes and a wall of trees.

And then there was silence, no one knowing what to say.

I walked over to April, put my arm around her, when Tornado started barking, high pitched, danger barks. He raced past us, ran in the direction Kendall and Beth had gone.

"What's wrong with Tornado?" April asked.

We heard screaming, then thrashing, then the roar of something inhuman.

All of us, Potter, Jonny, Angie, Greg, Daniel and Oliver ran toward the blood curdling, terror-filled screams. And as I ran, I realized those shrieks and cries belonged to Kendall. We all came to a halt, and in front of us was the horrific scene of a huge brown bear, standing on his hind legs, his head elevated ten feet in the air. Growling at the bear was Tornado, just below him, teeth bared, paws dug into the dirt, appearing ready to leap in defense of Kendall.

"No Tornado! No!" I screamed. Not wanting my dog to have another brush with death. Besides, it appeared far too late to do anything for Kendall. The bears long, sharp claws dripped with the same blood that squirted from Kendall's throat, the blood that painted her face and hands as she writhed in the dirt, grasping at her neck, attempting to hold close the rip the bear tore in it.

I yelled again, "Tornado, down!" But he leapt at the bear, attacking him high, sinking his teeth into the bear's shoulder. Both animals fell to the ground, rolled around in a cloud of dirt and dust, and I knew the animal would rip poor Tornado to sheds if nothing was done that second.

Greg stood beside me, his rifle already trained on the bear, the barrel moving to track the huge animal.

"Kill it!" I screamed.

"I don't want to hit Tornado!" he yelled over the bear's growls, squinting an eye, his cheek to the stock of the weapon.

"Kill him now, or Tornado's dead!"

The rifle kicked in Greg's grasp, as two shots erupted from it, echoing off the rocky cliffs on either side of us, then both animals went down, lying still.

"Tornado," I cried, taking a step toward the animals, when I saw movement. It was my dog struggling to free himself from under the huge arm of the dead bear. Tornado barked, and wrestled more.

"C'mon, boy! Come!"

He fought his way out, ran toward me and jumped in my arms. Some of his hair was stained with blood, and after quickly feeling for injuries, I realized the blood was not his, but Kendall's. She lay in the dirt surrounded by Beth, Potter, Toni and the girls we rescued. Beth kneeled beside her, pressing her hand into Kendall's throat, trying to stop her carotid artery from belching out every drop of her blood.

"Hold on, Kendall! Don't die! Don't die!" Beth cried.

We all stood watching, horrified, as Kendall's body jerked and shuddered, her heels kicking about in the dirt. Nothing could be done for her; there was no hospital to rush her to, no doctor to stich her up. We watched Kendall's feet come to a stop, her bloody hands fall from her own throat, her eyes close and her body fall still.

At my left leg, Tornado whined his apology for not being able to do more.

# 29

The ceremony was a quick one. We dug the grave, placed Kendall in it, and covered her, not risking the chance of other animals picking up the scent of blood and come looking to feed. We stood around her grave: two sticks, crossed and tied together, pushed into the soft dirt. Heads lowered during a moment of silence, I heard Beth sobbing softly, and looked up to see April doing her best to console her big sister, but was unable.

"Does anyone have anything to say before we get back on the road?"

Beth, in her state, couldn't to speak for her friend; no one else made an effort, so I stepped forward, looked down at the mound of dirt, visualizing Kendall lying beneath it, and couldn't help but feel sorry that she was gone. I allowed everyone another moment of silence, lifted my head, opened my eyes and said, "I think it's time we move."

We'd been on the road for three hours when I stopped at a two-lane exit ramp, fifty feet in front of us. There were signs posted on the side of the interstate for Hardees, McDonald's, Wendy's, Burger King, Taco Bell and Arby's.

"Keep going, or turn off onto that road to look for food?" I asked of the group.

"I say we keep going," Potter said. "We'll never make it there if we keep stopping."

Toni eyed him, seeming not to like his answer. "Can we starve out here?" she asked.

"We can starve anywhere without food," Greg said.

In the days we'd been on the road, we had found nothing to eat. The little food we all carried was desperately running low. Soon we'd have nothing left.

"All those who vote to see what we can find on the exit," Greg said. "Raise your hands."

Every hand rose, but Potter's.

We walked the half a mile, went through the kitchens of all of the restaurants, throwing open huge freezer doors that were hotter than the air outside. We searched cabinets, basement storerooms and closets for anything edible, and found absolutely nothing. We searched the rest of the small town: the library, and the post office, still coming up empty. We walked to the high school: a small, one story brick building—one of the front double doors appearing ajar.

"So," Daniel said, all of us standing on the overgrown lawn in front of the building. "Do we go inside?"

"There was no food anywhere else," Potter said. "What makes you think there'll be any in there?"

He had a point, but looking at the starving faces of our group, and hearing the gurgling of someone's stomach growling, I said: "We need to at look."

"We'll never know if we don't try," Angie said behind me.

We all moved inside a wide foyer that fed into a long hallway, several doors on either side of it. The moment the front door closed on us, I knew this was some place we didn't belong. The stench inside was overpowering, had those of us who still had bandanas or masks, pulling them up, trying to block the stink from entering our lungs.

"What do we do?" Tracy asked.

"We should find out where it's coming from," Jonny said.

I put a hand on April's shoulder. "Go outside and wait for us."

"No!" April said. "I wanna go."

"You're too young to—"

"She was too young before all this happened," Beth said. "She's old enough now. Whatever this is, she needs to see it."

I felt Greg's eyes on me. Glance at him, then back to Beth and said, "Okay."

We started down the hallway, having agreed that some of us would open the doors and check the rooms to the right, the others checking the left side doors.

The plan changed when Jonny said, “Wait! What’s that on the floor down the hall?”

Down the fifty-foot long hallway, shrouded in darkness, I could see something littering the floor around the double doors at the opposite end.

Daniel and Angie had their flashlights out, shined them in that direction.

“Shoes?” Oliver said.

“C’mon,” Greg said, already taking strides in the direction. Reaching the doors, we confirmed what Oliver had guessed: stacks and stacks of shoes: all sizes, tennis, hard bottomed and sandals, scattered about the floor in no particular order.

“What is this?” April said.

“It can’t be good,” Potter said.

“Do we go in?” Daniel asked.

“We have to see,” I said, stepping over the shoes, pushing past Daniel and Greg to grab the doorknobs. “Anyone who doesn’t want to see this should leave now.” I scanned the faces of our group, everyone appearing certain of what we were about to do. I turned to the door, grabbed the knob, shut my eyes, and prayed that this wasn’t what I knew it would be, then threw open the door of the school’s gymnasium door. Not an inch of the hardwood floor could be seen; it was covered, from wall to wall with dead bodies.

I staggered backward, screams coming from somewhere behind me. I was more startled than I thought I would’ve been, the sight more gruesome than I ever could’ve imagined.  I looked back to see Tracy running away, down the hall, toward the school’s exit, her sister Amy following behind her.

“Could this have been where they stored their dead when the air turned?” Greg said, beside me.

"No," I said, looking down at a blonde girl with freckles on her cheeks, lying dead at my feet. She couldn't have been a day older than April. "They're too young."

"Are those cups?" Beth said, walking around us, into the room, carefully stepping over bodies. "Did they—"

"They killed themselves," Angie whispered into my ear.

She was right. There were just as many white Styrofoam cups as there were bodies: easily a hundred of them littered the room.

We made our way in trying not to gag on the stench of decaying flesh, feces and urine, as we stepped over kids no older than Sloane and far younger than April: little bodies, children the age of five or six.

Fighting emotion, I leaned over several of them, pulling down the collars of their shirts, checking for the ligature marks I saw on Tommy's neck, trying to rule out murder; there were none.

I gathered wallets from those that carried them, checked the ages on the ID cards, and just as I suspected, no one was over the age of 19.

"No! What are you doing?" I heard Beth yell.

I looked up, saw her going after Potter, trying to take something from him. He held her by the wrists, trying to calm her down.

"Hey!" Hey, what's going on over there?" I called across the gymnasium.

"I saw him take something from one of the bodies and put it in his pocket," Beth said, pointing at Potter.

"And I thought you couldn't be any slimier than you already were," Oliver said. "Who would have known?"

"Screw you, Oliver!" Potter shouted back.

"Take it out of your pocket, Potter. Whatever it is," I ordered.

"It's a watch. I don't have one. And a couple of dollars, and I'm not doing a damn thing, Shea," he said, defiant.

I marched toward him, carefully stepping over the bodies strewn across the floor. "Whatever you took, Potter, drop it!" I said, nearing him.

"Or you'll do what?"

Staring into Potter's eyes, I said, "Or I'll drop you." I had drawn my gun, had it aimed between his eyes.

A sick, taunting smile widened across his face. He took a step to me, leaned forward, pressed his forehead against the barrel of my gun. "I'm getting so tired of you. C'mon, Shea. Be a man. Pull the trigger."

"Shea!" Greg yelled from a corner of the gym, hurrying over. He wrenched the gun from my hand. "What are you doing?"

"He's taking stuff from these people that doesn't belong to him."

Greg turned to Potter.

"They're dead. They have stuff. We're alive. We need it more than they do," Potter reasoned.

"He's right, Shea."

"What?" I said, lunging for my gun in Greg's hand. "I don't care that—"

Greg took me by the arm, stared me in the face. "I'm sorry these people are dead. I'm sorry we found them, but they obviously chose to die this way. Not taking the things they left behind won't be showing them respect, and it surely won't bring them back." Greg took his hand from me, turned and addressed everyone standing in the gym. "If you want, you all have five minutes to take what you can find. After that, we're moving out."

Greg pushed my gun back into my hands then left me. I holstered it and watched Potter go about searching other bodies.

Beth stood off in a corner, her eyes glazed over, her arms wrapped tightly around her body, gently rocking from one foot to the other.

I walked over to her. "Beth! You okay?"

"How long do we keep on, as though we believe any of it will matter?"

"We can make a difference. You just have to—"

"Kendall is dead," she said, looking seriously at me. "And now this."

"It's terrible what happened to Kendall, and I wish we could've stopped this from happening. I feel so sorry for them."

Beth looked over the dismal scene stretched out before us, arms and legs twisted and crossed over neighboring bodies, the few of us who chose, rummaging through their clothes for trinkets.

"Why feel sorry for them, Shea?" Beth said. "These people are free. Maybe it's us you should feel sorry for."

# 30

It had been six hours since a word was spoken about the bodies we found in the high school. The group of us sat huddled around a fire of the campsite we chosen for the night. We were exhausted and starving.

I stared angrily at the stolen watch Potter wore on his wrist—a nagging sign that we were now no better than the people who threw bricks into store fronts, who robbed people on the streets, or no better than the boys who forced their way into my home and attempted to take from me and my sister.

My knee was nudged. I turned to my right to see April shaking her head at me.

"Just don't think about it," she whispered.

"What?"

She looked in Potter's direction, at his wrist, letting me know she had been watching me anguish over what happened hours ago.

"Just let it go. Continuing to think about it won't help anybody."

April was right.

"What are we doing?"

I looked up to see who asked the question, and through the high burning flames between us, I saw Beth standing. She looked lost and desperate, how I imagined we all felt.

"Why did we even come out here?" She looked around for anyone who would sympathize with her.

"Yes, we were gonna eventually die at home, but we would've been safe," Beth continued. "But now Kendall is dead, Tracy's sister is dead, and the boys Daniel and Greg killed are dead. How long before someone else dies because of this stupid trip to the capital?" Beth smeared tears from her cheeks then in a high-pitched voice asked, "How long?"

"Beth," I said, standing, trying to calm her down before she excited anyone else. "I know what you're feeling right now."

"Do you, Shea? Tell me what I'm feeling."

"Look, I just lost my sister and—"

"And what did you do? Dumped her in a hole, threw dirt on her so you could take us out here to die."

"Hey, hey now, Beth," Angie said standing, as if to stop me from jumping Beth, knowing what was just said might've caused that reaction. "Maybe you ought to calm down and watch what you say."

"Maybe Beth has a point," Toni said. She was up, rubbing her belly. "We're out in the middle of nowhere, starving, not knowing if we're even heading in the right direction."

"We're going the right way," I said.

"So how much longer till we get there?" Potter said, his arm around Toni, like the loving soon-to-be-dad we all knew he wasn't.

"Soon. I don't know. We'll get there," I assured.

"Not good enough," Potter said. "You're supposed to be the leader. You're supposed to be taking care of us, and you can't even tell us when we'll no longer have to go hungry and sleep and piss and crap in the dirt. We should've never trusted you and we should've never left."

They were ganging up on me. It was only a few of them, but I could see their sentiment catching, causing everyone to distrust me.

"Look, we're doing the right thing. I know some of you might not think so, but—"

"If we make it to D.C., what makes you so sure things will be better there?" Jonny said, and I was surprised to see that he would pile on, considering how deep in the hole he was with me, how supposedly thankful he was for letting him come with us. "Maybe Beth is right. Maybe we should just turn around and go back. At least we know what's back there."

"Right!" Potter said. "We go back. At least my son will be born at home."

I saw Toni nodding, Beth agreeing, and Potter started a chant of "Let's go home! Let's go home! Let's go home!" which half the group, including the rescued girls took up.

I looked to Greg, who returned my glance, shaking his head, as though there was nothing he could do. They got louder and louder. The last thing I needed was for this to evolve into a mini-riot, where Potter and the gang, yanked burning branches from the fire, setting blaze to our tents as they danced around them, screaming wildly that we should go home.

I went to my tent, and when I returned, I chose not waste my breath trying to out yell everyone. Instead, I pulled my gun, pointed it high in the air, and fired a deafening shot. The yelling and chanting ceased. I dropped the satchel filled with Mom's notes in the dirt at my feet.

"This is why we're going to D.C. This is why we're risking our lives to get there."

There was total silence, save for the crackling of the fire. All eyes were on the old brown leather satchel.

"And exactly what is that?" Potter said.

"Our future," I said. "My mom and her team were working to find a cure for whatever this is."

"You saying the cure is in that bag?" Oliver said.

"It might be. My mother said she was close, so yeah, I think the cure might be in here."

Revealing the news about the papers had raised morale some. After my announcement, there was no longer hopeless silence, but what sounded like almost cheerful chatter about getting to D.C. as quickly as possible so the hunt for a cure could be started. Greg even came up to me afterward.

"Is that for real?" he said, nodding to the back slung over my shoulder. "Or just some false hope you're giving to try to get everybody through this?"

"They're real."

He nodded and looked away. "It'd be a good thing if your mom did figure this stuff out. I mean, I'm not afraid of death or anything," he said, looking me in the eyes. "But it'd be nice to have more than just a couple of years to do...I don't know, to do whatever." His eyes didn't move from mine, and I got the sneaking suspicion that I could've been included somewhere in those "whatever" plans.

"Yeah, that would be nice," I said.

## 31

After taking Mom's notes back to my tent, and everyone broke off to do their own thing, I decided I needed a moment alone to clear my head. It was something I liked to do before the air turned: sit by myself in our backyard, and stare up at the trees, while I sorted things out in my mind.

Walking through a cluster of trees, I was searching for the perfect spot, when I heard talking. I hid behind a tree then peeked out and saw Oliver and Toni standing with their arms around each other.

"I'm tired of this. We need to just tell him. What could it hurt?" Oliver said, more angry and forceful than I'd ever saw him.

"What could it hurt?" Toni said, sadly, laying her head helplessly on Oliver's shoulder. "He'd go crazy if he were to ever find out."

I assumed the "he" they were talking about was Potter. I needed to know more, took a step, trying to get closer, when I lost my balance. I got it together, managed to hide myself again, but not before Oliver's eyes met mine.

"What was that?" I heard Toni say. "Is there someone out there?"

"No," Oliver lied. "Just a squirrel. But maybe you should go back before Potter misses you," Oliver said with attitude.

I watched Toni go. Oliver kept his back to me.

"Why'd you follow us, Shea?" he asked, not turning around.

"How you doing, Oliver?" I said, ignoring the accusation.

He turned. "The world is coming to an end. How you think I'm doing?"

"What's going on between you and Toni?"

"None of your business."

"I think it might be. Toni made it sound like whatever you guys are hiding could turn out to be a really bad situation."

"What did you hear?" Oliver said, taking steps toward me. "What do you know?"

"Only that you two share a secret that Toni wants to keep and you don't. What is it?"

"I told you, none of your business."

"Fine, but if it involves Potter, like Toni said, you'd be smart to keep it to yourself. You don't know Potter. He doesn't just act like a bad person; he is one."

"I'm not afraid of him."

"Didn't say you were, but maybe you should be," I warned.

Oliver smiled, but I could see the fear in his eyes.

"It's not funny."

Oliver turned back around. "Goodnight, Shea."

"Oliver, I would seriously think about—"

"Goodnight, Shea," Oliver said, raising his voice over mine.

"Have it your way," I said, leaving him alone.

## 32

The next day, after having completed our ten hours of walking, I sat nibbling on the last of the food I had left, while at the same time, keeping an eye on Potter, because I felt his constant stare on me.

Watching him sit on a rock, his knees almost hitting his chest, he looked like a full-grown man, sitting in a baby's chair as he took tiny bites from a bar of Laffy Taffy. Beside him, Toni ate nothing. I watched as she stared at the father of her soon-to-be-born child, happily eating and paying her no mind.

"Can I have some?" She had leaned in to him, attempting to whisper so that no one else would hear.

I looked over, spotted Oliver anticipating Potter's answer as I did.

"You had yours. Now let me eat mine," Potter said.

"But I'm hungry. I want—" Toni whispered even softer.

"Who ain't hungry, Toni?" Potter said, taking a bigger bite of the candy.

My eyes were on Oliver again, attempting to move before he did.

"Toni—," I started.

Oliver stood, held out the little bit of food he had left: a plastic bag, a dozen or so salted peanuts on the bottom of it. "Take mine. You can have it all."

"Sit down, Oliver," I said.

"Hold it. What did you say?" Potter said, holding his candy in his fist, no longer chewing. "You offering my girl your food? Why?"

"Because she's hungry, and you're too freaking stingy to give her some of yours even though you know she's starving."

"Sounds like reason enough to me," Jonny said.

"Stay out of it, Jonny," I told him.

"You know, I've been sick of schoolboy over there," Potter said, referring to Oliver. "But I'm really starting to get just as sick of you."

Jonny stood. "Then do something about it? Or try."

"I can fight my own battles, Jonny," Oliver said. "I don't need your help."

"Fight?" Potter said, about to hand Toni his taffy, thought another second, then shoved it in his back pocket. "Is that what you want, sissy?"

"I think we should all just calm down right now," Greg said.

"I'm calm," Oliver said. "Was just offering my food to Toni. That's all."

"Oliver, please! Just sit down," I said again.

"If Toni is hungry and Oliver wants to share his food because Potter is too insensitive to," Angie said. "Why not let him?"

Potter cut his eyes at Angie. "No one asked you. You need to mind your own business."

"Or what?" Angie said.

"Everybody!" Greg yelled, stepping in the center of all of us, waving his arms. "Take it down a notch and calm down!" He looked at Toni. "You still hungry?"

Toni nodded.

"You don't want her to have any of your food?" Greg asked Potter.

"She's eaten hers. I need to eat, too," Potter said.

"Fine," Greg said, turning to Oliver. "If you want to give her some or all of your food, do it."

"Try it and I swear you'll be sorry," Potter said, giving Oliver the death stare.

"Oliver, I don't want the food," Toni said, finally speaking up. "I'm not hungry anymore."

Oliver continued to hold out the food to her.

"Stay back," Potter warned Oliver again.

Boldly, Oliver took a step closer to Toni. "You can't care anything about her, or the baby that she's carrying."

"What did you say about my baby?" Potter said. "You don't talk about my baby!"

"Oliver, just stay back!" Toni said, her voice quivering.

"Listen to her," Potter said.

Oliver stood his ground in front of Toni, not taking a single step back. He looked lovingly at her; that moment his love for her was undeniable. "Here Toni, just take it."

Potter reared back, and with an open hand swung at Oliver, slapping him hard across the side of his head, forcing the food from Oliver's hand. He tumbled backward, and landed in the dirt on his belly.

"What is your problem?" Potter said, stepping up on Oliver, standing between his splayed legs. "I've seen the way you been looking at my girl. You got something to say?"

Oliver pulled himself up to his knees, patting the ground around him, looking for his glasses. "She's not your girl," Oliver said, squinting at Potter.

"Stop all of this now!" I ran to Potter, put my hands in his chest, tried to stop him from moving forward, but he continued trying to get past me, continued taunting Oliver.

"Yeah, she's my girl. That baby growing in her belly—my baby—says she is."

"That's not your baby," Oliver said, finding his glasses, pushing them back onto his face with both hands. And then he stood and said the words I would've never expected out of his mouth. "That's my baby. Toni is having my baby."

I waited for the deafening explosion, the mushroom cloud and the blinding light that came with this news, but there was nothing: silence, and nothing.

Potter turned to Toni, looking for confirmation or denial of what was said. She appeared exhausted, tired of playing the game, of supporting the lie. She didn't admit it, but judging by the guilty look on her face, she might as had confessed to her affair with Oliver.

"So is it true?" Potter said, seemingly needing to hear the words.

"Yes," Toni said, shutting her eyes.

It was out. And there was nothing to do now but talk about it, come to some understanding, so we could concentrate on finishing the trip to the capital.

Potter must not have felt the same way. Before I could react, recognize that he was reaching, his hand was around my gun. Potter snatched it from my holster, aimed it at Oliver then fired. A small red dot appeared in the center of Oliver's forehead, his brains simultaneously erupting out the back of his skull. His knees buckled and his body crumpled upon itself. His eyes remaining open, staring at me, he fell face forward into the dirt.

I staggered backward, mouth open, dizzied from shock, barely able to hear the screams, the cries and gasps, as Potter turned the gun on Toni. He pulled the trigger a second before Angie and Greg tackled him.

Screaming, tears streaming down her cheeks, Toni was still alive. That was only because the hammer had fallen on an empty chamber when Potter fired the gun.

# 33

We buried Oliver. April and Toni wept during the funeral, me and the boys did our best to hold back our tears. We weren't successful.

After Potter pulled the trigger on my empty gun, he was taken to the ground, his arms wrenched behind his back, and the cuffs he had found, taken from his pocket and clasped tightly around his wrists.

When Oliver's funeral ended, we stood Potter in front of all of us. There was no reason to hold an informal trial. We all knew he was guilty.

"So what do we do?" Angie said.

Potter stared defiantly at me, his hands cuffed behind his back, as I tried to answer that question. "What?" he barked. "The boy had it coming! He took my baby, my future from me."

"Oliver took nothing," I said. "That was never your baby, and because of what you did, we're gonna decide what future *you* have left, if any."

"You would've done the same thing," Potter said.

I shook my head, walking away from him.

"Then you would've," Potter said, shouting at Greg. "And you," he yelled at Daniel.

The three of us huddled around Angie.

"So, we handle this how?" Greg asked.

"There are only two options," I said.

"Those are?" Daniel asked.

"Take him with us?" Angie guessed. "Or, considering what he did to Oliver, we..."

I nodded, sadly, knowing Angie was suggesting a death sentence.

"I don't think we should kill him," Daniel said. "If we take him with us, maybe he can get an actual trial in the Capital."

"He killed one of us," Angie said. "You want to risk him doing it again?"

I looked over at Toni, still weeping, holding a rag to her face. “Maybe this isn’t our decision to make.” I turned back. “Give me a sec, okay.” I walked over to Toni, hugged her.

“Why did he have to tell Potter? I told him how he’d react. I just didn’t think that Potter would—“

“Was Oliver right about what he said? How would he know? Are you carrying Oliver’s baby?”

Toni nodded her head. “Potter didn’t know, but I was seeing Oliver for the past year. That month that Potter was out of town, that’s when I got pregnant. I loved Oliver. I was going to break it off with Potter, and then the air turned and...” Toni broke into a fit of sobs.

I took her by her shoulders, squeezed just enough to get her attention. “Don’t feel bad, Toni. None of this is your fault, okay. But there’s a decision that has to be made about what’s going to happen.”

Toni sniffled, dabbed around her eyes, clearing them to look at me. “What decision?”

“We bring him with us,” I said. “There still must be some form of judicial system left in capital. I might get a trail of some sort there. But if you want this to be over now, we can do something else.”

“What is ‘something else?’” She asked, the rag still pressed to her face, as though hiding behind it, afraid of the answer.

“I think you know.”

## 34

Potter marched along with us at the back of the group, his wrists cuffed, Daniel, Angie, Greg and me, taking turns walking behind him, a weapon always aimed at the back of Potter's head, or the space between his shoulder blades.

It had taken Toni quite a while—smearing tears from her face, sobbing aloud—to decide that she didn't want us harm Potter.

"Make him suffer with us the rest of the way to the capital," Toni said, sniffling. "We'll let whosever there decide what to do with him."

We had been on the road for nearly five hours when I was startled out of my trans-like state by Jonny's high-pitched scream.

"Hey? Look! Everybody! Look! It's a house! And I think they're people inside of it!"

Starving and without thought, all of us hurried through the waist-high grass toward the house, Tornado leaping and barking happily in front of us.

Only feet away from the front porch, breathing heavily, we stood staring at each other wondering what to do next. Greg moved to the climb the first stair when we heard the cocking of shotguns: one in front of us, another from behind. Flashlights were shined in our faces.

"Who are you? What do you want?"

That voice belonged to a boy. I couldn't see him behind the glare of the light.

"We don't mean any harm. We're just on our way to D.C." Greg said.

"And?" A girl standing behind us, holding another shotgun asked.

Squinting, I said, "We're out of food and we're starving."

"I said we can't help you," the boy said again. "You need to go."

The weight of Greg's stare had me turning to face him.

"We need food, and they have some," he said.

"So?" I whispered. "They also have guns."

"So do we. We're hungry and—"

The barrel of the girl's shotgun was in Greg's face before he could finish his sentence.

"Go! Leave now!" the girl said. "All of you have to leave now."

"I'm pregnant!" Toni said, desperate. "We go any longer without food..." her voice cracking with emotion, she continued. "I don't want to lose my baby."

We heard the locks of the security gate being undone, and the door opening. We turned to see a girl step out wearing boots, cargo pants, and a turtleneck sweater. A hunting knife was strapped to the thigh of her right leg. Average weight and height, no older than me, she had dark hair that was parted down the middle, two braids dangling from each side of her head. To the surprise of all of us, she carried a two year-old toddler on her right hip. The baby bounced and giggled, playing with one of the girl's braids. "Lizzy, Dylan," the girl on the porch ordered. "Put the weapons away. I really don't think they're trying to wage a gun battle out here."

Inside, the house appeared as secure as mine had been. There were stacks of boxes everywhere. Some piled nearly to the ceiling, filled with what Nina said were supplies that could keep them going for years if need be.

We all sat in the large dinning room—the nine from my group, (potter was locked in a barn outside) and the seven people who lived here—to include little Sophie, who Nina had informally adopted when the mother succumbed to the air. We all sat at a long table set with plates of food: green salad, sautéed vegetables, hot roasted chicken with roasted potatoes and barbequed corn on the cob.

"Where did all this food come from?" April asked, before we all dug in.

"We grow the vegetables on our farm," Nina said. "And we raise cows, pigs, chickens and ducks. We are totally self-sustainable here."

Plates balanced on our knees, heads lowered, stuffing the delicious food in our mouths, our cheeks shiny with chicken grease as we licked our fingers and made noises reserved exclusively in the past for dinner served on Thanksgiving and Christmas, I couldn't believe our good fortune. We were even served sweet potato pie.

After dinner, Nina started a fire in the huge, brick dining room fireplace. It roared, cracked and popped loudly, warming the entire house as we all relaxed for the first time in days.

"You never thought of going to D.C.?" I asked.

"For what?" Nina said.

"Because the president asked everyone to," I said. "To help re-organize, repair and rebuild."

"Rebuild what?"

"I don't know...our government, our way of life."

"Our government was who killed all of our parents," Nina said. "They knew what was happening to our air, yet they chose to stand by and watch until it was too late. Why would we want to rebuild that?"

"It can be different. We can make it better," I said. "We have a new president."

"And she's a child, like most of us. Knowing that, what's to stop any heavily armed group from here or anywhere in the world, making a run on the White House, attempt to topple the flimsy little government that's left, and take control of our new world?" Nina stared me in the eyes as if waiting for an answer. "I'll take my chances here," she said.

"Anyone ever try to break in?" Greg asked.

"Twice in the six months we've all been here. One of the guys managed to get in," Dylan said.

"What happened?" Daniel asked.

"He's buried out back," Dylan said.

"No he's not," Nina said, waving Dylan off. "Dylan was a drama major before all this happened. Yes, somebody did get in, but we got him out without having to fire a shot. Dylan just misses performing in front of a crowd."

I glanced back at the red haired boy, and saw that he was smiling.

Sarah, one of the younger girls living here, her palms pressed together, asked Nina if April could please spend the night in her room. They had become new BFFs just that fast. Nina, of course, said yes, and two hours later, through the ceiling, Greg and I heard the girls playing and giggling.

Toni slept in the den on a reclining E-Z chair. I didn't know where Angie or Daniel were, but I had the sneaking suspicion they were together. Jonny, Beth and Sarah, camped out in the remaining spare rooms upstairs. I took the living room sofa, and Greg made a pallet just below me, while Tornado curled up on the floor, in a corner, fighting sleep, one eye open, watching me.

Only glowing red embers left burning in the fireplace, Greg said, "Did you hear what Nina said?"

Stretched across the sofa, eyes staring wide at the ceiling, I said, "She said a lot of things."

"'If I'm going to die anytime soon, this is where I want it to be,'" Greg reminded me.

It was a comment Nina made that had caught all of our attention, had Toni staring at her as though jealous that Nina had a home, a place where she knew she'd comfortably and safely live out the rest of her days.

"I heard it," I said, softening my tone, folding my arms over my chest.

"We could do that, you know."

"Do what?"

"We could stay here," Greg said.

I sat up on the sofa, looked down at him on the floor. "I don't understand."

"I was talking to Dylan earlier. They lost six people to the air in the last three months. He said he would have to clear it with Nina, but he knew she wouldn't mind if we stayed here."

"For how long?"

Greg turned his head on the pillow to look at me. "Forever, which is not very long anymore. But forever."

"No!" It didn't even take me a second to think about it.

"Look, before you say no."

"I already did, Greg!" I whispered harshly, yanking the throw off me, pulling my boots on and walking to the front door. I undid the bolts and stepped out, sensing Greg and I were about to have a debate that might get loud. I stood on the porch, looking out on the farmland that stretched for miles in every direction.

"How many have we lost so far?" Greg said behind me.

"No," I said. "We're not doing this."

"Kendall, Sloane, and the girl we tried to rescue," he answered his own question. "How many more will it take?"

I didn't answer, just shook my head at what he was trying to do.

"Do you really wanna go back out there? Walking, starving, scared that we might roll up on the wrong people, and—"

"No, Greg! No! I don't want to do any of that."

"Then we should stay," Greg said, sounding more passionate about his position. "We won't have to fear for our lives anymore, won't have to worry we'll wake up with everything around us on fire, and you and I can—" he stopped himself, looking as though he might've said more than he wanted.

"You and I can do what, Greg?"

"Nothing," he said, shaking his head, turning away from me.

I hurried to him, spun him around, needing to know what he was suggesting. "We can do what?"

He stared past me, looked to have been wrestling with the thoughts in his head. "What you did to me, I don't know if I can ever forgive you for that. I don't even know if I can stand you anymore, but this place..." he said, looking out over the balcony, as though imagining himself working the land, harvesting vegetables beside Dylan on a warm evening. "If we don't have to worry about food, about being killed, this place might allow us to get to know each other again, start over and..."

They were the words I wanted to hear: that he would try to forgive me, that we might be best friends again, and maybe more. But there was no way that could happen here.

I shook my head. “We can’t stay here,” and despite wanting exactly what Greg was proposing, I said, “You know what we’re doing is more important than you and me, or any of us. You know what we’re trying to get to the president.”

“The notes? Your mom’s notes?”

I nodded.

“What makes you know they aren’t as worthless as the paper they’re written on?”

“I’ll guess we’ll find that out when I deliver them.”

“Stay here with me, Shea. You said I used to mean something to you.”

“You still do.”

“Then stay.”

I thought of what life would be like here with Dlyan, Sophie, Nina and the other members of her group. I could convince all of my friends to remain here with us. We’d be stronger, more productive, safer, and Greg and I would grow closer. One day he’d forgive me, we’d fall back in love and live out each day happily and content. But while we did that, people in D.C., around the country, and around the world would continue to die from the air, when I knew there was a chance I could’ve stopped it.

“And what if I don’t?” I asked Greg.

He closed his eyes, shook his head as though he took my indecision as a personal insult. “Then I guess we’ll see what happens tomorrow.”

## 35

After breakfast, Nina asked if I'd like to come out back and check out some of the animals.

"Sure," I said, pushing away from the table, feeling there was something she wanted to talk about.

Out back, there were the cows, chickens and pigs she spoke of last night. It wasn't anything I hadn't seen before. Afterward, Nina closed the barn doors, slipped the two by four back into the catches then we walked lazily, the fifty yards back to the farmhouse.

"Dylan said that Greg told him you're a Legacy cop."

"My dad was a sheriff," I said, dragging a skinny branch I had picked up behind me. "But I don't do that anymore."

"But you know how to use a gun. He trained you how to protect yourself and others. Right?"

Yeah, but like I said..."

Nina stopped in some of the knee-high grass. "I wasn't trying to listen in on you two, but my bedroom is right over the front porch. Greg told you that I want you all to stay. It's not safe out there. I'm actually surprised you guys made it this far."

"We can take care of ourselves," I said.

"Obviously, and I didn't mean to say that you weren't able," Nina said, picking up on my tone. "But the people out there, all they want is what they can take from others."

"Everyone's not like that."

Nina took a few more steps then stopped again, turning to face me. "What Dylan said last night was true. There were two attempted home invasions. We fought them off, but..."

"But what?"

"That freshly plowed area right there?" Nina said, turning, pointing to an acre plot of just turned over dirt, fifty yards and to the left of the farmhouse. "Those used to be crops: corn and wheat. One night it was on fire. Before we had a chance to put it out, we noticed we were surrounded by the Crazies, with their white painted faces and their fetish for fire."

A chill sped the length of my spine. "You mean Burners?"

"Burners," Nina nodded, smiled a little. "You can call them that too, I suppose. We were surrounded. We had guns, they didn't. We shot in the air. All but one took off. The one that stayed managed to strangle one of our friends before we could get a shot off and kill him."

"I'm sorry."

"We buried ours and the Burner too, even though some of us thought we should've just left him out to rot." Nina walked closer to me, her eyes even more serious than before. "You call them Burners, but they do more than just set stuff on fire. They're killers, and they're out there: crazy with their death mission, chalk crosses on their faces, and those burning cross brands on their arms. Shea, if you don't have to go to D.C., you really might want to—"

"Hold it! What did you just say?" I asked.

"I said you should consider staying here, if you don't—"

"No, about the brands. You said the Burners have brands."

"When we buried him," Nina said, rubbing the side of her own bicep, showing me where the brand was located, "I saw it. It looked like a cross, with a flame burning behind it. I saw the same brand on a couple of the others, the ones with their arms exposed. They had the same thing."

I ran up the steps, stopped on the front porch, breathing heavily. Nina grabbed me by the arm.

"Shea, what's going on?"

Hearing people talking and laughing just inside the house, I gave Nina no more information than I believed necessary.

"You need to tell me what's going on. This is my house, and—"

"I'll tell you everything," I said, grabbing the wrist of the hand Nina held me with. "But right now, there's not enough time. I just need to go upstairs, and if anyone tries to follow me, make sure they don't. Can you do that for me?"

I needed confirmation, something to prove to me that he wasn't the monster I thought he could've been.

I rushed over to the bags, unfastening the bigger one first. I tried sifting through it without disrupting his stuff, but with the little time I had, that proved too difficult. I dumped the bag on the floor, having no idea of what I was looking for. Matches? Black face paint? White clothes? A Burner nametag saying, "Hi, I'm Jonny!"

Finding nothing, I shoveled all of Jonny's crap back into his bag. I was about to leave without checking the smaller satchel, but stopped, knowing I would continue to question myself if I hadn't checked everything.

I grabbed the satchel, started searching the pockets and pulled out a single folded sheet of paper. There was a diagram on it and some writing. I shuddered, realizing it was a drawing of the earth, passing through three stages. In the final stage, all of earth was on fire.

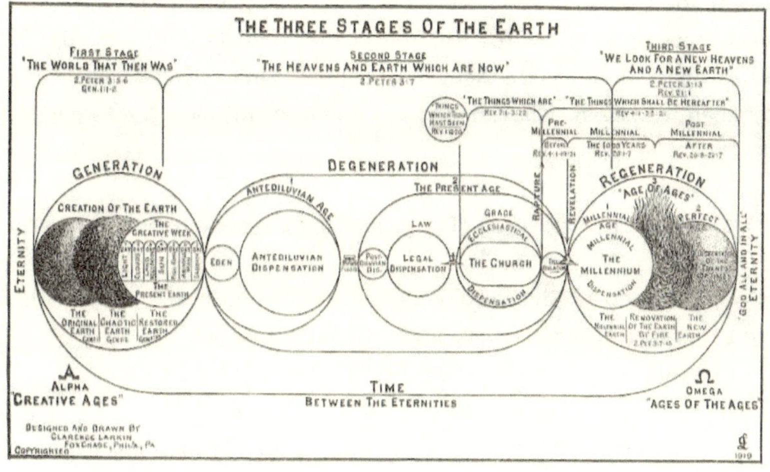

Jonny was one of them!

Twenty minutes later, the ten of us stood at the bottom of the stairs, thanking Nina, her friends and family, who waved sadly from atop the porch.

I was surprised to have seen Greg among our group. When I walked toward him to thank him for continuing on with his, he turned his shoulder, spoke to Daniel, letting me know he had nothing to say to me.

We were well rested and well fed, to include Tornado, who had happily feasted on scraps from the table, and the leftovers from both dinner and breakfast. Nina allowed us to take a little bit of food with us, packed in plastic bags. Even though it wasn't much, we were much better off now than we had been coming here.

"Everyone ready?" I asked.

"Wait," Toni said, hurrying back up the stairs, over to Nina, who the toddler, Sophie in her arms. Toni leaned over, kissed both chubby cheeks of the baby, told her how much she was going to be missed, then hurried back down the steps to us.

We started off, stepping reluctantly off the land we all knew provided us with food, security, and a feeling of home: things we've all missed and would never have on the road. In front of the group, I turned around, walking backwards to face them. "Just another couple of days," I yelled confidently, showing what I hoped was a smile on my face. "And we'll be in the capital."

"Wait!"

The group stopped, all of us turning our attention to Toni, who gave the order.

"I can't do it." She had already taken off her backpack. It was in the dirt at her feet. "No more walking. No more on the road."

"What are you talking about, Toni?" April said, taking her hand, pulling her along. "Shea said we only have a few more days."

"I can't make it another few more days, April." Toni shook her head.

I pushed through the group, walking toward Toni. I saw that from the porch, looking concerned, Nina handed Sophie off to Liz, came down the stairs and approached Toni. We stood on either side of her.

"Toni—" I said.

She shook her head again, as though to decline whatever I offered.

"It's too hard out there, Shea. Oliver's dead. I'm not going to walk another two days beside his murderer, sleeping on the ground, crapping in the woods, looking over my shoulder, fearing for my life and the life of my baby."

"Then what about your baby?" I said.

"We'll care for her here," Nina said. She had a hand on Toni's shoulder, like they were old friends. "If you want to stay."

"Toni—" I said, not really knowing why I continued trying to convince her the journey was better for her, when it wasn't.

Toni grabbed me by the hand and squeezed. "Shea, you've been the best friend I could've asked for all these years, as well as a savior. But you can't save us all." Tears spilled from Toni's eyes, as I felt her releasing my hand. "I'm gonna be fine here." She glanced at Nina, as if looking for confirmation of that. Nina nodded her head and smiled.

Back on the interstate, Tornado pulling harder on his leash than normal, as though as tired of being on the road as everyone else, and wanted to get to the capital as soon as possible, I looked over my shoulder and saw no sign of the farmhouse. Silence hung over us like the regret of a badly made decision. We had lost Toni, and we all felt the void she left. But she wasn't the only one. We lost Amy and Tracy too.

As we marched away from the farmhouse, the girls turned and ran back without saying a word, as though we would've run after them and tackled them, stopped them from staying if we had spotted them leaving.

"Hey," Angie said, nudging me. "I think we have two more defectors."

I saw the girls sprinting back to the farmhouse, their long hair, trailing in the wind behind them. Reaching Nina, I saw them say something to her, then Nina reaching out to hug them both.

"Shea…" Angie said.

"Just let them go," Beth said, standing next to me. "If they can't do it anymore, they shouldn't have it."

"So what you wanna do?" Angie asked.

I turned back around, continued walking, and said, "I just wanna make it to D.C."

# 36

We walked far enough to where I felt comfortable that no one in the camp would hear the gunshot if I had to use my weapon on Jonny. Walking, Jonny just a couple of steps in front of me, I believed he was getting suspicious of why I brought him out here. I had run out of things to talk about, and we'd been silently walking for the last five minutes.

"So why'd you really bring me out here?"

I stepped back, making sure there was at least ten feet between us. "Raise the sleeve of your right arm."

"Why, Shea?"

"Just do it."

He looked at me as though he didn't want to, but started to roll the sleeve cuff anyway. "Exactly what are you looking for?"

"I'll know when I see it," I said, trying to visualize the description of the symbol Nina had told me about.

"I said it was nothing. Why don't we—" Jonny said, exposing the bottom tip of his keloid skin.

"Keep on," I said, as he revealed the entire brand. Shocked and saddened, I stepped back, stumbling on a rock. Almost falling, I grabbed my gun as I saw him starting toward me. I regained my balance, pointing the Walther at him. "Stay right there! Don't move!" I said, surprised to hear my voice quivering. I always sensed there was something not quite right about him, but I never thought he could've been a killer—a Burner.

Jonny stopped, raised his palms. "You were about to fall, I was just trying to—"

"Shut up!" I yelled, slowly circling him. "You're one of them. That's why they've been following us, why we can't shake them, right?"

"Shea, no," he said.

"Turn around!" I ordered, jabbing the gun at him. "That brand. It's on all their arms." I thought about how foolish I'd been letting him travel with us, sleep with us. I put the welfare of the entire camp in jeopardy. "Face me!"

Jonny turned.

"Where are they? They camped near us? Have you been communicating with them?" I quickly rattled off questions, feeling that Burners could've been watching my camp that moment.

"Shea, I'm not one of them."

"The brand says you are!" I yelled, pointing toward it with the gun then setting the site back on him.

"I was, but not anymore. I swear!" he screamed, his chest heaving. "I was with them, but for not even that long. I thought I believed what they stood for. I thought they were a group I could've belonged to—a family. But not after what I saw them do—not after what they wanted me to do."

"Tell me."

Jonny reiterated the fact that he couldn't make it on the road. After being alone for two days, he had been robbed twice, and knew he needed to be with a group in order to survive—any group. He fell in with the Burners when they found him shivering, bawled up in a storefront doorway.

"They took me in, said I could travel with them," Jonny said. "I didn't know who they were at the time. Yeah, they looked weird—the crosses and stuff, but they gave me clothes and food, and seemed like decent people." He said, in order to stay with them, he was branded. "It burned like hell. I could smell my own flesh cooking, but I was happy, because I felt safe."

"Then why leave?" I said, still not satisfied that he wasn't lying to me.

He told me that two other boys were taken in the day before they found him. There was a task they had to preform to become fully accepted among the Burners.

"That evening, we stood behind the trees, watched a couple, probably girlfriend and boyfriend, maybe sister and brother—I don't know. But they weren't hurting anyone. Then all of sudden, we were surrounding them, right up on them, before they even knew we were there. The two new guys took them around the throats," Jonny said, seeming to have a hard time describing the scene, shutting his eyes, shaking his head. "The girl begged, pleaded for her life, screaming as the boy fought like crazy, but they killed them anyway. Afterward, I watched the other Burners set fire to them, to the leaves and the trees around them, and like in those stupid movies where the guy walks off all slow after a building explodes, we did the same thing. Just walked off and didn't look back, everything going up in flames. They wanted me to do it next: kill for them, but that night after everyone fell asleep, I ran off. After a couple of days, I found the group that broke into your house."

"Guess you're no good at finding groups," I said, believing Jonny's story enough to holster my gun.

"Until now," he said. "You have good people, Shea. And I need you to believe I'd never knowingly put you guys in danger like that."

"You don't have to know it for us to be in danger. Could they be looking for you? Is there some Burner code that you're not supposed to sneak off in the night after you receive the stupid arm brand or something?"

Glancing up from his hands, Jonny nodded, apologetically. "I guess. Somewhere I got the impression that once you're a Burner, the only way you're not anymore is if you're dead."

"Good job, Jonny," I said, standing from the tree. "Get up. We're heading back."

# 37

"I don't want anyone to be alarmed. No one is in danger, but Jonny is a Burner," I said, feeling the need to just get it all out.

"Yeah, Shea," Daniel laughed. "Where's the cross on his face?"

"The face cross isn't permanent," I said. "But the brand Burners have is. Show them, Jonny," I said.

Jonny attempted to pull away from me.

"Show it, Jonny!" I ordered.

He stopped fighting, lowered his head, slapped a hand on his arm then pushed his sleeve up to expose the brand.

Angie gasped loud enough for all of us to hear. It was the only sound, for the mouths of everyone else either remained closed, or hung slightly open, eyes staring shocked at me.

"I told you!" Potter yelled, standing from the base of the tree. "I knew there was something not right with that kid!"

Out of my periphery, I saw Daniel step a number of feet away from Jonny and unsling his rifle. Angie and Greg did the same, stepped back, pointing their weapons at Jonny.

"No, no, no, no!" I said, rushing in front of him, hands up.

"Get out of the way, Shea!" Greg said, squinting down the sight of his weapon. "He has to go! He killed those people!"

"I didn't kill them," Jonny screamed.

"Then your people did," Potter yelled.

"We have to hear him out!" I held out my arms, stepping in front of Jonny each time Greg tried to aim past me. "We hear him out, take a vote and decide what to do. That's how we do it, right? A democracy: isn't that what we decided," I yelled over the chaos.

Jonny was given time to talk, telling our group everything he told me, all the while pleading for understanding and mercy. When he was finished, he stood quiet, staring down at his feet, awaiting our decision.

"So we vote now," Greg said.

"We aren't going to hurt him," I said, feeling strangely protective of him, knowing I put him in the position he was in.

"We vote whether he stays or goes," Greg said. "All in favor of us allowing Jonny to continue on with us to D.C., raise your hands."

The single hand that was elevated belonged to me.

I glanced at April, at Angie, even Beth, trying to convince them to trust me and spare Jonny.

"All those in favor of getting rid of him..." Greg said.

The seven remaining votes were cast in favor of sending Jonny away.

There was no time wasted in executing his punishment.

Angie, Greg and I walked Jonny, blindfolded, a mile away from our camp. After we were far enough out, weapons were pointed at him and I was allowed to pull the scarf from around his eyes. Jonny blinked against the sunlight, turned and looked around to get his bearings.

"Shea?" he called, desperately, starting toward me.

All weapons were raised again, stopping him in the dirt.

"I'm sorry, Jonny," I said. "But the vote was taken and the decision was made."

"You have to go, and if you try to follow us, if anyone sees you...you'll be shot," Greg said.

Jonny stood in front of us with just the clothes on his back, no supplies, no food, palms open, appearing frail and frightened, looking worse off than when we found him.

"But I have nothing."

"I'm sorry," I spoke softly, knowing he would be eaten alive out there by himself.

"And don't go back to Jessie's farm. I had told her I suspected you of being a Burner. She'll shoot you on sight if she sees you again."

Jonny stared at me, not with anger but sadness, as though he knew I did what had to be done, but regretted the way things turned out.

"Goodbye Shea," he said, turned, and walked off.

# 38

We had gotten rid of Jonny. But solving one problem only meant there was more time to pay attention to others.

Since Kendall was killed, Beth dragged along, silently behind us, her head down, seeming not to care about anything. I knew that Beth's wellbeing was somehow tied to Kendall, but never thought Kendall's death would have the overwhelming affect on Beth it had had over the past few days.

Since we had buried the girl, April stuck by her sister's side, telling Beth corny jokes, reminding her of the times they enjoyed before the air turned: memories with their parents, hoping to trigger something in Beth that might make her realize there was life after Kendall.

Nothing worked.

"Can you talk to her?" April asked me.

"She's mourning, April. She lost someone she cared very much for."

"What about me? I'm still here! When I try to talk to her, she's sad and looks right through me, like she'd rather be dead. Please, Shea," April said, grabbing my arm, tugging on me. "I know Kendall was, like, my sister's whole world, but can you tell her there are still people here that love and need her."

It was during a break from our walking that I decided to do as April asked. When I approached Beth, she was sitting on the guardrail, under the shade of some leafy branches.

"You mind if I sit with you a while?"

Beth looked up at me and hunched her shoulders.

"We're gonna get through this, you know," I said, sitting.

Beth didn't respond.

I thought about mentioning what April had said, but figured since April herself couldn't get through to Beth, nothing I told her she said would matter.

"I'm sorry about Kendall."

Beth squinted against sunlight that found its way through the leaves. "I loved her, you know."

"We all loved—" I said, about to lie, only to make Beth feel better, when she cut me off.

"No, I was in love with her. I know she wasn't the nicest person, and I know she didn't look my way twice before the air turned, but since then, she needed me. She made me feel I had purpose, that she couldn't live without me. Over that time, I fell in love with her, and I think she loved me too." Beth smiled, wistfully. "Now that she's gone, I'm wondering why I'm doing all of this."

"You know why." I said, feeling as though I should've realized that was the bond between the two of them, but shocked to hear it. "To survive."

"Surviving. That's different than living, isn't it?"

It was. I knew that, but I wasn't going to give Beth the answer she was looking for. "Guess it's all how you look at it."

Beth nodded, knowing the game I was playing. "It's a lot worse. I'm not sure if I like just surviving."

"What do you mean?" I asked.

Staring out across the interstate, her palms pressed between her knees, she said, "What we're doing...the struggle, the pain, the loss, with nothing to look forward to but that horrific, tragic end."

"Beth—"

"Do you know how they go? How it takes us when the air does what it does."

I knew. I felt I had seen it a thousand times, but said, "How we die?"

Beth shook her head. "Not dying. That word is too peaceful. Killed, strangled, tortured maybe. But whatever it is, it's frightening to watch. Imagine how terrible it must be to experience."

"You can't just check out. What about April? She needs you."

"At 11 years old, April is stronger than I am now. Besides, she has you. You're the one she looks up to."

"Don't put that on me, Beth. I can't—"

"You can." Beth grabbed my hand. I tried pulling away from her, not ready to be some kid's wilderness Godmother. Beth held tight to me.

"I'm not one hundred percent sure of it, She, but I'm pretty sure I'd rather end things my way than go out like everybody else. I'm not brave enough or strong enough for that. So if that day comes, promise me you'll watch over April—be the big sister I wasn't able to be."

"Beth, think about—"

"I have. Now promise me, Shea."

"It's not guaranteed, Beth. We might have the cure, remember. And—"

Beth chuckled. "In high school, you always seemed kind of pessimistic. Now look at you: all about hope and harmony. What happened?"

"I don't know," I said, feeling as though I didn't owe Beth an explanation. "But without hope, we have nothing. Right?" I said, setting a hand awkwardly on Beth's wrist.

She looked down, letting me know I failed in whatever gesture I was making, then said to me: "I guess I have nothing left."

# 39

That night, I watched as April stomped over, kicking dirt as she came. She had been attempting to set up their tent for the night, and it appeared as though Beth wasn't being of much use to her.

"You talked to her, right?" April said, her fists on her narrow hips.

"I did, but to be honest, I don't know if it did much good."

"I'm tired of it," April said. "She acts like she misses Kendall more than Mom and Dad. She does nothing but mope all day, and now she won't even help me pitch our tent. She's useless!"

Angie walked up. "I'll help you."

"No," April said. "You have your own tent to do. Beth is supposed to help me, and that's what she's gonna do!" April marched back toward her sister.

"I hope this doesn't turn out like I think it's going to," Angie said.

"Same here," I said under my breath.

April stopped in front of her big sister who sat slumped on a big rock. Waving her hands about, I could see that April was telling Beth off. I couldn't really make out words, but the tone I heard was definitely forceful and demanding.

"She's letting Beth have it," Angie said.

April grabbed the tent that was still rolled up, dragged it over, kicked it toward Beth's feet, and continued giving her the business, her voice much louder.

"---your responsibility! But you're not only giving up on life, you're giving up on me!" April yelled.

"Wow," Angie said. "She's really going in."

April pointed her finger at Beth's face, an inch from her nose, continuing with all the ways Beth had let April down.

"I should go over there. Looks like it's getting out of hand," I told Angie, getting up. Before I took a step in that direction, Beth stood, as if to intimidate her sister into backing down. April didn't let up, only raised her voice louder, for all the camp to hear. "Then if you're so sick and tired of living, why don't you do us all a favor and just kill yourself, already!"

Beth's reaction to the comment was immediate. She hauled off, slapped April like an abusive mother would her mouthy child, and April hit the ground, lay prone in the dirt, on her forearms, staring angrily at the dirt. After a second, she pulled herself up, stood in front of Beth, a hand to her cheek, disbelief on her face, then ran off into the woods.

# 40

High up in the mountains, the air was crisp, the sky clear. The last of us struggled up the steep incline, on the plateau. We looked out, breathing heavily, our hands on our knees, bent over, physically tested and saw for miles and miles out into the distance, over trees, streams, lower mountains and down to a body of the bluest water I've seen in years.

"I hate hills," Angie said. "Unless I'm going down them."

I chuckled in agreement.

"I know what you mean," April said. "Right Beth?" April was trying to engage her sister. She had been attempting that every since the incident at our campsite last night.

Marching ahead of them on our way here, I couldn't help but overhear April ask for Beth's forgiveness.

Beth had nothing to say to her little sister. I glanced over my shoulder, saw that Beth stared straight ahead, as if the girl wasn't walking there beside her.

"I'm not a huge mountain fan, either," I said. "But it was worth climbing this one to get to this view," I walked to the ledge of the plateau, my hands on my hips "It's beautiful up here."

"It is, isn't it," Greg said, stepping up beside me, holding a hand over his eyes as a visor against the sun. "This alone almost makes the trip worth it."

"Don't know if I'd go that far," Daniel said, picking a rock from the ground and slinging it. "But it is kinda cool. How much farther to D.C.?"

I glanced down at the roadmap I had just unfolded. "If we keep the same pace, just another few days," I said looking over at April. Her head hanging, I could tell she was still disappointed about the situation with her sister.

"You wanna see the view, Beth?" I asked.

Beth turned to me, raised a brow, as though my question was the most ridiculous one she's heard in her lifetime. "Why?"

"Because she asked you, that's why?" April shouted. "Because what the hell else are you gonna do but mope some more, cry, feel sorry for yourself some more, and let everyone know how sad you are that poor Kendall is gone. Well I don't care, Beth."

"April—" I said, not wanting to see a replay of last night.

"No, Shea," April said, holding up a hand.

"No one wanted this to happen, Beth. Everyone has lost at least someone to the air. They're dead now and there's nothing we can do about it. But I'm not ready to lose my sister when she's standing right in front of me. You're all I have left!" April said, her voice cracking and high pitched. "I need you to snap out of this. Life is still worth living."

"No it's not." Beth's voice was low.

We all stood silent.

"It is!" April said. "I need you!"

"But you said..." Beth started, looking past April, at the view behind her sister. Beth's eyes softened, as if only just noticing the beauty around her. "You said you didn't."

"I didn't say that," April said.

"You said that I might as well kill myself."

"I..."

"It's okay," Beth said, then an actual smile came to her face and she looked up toward the sky and took a deep breath in. "You were all right. It is beautiful up here."

"That's right," I said, happy and relieved that finally Beth might've been coming out of her funk.

"But this is it," she said. "As beautiful as the world will ever be again."

"We don't know that," April said.

Beth walked over to her sister, the smile still on her face. She placed a palm to April's cheek. It was the same hand Beth had struck her with in anger. "I'm sorry I hit you. But you're gonna be okay, aren't you?"

April nodded, appearing as though she didn't fully understand the question, but agreed anyway. "Yeah."

"Shea'll take care of you when I'm gone. Won't you Shea," Beth said, glancing at me.

"When you're gone?" April said, taking the words out of my mouth.

What was happening?

Beth leaned in, kissed April's cheek, stepped back, stared at her sister as though imprinting her image on her brain so as to never forget it, then turned in the direction of the plateau ledge and started running.

Not until that very moment, when I witnessed Beth digging her feet into the dirt, kicking it up as she ran as fast as she could, total determination on her face, did I realize she had been planning this end, but had been waiting for the right moment.

Tornado started barking and took off after Beth.

"Stop her!" I yelled. "She's going for the ledge!"

Daniel went after her, grunting as his boot heels kicked up chunks of dirt, his body leaning forward, an arm outstretched. He would catch her, I told myself, force her to the ground, wrap her up so she could not move, then we'd all go to her, and after she stood, we'd embrace her, tell her how much she meant, not only to us, but to all those who survived. But Daniel had lost his footing, slipped, tripped, stumbled, slowing him a fraction of a second. He recovered, continued his chase, Beth not an inch from Daniel's outstretched hand. Then Beth planted a foot on the last bit of flat earth before it dropped off at a ninety-degree angle, and then leapt. Daniel caught her, his hand wrapped around the scarf that whipped in the wind behind Beth, he held tight to it, but it unraveled from around her neck, as she disappeared over the mountain's edge.

The shriek from April was deafening.

We ran, fell to our bellies on the ledge of the cliff, hoping that Beth had fallen to a soft, grass covered shelf just bellow, gotten hung up on branch—cartoonlike: Wyllie Coyote style—by the back of her shirt collar.

That didn't happen, for we saw her falling, arms and legs stretched out, plummeting downward, backward, facing us, hair flying, flapping about her face. I don't know if I had actually seen it on her face, or if it was just my imagination. Nevertheless, I know I will never forget the expression, real or imagined, of peacefulness and contentment as she fell to her death.

Still screaming, April ran toward us. I spun around, got to my knees, reached out, snatched her in my arms and held her tight, fearing that in her frenzy, without thinking, she might have tried to follow her sister down.

# 41

We had lost Beth, and as to be expected, it had a horrible affect on April. If we weren't in the middle of nowhere, exhausted, running out of food, and needing to make it to D.C. before I feared we'd all just give up and die, I would've suggested we stop—give April time to mourn her sister's loss. We didn't have that option. So we pushed on, members of the group taking turns, walking beside her, an arm around her shoulder, speaking softly to her.

Over the course of the day, I marched with the group—sometimes up front with Greg and Daniel, sometimes in the rear alongside Potter—always with my hand resting on the butt of my weapon, because I knew we were being watched. That wasn't a hunch, a suspicion, or a gut feeling, like most times. That was confirmed when I had turned around to see the outline of a figure in the trees a half dozen times. I thought there was reason for concern, was going to tell Greg, Daniel and Angie, come up with a plan to nab the guy, whoever it was, until an hour ago, when I looked over my shoulder, and behind us, twenty yards away, I spotted the figure again. He ducked quickly back behind the cover of a tree, but not before I was able to identify him.

After the group dug in for the night, had set up our tents and built a small fire, I told Angie I was going to check the perimeter. It only took me ten minutes to find who I was looking for. I stepped out from behind a tree, my gun drawn, pointing at the back of the shivering figure sitting on the ground.

"Turn around, Jonny," I said.

He looked over his shoulder, and paying close attention to keep the thin, ratty blanket around his shoulders, he got to his knees and stood.

"You here to shoot me?" Jonny asked, holding up one of his hands, the other busy grasping the ends of the blanket together under his chin.

I knew he had been following us.

"Not gonna shoot you, Jonny," I said holstering my gun and setting down a thick blanket and the little bit of food I had brought for him. I watched him race toward the offering. He grabbed the blanket and draped it around himself, covering the much thinner one he already wore. He took the plastic bag of trail mix, turned it up, munching on the nuts and berries as they fell into his mouth. He turned to me still chewing, lowering the bag from his face, leaving half of what I had given him. "Can I keep what's left if I don't eat it now?" he asked, rolling the top of the bag closed.

"You can have it," I said. "I brought it for you. Take care, Jonny, I said, turning to go, still feeling guilty about him being exiled.

"Shea..."

I stopped, looked back at him.

"You should be proud of yourself for doing this."

"Doing what?"

"Getting your friends to the capital, and trying to save the human race.

People will remember you." He smiled. "I'm nineteen now, so I won't be around for that much longer. But if I had to do it all again, that's what I'd wish for: to do something meaningful, something that people would remember me for."

I blinked my eyes quickly, holding in my emotion. I wanted to bring him

back to camp, sit him in front of the fire and let him warm himself, talk to him, and maybe the two of us could come up with something that would make his memory last in the minds of our group members. But I knew I had to leave him here.

"Goodnight, Jonny," I said, walking away, forcing myself not to look back.

## 42

Almost everyone had gone to sleep a couple of hours ago. I stood outside my tent, staring at the boy that watched over us for the night, his back was to me.

Hearing me, Greg stood from his rock, turned, his rifle leveled on me.

"Shea," Greg sighed and lowered his weapon. "What are you doing out here?"

"Couldn't sleep." I walked over to him, stopped a few feet shy. "Can we talk?"

"Go back to bed, Shea." Greg turned away and took his seat back on the rock.

I stood in front of him. "I want to talk."

"Nothing to talk about. I have nothing to say to you, okay."

"About what happened at Nina's. You could at least—"

"At least what, Shea?" Greg raised his voice, standing from the dirt. "We had an opportunity to have a better life, to be...to be...something, but you didn't want that. I got the picture. So now, I have nothing left to say to you," he said, turning his back on me.

"Then why'd you come on this trip if you hate me so much?"

Greg spun. "You really wanna know?"

"It's why I'm asking."

Shaking his head as though not sure he wanted to say what was on his mind,

Greg said, "Sloane asked me because she didn't know if she would live long enough to make it to the capital, and she wasn't sure you had what it took to get these people there safely."

"No," I breathed, not believing him. "She said that?"

"Yes. She practically begged, needed me to go so she wouldn't have to worry about you getting hurt, robbed, or killed. She knew I wouldn't let anything happen to you."

"Sloane lied to me?"

"It wasn't the only one," Greg said, seemingly taking pleasure in how much his news hurt me.

"What else?" I asked, not sure I wanted to know.

"She had no friend that had made the trip and came back. That was a lie to make everyone believe it was safe to go there. The White House, the Smithsonian, the Lincoln Monument, all the streets of D.C., could be burning this second."

A tear sped down my check. Sloane asking Greg to go on this trip, I knew, was only because she cared for me. I could understand that, but to have lied to my face when I thought we kept no secrets was almost unforgivable. I walked right up to Greg and asked him, "What's the point in telling me all this?"

He looked angrier than I had ever seen him, his jaws clenched, fists bawled up against the sides of his thighs.

"So you'd know how it feels to be betrayed by someone you thought cared about you."

Silently, I nodded, acknowledging his pain as I dug into my backpack and pulled out a stack of unopened letters I had written to him over the two years he had been gone.

"I'm sorry about what I did. It doesn't mean I didn't care about you. It was just a really stupid mistake." I set the letters in his hand, and started away from him.

"What's this?"

"Two years worth of me telling you how much you meant to me, how sorry I was.

He stood silent.

"Read them or throw them away. They're yours," I said. "I guess I don't really care anymore."

## 43

It had been a full day since I'd given Greg the letters: the same amount of time since he had spoken a word to me, or looked in my direction.

We marched most of the day and took two of our three breaks, Greg never coming over to tell me what he thought of what I wrote.

"What'd you do to him?" Angie said, sitting next to me, staring over at him, his head down, reading from a sheet of paper. "He seems really pissed at you, girl."

"I didn't do nothing," I grunted, and watched as he turned away when he saw that I was staring at him. I assumed that he was reading one of my letters.

We got back on the road for the last three hours of our days requirement.

I glanced over my shoulder only twice to see Greg lagging behind the group, head down, holding another page between his fists as he walked.

After all of us agreed on the spot where we'd pitch camp for the night, I was startled when someone grabbed me from behind. I spun around to see Greg.

"I finished the letters," he said. "I need to speak with you later, okay?"

"About what?"

"I'll come to you," he said, walking away.

Later, I lay inside my tent, wide-awake.

I pulled the top of my sleeping bag up over my shoulder, shut my eyes and told myself to go to sleep. A minute later, I heard my zipper door being undone and someone crawling in.

"Shea?" Greg kneeled next to me, so close I felt the warmth of his breath on my face. "You awake?"

"Greg?"

"I finished the letters."

I shimmied out of my sleeping bag. "And?"

"Seems you had a lot to get off your chest."

"A whole lot," I half smiled. "How many letters were there, like fifty?"

"There were a lot," Greg said. "I'm glad you were able to make yourself feel less guilty for what you did to me. Good night, Shea." He turned and started crawling toward the tent door.

"Wait!"

He stopped, looked over his shoulder. "What?"

"How many times can I tell you I'm sorry before you let me back in?"

"Sorry wipes away all the humiliation you caused me? The shame I felt. I was already a joke in everyone's eyes, but that didn't matter to me as long as I knew you were my friend."

Leading up to the dance, it was all Greg could talk about. Smiling in my face, he would tell me he was going to get fitted for a suit and asked if I wanted to come, or that he was practicing dance moves so that he wouldn't embarrass me on the floor. He told me how excited his father was that I was going with "the prettiest girl in the whole high school".

I was honored that he was so excited about going with me, and I was just as excited, until I had made that deal with Kendall; until I knew on the night Greg looked so forward to, I would deceive him.

At the dance, fifteen minutes after we had arrived, I excused myself from the table to go to the restroom. I stood, staring at myself in the mirror, corsage that Greg had given me, pinned to my chest, the makeup Sloane helped me apply, doing nothing to stop the nervous sweat from beading on my forehead.

The restroom door opened, startling me. It was Kendall and a friend of hers I had seen a thousand times around school, but had never spoken to.

"You all set?" Kendall asked, beaming, clip-clopping toward me in super high heels and a form-fitting aqua blue gown. "Undo the top of your dress. My girl is going to wire you for sound."

I glanced at Anna: that was the girl's name. Her dark hair curled, stacked on top of her head, and frozen with hair spray, she went into her clutch and pulled out what looked like a small battery pack, a wire attached to one end, a tiny microphone on the other. She held it in front of me, like she was a surgeon about to implant it inside of me. I stepped backward, thinking of ending the arrangement that moment.

"Shea!" Kendall snapped, rattling me. "Do you remember our deal?"

I nodded, still deciding how badly I would be regarded if I bailed out then.

"Good," Kendall said. "So do you still want to be part of our clique and do you still want to date Markham Jennings?"

I had felt like the hopeful fool since I had paid for Markham's lunch, thinking he'd somehow find my phone number or email address or Facebook page, and text, mail or message me to ask me out. That had never happened.

"You sure he said he'd go out on a date with me, because it doesn't feel like he will."

Kendall shook her head, blew out an exasperated sigh, then turned to Anna, gave her instructions and pointed toward the door. A moment later, Markham Jennings sauntered into the restroom, wearing his black suit and tie, enveloped in an aura of royalty. He stepped around Kendall, reached out, took my chin in his hand and told me if I did this one little thing, he would take me wherever I wanted to go.

"Will you do this for me?" he asked.

A stupid grin on my face, half in a daze, I nodded. Magically, he was gone, and Kendall was standing in front of me again.

"Now unzip your gown, and let's do this," she ordered.

Half an hour later, Greg and I were in the storage room off the gymnasium, sitting shoulder to shoulder on the small sofa, unable to see our hands in front of our faces; the only light, a strip from the hallway outside, spilled in from under the door.

"Why are we in here?" Greg asked, his body rigid beside me.

"Just thought you might've wanted to get away from all those people."

I heard him sigh. He was relaxed, more so than I think he's ever been with me.

He, like almost everyone at the dance, had had a couple of glasses of the spiked punch.

"Would you mind if I tell you something?" Greg asked.

I spoke softly. "If you want."

I felt his hand fumbling about on the sofa, touching my knee, crawling up my thigh like a huge spider. I smelled the alcohol on his breath as he neared me, telling me he had always thought me beautiful, always had a crush on me.

"It's okay, Greg," I whispered, trying to quiet him with a squeeze of his hand, hoping the microphone pinned just inside the strap of my gown wouldn't pick up what I was saying. I knew everyone in the gymnasium would hear, was probably listening in at that point, leaning forward in their chairs, hands cupped to their mouths, waiting with suspense-filled eyes for what was to happen.

Without notice Greg told me he loved me, leaned forward, grabbed me and pressed his mouth to mine. I wasn't shocked. I had always known there was a possibility of this happening at anytime: while we walked to school, in the cookie aisle at the local grocery store, or after we had jogged a few miles, leaning bent over, palms pressed on our knees, huffing, our faces nearly touching. But I was surprised that I wasn't grossed out when it actually did happen, that his kiss wasn't awkward, hurried or frantic, and unlike the Spiderman kiss in the tree, this actually felt right.

I was lost in the moment, allowed him to continue kissing me, quickly forgetting all that was around us. Then a second later, I remembered: the cameras, the microphone, the potential embarrassment and humiliation.

“Greg. Greg!” I said, pushing my hands into his chest, feeling him grab me tighter around the shoulders, trying to pull me back to him. Breathing heavily through his nose and mouth, he thrust his pelvis into me several times, then suddenly rolled away, crying out, doubling over, grabbing his middle, as though I had accidently kneed him in the groin.

That’s when the lights flashed on.

We were blinded. Then I had heard them, what sounded like hundreds of kids standing in the room with us, many still piling in, camera phone flashes going off, red cell phone recorder lights blinking as video was taken of the two of us.

Greg was still folded over as though hiding something, while the students heckled us—him mostly—crowding around, taunting, mocking and poking him, forcing him to stand to get away. And there, in the center of his light colored slacks was a huge dark, wet stain. Everyone saw it. The crowd jeered, and squealed, Markham Jennings, standing in the middle of them, his hand to his mouth, laughing so hard he looked as though he was about to cough up a lung.

Greg broke through the crush of laughing, mocking students, separating them with his arms. The girls fell away in disgust, hands pulled back as though touching him would contaminate them. The boys howled, some of them slapping Greg on the back, others tugging at the pockets of his pants, saying cruel things like, “Water balloon bust in your pocket, or were you just happy to see Shea!”

“Greg, I’m sorry. I was wrong. I was just...just caught up in the moment,” I said, still trying to stop him from leaving my tent.

“The moment? That’s all it took to undo all the years we were friends? That moment almost cost me my life.”

“What?” I asked, having no idea what he was talking about.

“You wanted to know why my parents sent me away, why they never talked about what happened to me,” Greg said, unfastening the buckles on the wide leather wristbands I had never seen him remove since his return. He pulled one off, then the other, let them both fall to the tent floor. He shoved his wrists at me, the butts of his palms facing up. I looked down, could barely see them in the small, dark space.

"Grab my wrists," Greg ordered. "Feel them."

I did as he told, the tips of my fingers feeling lines of raised scar tissue, each about two inches long, running vertically up his wrists. A split-second image of his veins opened, spewing blood, skittered across my brain. I grabbed his wrists tighter, as if to hold closed the imagined open wounds.

"Mom found me bleeding on the bathroom floor. I can still hear her screaming," Greg said. "They sent me away after that." He eased his wrists from my grasp. I didn't want to let them go. He blindly searched the floor for his bands, finding them, fastening the buckles back on his arms.

"Every time I look at the scars, I hate them, and I hate you even more. That's why I wear the bands. I got tired of hating you, Shea. Hating you, even though I still loved you."

At the dance, after Greg left the storage room, I couldn't find him. At home, I stood on the sidewalk, staring at his house, at the light on in his bedroom window, knowing I should've gone over there, apologized for the unforgivable thing I had done to him, but was too ashamed to ask his forgiveness, too afraid to put myself in front of him, knowing the anger that would be directed at me.

I hadn't spoken to Greg the entire weekend, and the following Monday at school, I hoped there would be no mention of what had happened, that all would've been forgotten, and Greg and I could've gone back to being the social nobodies we'd always been. We weren't that lucky.

As soon as I walked into the building, it felt as though everyone stopped in the hallway, mid-distance to their next class, and stared at me. I heard whispers then laughter, and then I noticed the t-shirts: a silkscreened photo of Greg from prom night, face bawled up like an infant who had wet his diaper: the dark stain in the crotch of his pants, me just behind him, humiliation all over my face, reaching out attempting to save him from his embarrassment. It looked as though nearly all the students in the hallway wore the shirt.

I lowered my head, worried about where Greg was, hoping he had not already endured this. I hurried to class, but on the way there, taped to many of the locker doors, I saw the same photo, 10 by 12 inch, glossy prints.

For the entire day, there was talk of what had happened that night, and sometime just before lunch, I found the courage to go on line, watch the video that I had been hearing had been uploaded to Youtube. It was there, and had already had fifty thousand views.

I had gone to Greg's last period class, waited for him by the door, but he had not shown; I figured he had already had enough, and had gone home. At least, that's what I had hoped. But when I walked outside, I saw him on the campus grass, surrounded by a crowd of laughing, yelling students. I pushed through the press of bodies, into the clearing where Greg stood with Kendall and Markham.

"And look who's here," Kendall said to the crowd. "The other half of the beautiful prom couple, Shea Kennedy!"

I heard both applause and boos from the seemingly growing gaggle of students. I rushed to Greg, who looked lost, humiliated and afraid. I reached for him, tried to take his hand, pull him out of there, but he yanked away from me.

"He's pissed at you, Shea," Markham laughed. "Because he knows you helped play the prank on him. And you wanna know why she did that to Gruesome Greg?" Markham asked of the crowd.

They simultaneously asked why.

"Because I told her I would date her if she did. And guess what?" he hollered, having a hard time controlling his laughter. "She believed me!"

More laughter erupted in my ears; grinning, mirth covered faces spun around me as Markham continued his rant.

"Why would I or anyone, for that matter, wanna date Shea Kennedy? She has a haircut like a little boy, her father will throw you in jail if you try and get in her pants, and then again, and considering how she humiliated her best friend the other night, why would anyone trust her?"

My head was spinning, my ears aching, and I thought I would just fall on the ground, roll into a ball and cry if I endured to much more of that. I needed to get out of there. I turned, looking for Greg to take him home, when I saw him confronting Markham for the things he had said about me.

Greg, standing six inches shorter than Markham, brought back a fist, appearing to take a swing at the bigger boy. Markham easily sidestepped the swing, causing Greg to stumble clumsily forward, at which time Markham punched Greg across the face. Greg whirled and teetered on his feet, then fell, bleeding, onto his side. The dense circle of kids exploded gleefully as though they had witnessed a first round knockout at a heavyweight championship fight.

I dropped to my knees, tried to take Greg's head in my lap, make sure he was okay, but he pushed me away, spat blood from his mouth, slowly got to his feet and staggered off without looking back.

That night, I went to his house, frantically rang the doorbell, pounded on the front door, but no one answered. Now I realized, they were probably at the emergency room, worrying whether Greg would pull through, while doctors tried to stich up wrists.

"You...you tried to kill yourself?" I gasped.

"I didn't see the point in continuing to be made a fool of by everyone at school, including you."

I reached out in the dark tent, wrapped my arms around him, pulling him into me.

"I'm sorry," I said, kissing his forehead. "I'm so, so sorry. Please just forgive me and let me back in."

"I'll never forget what you did to me, but I've forgiven you a long time ago. Accepting your apology isn't what's stopping me from opening up to you."

"Then what is?"

"I love you. I always have. But I can't do this."

"What? Why?"

"Every day I'm frightened that the next breath I take will be my last. Do you know how terrifying that is? I don't want to know what it feels like for us to 'be together', to be loved by you," Greg said, resentment he still had for me, undeniable. "Knowing that I would no longer have you would make facing death even more terrifying."

I felt him still trying to pull away, but I wouldn't let him go. "Stay."

"No. I told you—"

"Don't think about the future. We could all be dead tomorrow," I said, saddened by how true the statement was.

He kneeled quiet in front of me.

"Fine," he said, visibly torn. "But only this one night."

"Okay." I lowered myself to my back, reached out, taking his hand, urging him to come to me.

## 44

A smile was on my face when I awakened the next morning. That was until I reached over and noticed Greg was no longer lying beside me. I sat up looking for him, calling out as though he might've been just outside my tent. When I got no response, I slid into my boots, and climbed outside.

"Greg!" I whispered.

It was very early morning, the sky was dark, everyone still sleeping, their tent doors zipped closed.

"Greg!" I called again, walking toward his tent; it was no longer there.

"Shea," I heard Daniel call. He trotted toward me.

"Where's Greg? And where's his tent? He didn't leave, did he?"

"Calm down," Daniel said. "He's not here."

"I know he's not here," I said, looking out over the camp as though I might see Greg dodging behind a tree, hoping not to be seen by me. "Greg!" I called again, this time, almost a full out yell. "Greg!"

"He's gone, Shea! And calling out for him, telling whoever might want to know where we are won't do us any good."

"Gone where?"

"He wouldn't tell me. He just said tell you that he could no longer stay."

"That's all he said?" I asked, crushed.

"Yes."

I yanked away from Daniel, ran back to my tent, came out with my gun belt, fastening it.

"Shea, wait!" Daniel called.

"Did he at least tell you what direction he was going?" I asked, not slowing for Daniel.

"No. And he doesn't want to be found or he would've told you where he was heading."

"I don't care. I'm going after him." I turned, backpedaling. "Don't wait for me. If I'm not back when you're ready to go, leave without me."

Ten minutes on the road, the sky was starting to lighten. I saw three older boys, thirty or forty feet away, strolling toward me as though they had no destination in mind and all the time in the world to get there.

The wind carried their laughter: rude comments they made about me. I lowered my head, marched harder, and told myself to mind my own business, but that I would let nothing stand in the way of finding Greg.

Ten feet away, a boy said, "Hey girl, you lost or something?"

I kept toward them.

Five feet, another boy said, "You need some help?"

I took four more steps, looking to step in between the sliver of space they quickly closed between their bodies. I stopped momentarily in front of the wall of dirty-faced boys, stepped to a side wanting to pass, but was grabbed around the arm.

"Please," I asked. "Just let me go."

"Maybe after you—"

Before he could finish his sentence, I grabbed the boy's wrist, spun around, and wrenched it downward till I heard it break. The other boys charged. I sidestepped one, stomped on his ankle, snapping it, then drew my gun, whipping around to find the last boy pointing a gun of his own at me. We faced each other, staring down the barrels of the other's weapons, his friends crying out at our feet.

"Let me pass," I said, one eye closed, the other, looking down the gun sight at my target. "I'll kill you if you try to stop me from what I need to do. I swear I'll kill you."

The boy looked down at his friends, back up at me, slowly lowered his gun, then stepped aside.

It was two hours later when I made it back to camp. I had run half an hour west, then doubled back, going another half an hour east, yelling

Greg's name. He could've been outside of earshot, or could've heard me coming, ran off the interstate just before I saw him, and hid behind a tree to watch me pass.

Back at camp, all the tents and bags were packed up. Daniel was shouldering his bag as he walked toward me. "Didn't find him, did you?"

"What do you think?"

"I'm sorry, Shea, but we have to move out."

"Then we move out," I said, walking past him.

## 45

A canopy of clouds hanging over us, obscuring the moon and the stars, blanketing us in almost complete darkness, I sat across the fire, staring at Daniel. It was at the end of another day of what seemed endless walking. Every other group member had long ago retired for the night, excited with the knowledge that tomorrow we would finally step foot into Washington D.C.

"Shea..." Daniel said. "You haven't said a word to me all day."

I looked up from the smooth stone I had been playing with. "Why did he leave? Did he tell you that he stayed with me last night? Was it because he regretted—"

"Shea, Shea, Shea, I don't know," Daniel said, compassion and sincerity in his voice. "But I'm sure it had nothing to do with you."

I tried to walk away, but turned right back around. "What does it matter?

He didn't care anything about me."

"Don't say that."

"Or you, or any of us, or he wouldn't have left, right?"

"Shea—"

"Right, Daniel?" I raised my voice, upset I couldn't find Greg, and couldn't shake the thought he was lying in a ditch somewhere after having been strangled by Burners.

Daniel didn't answer my question, but continued to stare at me with sympathetic eyes.

"Anything you need?"

I shook my head, realizing he wasn't going to tell me anything. "Sleep. Big day tomorrow, so I need sleep. I advise you to get some too."

I awakened early.

Rising from my sleeping bag, I saw that it was still dark, but I heard movement and the voices of our group. I slid on my boots, stepped outside to see that everyone was awake, standing in a small circle just beside the campfire, blankets draped over their shoulders, sipping coffee from plastic mugs. I glanced down at my watch. It read half past five in the morning.

I started toward my friends, but stopped, halted by the eerie feeling we were being watched. I gazed out at the perimeter of our camp, toward the walls of dense trees that surrounded us, then at the sky that looked more like night than early morning. I listened for movement; the wind was blowing hard, causing branches to creak and leaves to rustle, masking any sounds that would've alerted me of danger.

"Morning, Shea," April said, smiling.

"Hey April," I said, dismissing the uneasy feeling as paranoia. I walked over to her and lightly tugged on one of her pigtails. "What woke everyone up so early this morning?"

"Everyone's excited to finally make it to D.C., right?" Angie said.

April and Daniel nodded, agreeing with her. Even Potter, cuffed, to a nearby tree, seemed equally excited to get to the  capital, if only to have his fate determined.

"Yeah, you did it, Shea," Daniel said. "We set off on this crazy journey to D.C., and you got us there."

"Not yet," I said.

"Just a few hours away," April said. "Thanks to you. To Shea," she said, raising her coffee mug.

The wind blew harder, carrying a disturbing smell on its gusts. One in which I now associated with fear, pain and death.

"To Shea," Daniel said, Angie echoing him, both of them raising their mugs.

They drank in tribute to me, as the stench of burning wood and vegetation grew stronger, forcing me to ask, "Does anyone smell that?"

Daniel lowered his cup, sniffing the air. "Smoke." His eyes widened. "Something's burning."

Tornado stood, started barking ferociously, the hair standing needle-straight on his back. I saw a blur of white moving from one trunk to another in the trees before us.

No, I thought, panicking. We couldn't have been so careless as to let ourselves be surrounded. "Everyone!" I yelled. "Grab what you can. We need to leave! Now!"

"What's happening?" April cried.

I grabbed her by the arm, pulled her to me when I saw a flash of firelight in the tree line. The flame grew immediately to six feet tall within seconds, raced around the perimeter of our camp, the entire line of trees catching fire. As I held April closer, I could only imagine someone, under the light of the moon, wetting the ground with gasoline as we slept. But I didn't have to imagine, for they were in front of us now, just inside of the flames that were quickly crawling up the trunks of all the trees—three figures, then three more, crosses painted on their faces.

"Run, April! Run!" I screamed, shoving her toward what I thought was a break in the fire line.

I started toward my tent, whipping my head around, hoping to locate Angie. I saw her running to her tent, but was tackled just in front of it.

"Angie!" I cried, watching as one of the Burners threw himself on top of her, dragged her to her feet and started to strangle her.

Daniel! Where's Daniel, I screamed in my head, looking for him, only to find that he was on the ground, wrestling with a huge Burner the size of a grown man, his hands pressed down into Daniel's throat as my friend desperately struggled to tip the Burner off of him.

One step from my tent, I reached out to push through the mesh door, grab my guns when I felt the weight of someone slam into me. I was thrown to the ground, forced onto my back, and punched in the face, blood filling my mouth. I screamed, threw my arms over my head, attempting to block the blows, defend myself, at the same time get a glimpse of my assailant. All I saw were white face-shaped smears, black hateful eyes, and a mouth wrenched open, screaming.

I was snatched from the ground, forced upright, an arm that felt like an iron bar, smashed into my neck, cutting off my air. I heard Tornado coming quickly toward me: his paws striking the dirt, his furious growl becoming more menacing, then the scream of the boy that held me. Tornado's teeth were in his leg, but the boy whirled his arm around, striking Tornado on the head with his fist. Tornado howled, fell away then dropped to the dirt.

"No! No!" I screamed, fighting back, wildly throwing open hand slaps behind me, not knowing whether or not they did any good, as I frantically searched the camp to see if April had gotten away. I saw Potter by the tree, his arms still cuffed behind him, his face turning blue, his life being taken by the Burner strangling him. A moment of guilt struck me, wondering if I had not condemned him to those cuffs would he had lived through this—would he have helped to save all of us from dying.

Abandoning my efforts to beat the boy behind me off, I clawed at his forearm, digging my short nails into his flesh, still looking for April, horrified when I finally found her, suffering the same fate we all shared. She had been thrown up against a tree, her feet off the ground, heels wildly striking the trunk as a Burner stood in front of her, his arms outstretched, chocking the life out of who I now saw as my little sister.

"No!" I tried to scream, but I only gagged, the oxygen it took to speak, no longer in my lungs. I was lightheaded, my eyes swimming about in my head, seeing in the fire that consumed the trees around us, that I knew, once we were dead, would engulf all of us.

The wind blew harder, sweeping through my hair, blowing burning leaves into ten-foot high twisters from hell. I thought about Mom's notes in my tent, thought about the cure that would burn in the fire. What a failure I had been. Why did I ever take this on? What made me think I could've accomplished this? And then I saw Sloane's face, heard her yelling at me, telling me not to give up, that the world was depending on me.

Obeying her orders, I made a last attempt to live, grabbing at the arms of the boy who was trying to kill me. My hands slipped on the warm blood I had drawn when I pierced his skin with my nails. My boots kicking up dirt: trying to find his shins, his crotch, a whining, screaming, coughing coming from somewhere, sounding eerily like my own voice, I realized despite how much I tried, how much I wanted to live, this would be the day I died.

On the edge of consciousness, I glanced around the camp one final time—everything appearing blurry—hoping to in some way meet the eyes of my friends, apologize for the horrible fate I brought upon them.

Then I saw someone running toward me. I told myself I was hallucinating, for it looked like Jonny, sprinting full speed in my direction, screaming at the top of his lungs, a huge stone in his right hand, the cuff of his left sleeve and his entire left pant leg on fire. As he ran, the flames flapped around him, spreading up his torso and sides, clinging to his hair, entirely engulfing him, till he was no more than a speeding, human fireball.

Seconds before I thought I would die, I felt the enormous heat of Jonny's burning body near me, heard his screaming louder, then the sound of him striking the skull of the boy that held me, the "crack" of the Burner's head opening, and then the ground raced up, struck me on my hands and knees, where I almost drowned on the air that gushed into my lungs.

I needed to lie there, let the oxygen replenish my body, give me the strength to at least stand, but there was no time. I got to my feet, staggered about, seeing my killer on the ground, convulsing, bleeding from his head and Jonny, rolling about in the dirt, some of the flames being extinguished from his burning body. I wanted to go to him, rip off my parka, cover him, do everything I could to extinguish the flames I knew would kill him. But sadly, I knew he was already dead. My friends were still living, still wrestling with the Burners for their lives.

I had to get to my tent, get my guns so I could save them. I threw myself to the ground, about to scramble into my tent when I heard the crackle of a distant gunshot. Surprised and fearing for my life, I shimmied around the tent for cover. Another gunshot rang out, and I saw the head of the burner wrestling with Daniel, explode.

Another shot: the Burner strangling April dropped to the ground, releasing her, where she fell to her knees. Four more shots in all, the bullets of which ripped through either the heads or hearts of the remaining burners, putting them all down.

By that time, I had gotten to my feet, stumbled to Jonny, his body was blackened and smoldering, his eyes darting about in his charred face, as if from under a dark hood. I threw myself down, kneeled beside him. "Jonny," I gasped.

Unbelievably, he smiled when his eyes found me, and he struggled to speak. "Did I...save you?"

"You did, Jonny. You did," I said, doing my best to push back my tears.

"You gonna remember me, Shea?"

"We're all gonna remember you, Jonny. But we won't have to for a while. You're gonna make it through this."

"Shea..."

"Jonny, you made it this far," I said, hating the tears that spilled all of a sudden from my eyes.

"This was the best time of my life." Jonny coughed. "But I think this is the end." He held up a hand. It appeared the only part of him that had not been scorched by the flames. I took it, squeezed as tight as I dared.

"I'll never forget you, Sheriff Shea," he smiled again, wincing against the pain it caused him.

The tears still falling down my face, I couldn't help but smile with him. "So that's who I am now to you?"

"Something tells me that's who you've always been."

His eyes closed, a peaceful expression on his face. I didn't want to leave him, but the fire still burned wildly around us, and Angie was pulling at my arm.

"We gotta go, now, Shea!"

I stood, happy to see April in front of me. She looked shaken, but very much alive.

I saw Daniel kneeling over Potter's slumped body, Daniel's hand to his throat, checking for a pulse.

"Is he okay?" I called to him.

Daniel shook his head. "Didn't make it."

Another one I had lost, I thought, but I didn't have the time to beat myself up.

The fire had closed in us, trapped us in the center of the camp, trees falling around us. Tornado barked at them as they fell, as though they were our enemy and their intent was to harm us. I was glad to see that he was not seriously hurt.

"What do we do?" Angie yelled over the roar of the fire.

I quickly scanned the area, saw no opening, no path out, and yelled back. "I don't know."

"This way. This way!" I heard a faint voice call.

I turned in a circle looking from where it came, my eyes finally seeing the narrowest break in the fire, Greg standing inside of it, holding his rifle in one hand, waving us over with the other.

I grabbed my friends, pointed Greg out to them, pushed them all in that direction, and ordered Tornado to go with them. I started to follow, but stopped, needing to take one last look at Jonny, knowing if it wasn't for him, I would surly be dead.

When I turned to start back toward Greg, I shrieked when I saw someone behind him.

"Greg, no!" I screamed, about to tell him to turn around. Before I could, the figure I could only identify as a boy for I could not see his face, lassoed a forearm around Greg's neck, wrenched his head up as if to tear it off. In the boy's other hand, he held a huge hunting knife, the tip of which grazed Greg's temple. His face peered out from behind Greg's head, just enough for me to see the smeared cross, the dark hair and...the faded hazel eyes that belonged to my high school crush.

I staggered backwards, pulling my gun, leveling it, when I realized it was Markham Jennings. Had he followed us here? Tracked us, or happened upon us? I didn't know, but he was threatening the life of my best friend, and I couldn't allow that to happen.

"Let him go!" I screamed, my heart banging in my chest, sweat accumulating in my shaking hands.

Greg's arms were down at his side, his rifle on the ground.

"Take the shot, Shea!" Greg yelled, the sound of his voice barely making it back to me over the roar of the fire, the calamity of tree branches falling from the sky.

"No!" I yelled back to Greg. Then to the Markham: "I said, let him go! Drop the knife and let him go!"

Markham said nothing, but pointed the knife at my gun, then to the ground, demanding I toss it.

"Don't do it, Shea! You know this guy. He's a dick, and he hasn't changed. Kill him!" I heard Greg say, my eyes focused on Markham, on his efforts to hide—his knee, the hand of the arm that held the knife, and his head: bobbing in and out of sight, stealing glimpses of me with those haunting eyes. The flames around us were so bright I had to squint against the glare cast off everything, in order to maintain my aim.

Markham motioned again to the ground with his knife then pressed it against Greg's throat with just enough force to send a line of blood crawling down his neck. I looked in the Burner's eyes, knew he would kill Greg if I didn't do what he ordered. I froze with indecision. I had lost so many already; I couldn't afford to lose another—especially not Greg.

I pulled one of my hands from my gun, held my palm up. And against Greg's frantic shouts—"Shea! No, don't, Shea!" I pointed my gun toward the ground, and prepared to the toss it in the direction Markham asked, despite Greg's continued protests ringing louder and louder in my ears.

"I'm gonna die soon anyway, Shea!" Greg yelled, glints of flame reflecting off the tears that sped down his cheeks. "Just take the shot! Please!" he begged. "I'll always love you even if you miss and kill me. Just please, take the shot!"

There was a flash in my head, the course of the next year or eighteen months—however long Greg would've lived if I had done as he had asked and taken the shot—speeding by in a hair blowing blur; Greg not present in a single one of those scenes, because Markham had done what Dad's killer had in the gas station convenience store: lied.

Without another thought, I raised my gun, my targets already memorized. I felt as though I hadn't even aimed, just squeezed off three rounds in quick succession: the first bullet tearing through Markham's forearm, ripping open his skin, spraying blood in his face, forcing him to drop the knife. The next burrowing into his knee, sending him leaning to that side, fully exposing his face, where the last shot I aimed and sent speeding into the center of his forehead, at the intersection of the lines of the cross, leaving a tiny dark hole, closing his eyes, and dropping him to the ground.

Greg spun tremblinb, looked down at Markham Jennings, shook his head as though he regretted the boy's death, but knew there was no other way this could've ended. He bent, quickly grabbed his rifle from the ground and held out his hand to me.

"Come on, Shea!" he yelled. "Move it!"

I threw myself into him, kissing him.

The fire still blazing, the temperature around us feeling well over two hundred degrees, I felt Greg hesitate the briefest moment, then succumb, pressing his palms to my face and kissing me back. I held tight to him, feeling his heart bang against my chest, wanting to never let him go, realizing just how close I'd come to losing him.

"Why did you leave me? Leave us?" I said as though just remembering his departure in the middle of the night. Suddenly angry all over again, I tried to pull away from him. He held me tighter.

"I thought we were being followed," he said. "I couldn't risk us dying the way those other campers did."

I kissed him again then eased away, because I could literally feel my skin burning. "We have to go," I whispered.

"Wait," he said, digging a hand into one of his jean pockets, and pulling something out. "You left this because you didn't think you deserved it, but you do. You got us here; you've earned the right to wear this."

In his hand, was the sheriff's badge Dad had given me; the badge I had left on top of Sloane's grave; the badge that Greg must've taken before he followed me to the front of my burning house.

With the flames burning high, roaring loudly, Greg pinned the badge back to my chest as my father had done when he had deputized me.

"Thank you," I smiled proudly. Then grabbing his hand, I said, "But now we really need to go!"

## 46

Each day after the horrific day Jenna told me her father died, I expected to see a break in the evening broadcast, anchors pulling off their glasses, their voices quivering as they unbelievably read the news that President Sawyer had succumbed to the air. That didn't happen till a full month after his actual passing.

I guess our government feared what the rest of the world might do, knowing that our commander and chief was no longer in control. Or maybe the U.S. only decided to release the news after China, Russia and the United Kingdom informed the rest of the world that their leaders had all died, and felt that we were at no more of a disadvantage than the other superpowers.

When President Sawyer died, Vice President Johnson would've taken his place, if he too hadn't already passed. Instead, the Speaker of the House was elevated to the Presidency. He lived for another twenty days, at which time the Presidency was handed off again, and again, from the Secretary of State, to the Secretary of Treasury, skipping those who had died already, going all the way down to the Secretary of Agriculture and Labor.

After just three months of the air turning, all but one of the cabinet members had died: the man that sat at the bottom of the list—the Secretary of Homeland Security. It was he, an unassuming man of 53 years old, with a full head of premature white hair, Secretary Wilson Coin, that recognized if it was just those individuals of twenty years old and below that would survive, they would be responsible for carrying on tradition, for keeping order, for educating our children, for feeding and caring for our population, for defending our nation against threat, both foreign and domestic; it would be the responsibility of those twenty and below to preserve humanity. That goal would be achieved by something Secretary Coin termed The Legacy Appointment Act.

So, on the third month and the thirteenth day after the air turned, the first and only daughter, Jenna Amelia Sawyer was ascended to the level of President of the United States. The small ceremony, conducted in the White House Oval office was televised, tweeted, marked on Facebook, Youtube and every other social media outlet available.

News, and video, at least where the power and connectivity had not been lost, traveled quickly all over the world.

Sloane, Dad and I watched as Jenna rose her right hand, recited the oath, and gracefully, humbly and tearfully accepted the duties and responsibilities for the greatest nation on the face of the earth, and the dwindling number of survivors that still inhabited it.

She took the podium ten minutes later in the Brady Briefing room, surrounded by men in suits, dark glasses and earpieces, the majority of them under the age of 20 years old—the new secret service. The room was crowded with a small sea of reporters, the majority appearing equally as young. It was on that day, all the world watching, she made the call for those of us left alive to answer.

"Today is the saddest day of my life," Jenna started. "I do not deserve to be your president. I will do my best not to let you down in this horrible time of crisis. I can't do it alone, though. I'll need everyone's help. As you know, we have lost so many of our mothers and fathers, uncles and aunts, but they were also our doctors, and engineers, our policemen and farmers. For those of you who have performed those duties that made this country the strongest in the world, while there's still time, teach your children and those who will survive to perform those skills. As I've been appointed to this position, they will take your place."

I felt Dad's arm around my shoulder. He pulled Sloane and me close to him.

"And for those who have already lost those you've loved, I must ask a great favor of you. It is estimated that more than three quarters of our population in less than three months has died. We need to combine what knowledge we have, what skills we've learned. We need to be brave, endure whatever caused this onslaught of the generations that raised us, cared for us, and protected us. We need to prove to them, as well as to ourselves, that we won't just survive, but we will thrive. In order for that to happen, I need for those of you who can, to come to Washington, D.C. I know that I'm asking a great deal, but if we are all here, we can rebuild our government, our military, our medical care facilities. We will survive this," Jenna said, staring into the camera. To me, she looked lost. She appeared beaten and the worst, I feared, hadn't even begun. "God bless you," she concluded. "And God bless America."

We had survived the Burner assault on our lives, but in the process, lost two more of our own trying to get to the capital. Potter—someone who might've deserved his fate more than any other—was taken by the Burners, and Jonny did what I never imaged he would've: saved our lives, the five of us that remained.

We walked another six hours after the harrowing experience, all of us wanting to fall to the ground, but knowing we were so close, we pushed on keeping our complaints to ourselves.

The sky was darkening rapidly around us when Angie spotted the elevated metal road sign welcoming us to the nation's capital. We stopped in front of it, looking up, silently.

"It was all worth it, right?" Angie asked of no one in particular.

"We had to do it," April said.

I looked down at her. Her face was smeared with dirt, her clothes filthy, her hair tangled and working it's way out of the two rubber bands she had used to hold the braids.

"We had no choice," April added.

"That's right," I said, setting my hand on her shoulder.

"We lost a lot of people," Daniel said.

"They died for this cause. It wasn't in vain," I said, hiking up my pack on my back. "C'mon, this way. We don't have far to go."

## 47

We dragged ourselves down Pennsylvania Avenue, Tornado moving slowly by my side, his tongue hanging low out of his mouth, his ribs starting to protrude from his sides. All of us, our faces gaunt from lack of food and dirtied with soot, our clothes and hair smelling of smoke, we looked like coalminers who had been trapped underground for weeks. We were exhausted, but feigned attention, forcing our backs straight, holding our weapons at the ready, staying alert, just in case someone was watching.

We had made it to the capital: museums and old, brick government buildings, monuments and statues of our great forefathers regally posed, stared at us from every corner of every street. Yes, we had made it...but it was all on fire.

We continued walking—flames poking out the windows of every building—our eyes straight ahead, taking second-long glances at each other only to confirm the horror that we all saw, but could not believe was real.

Following tourist signs to the White House, we kept walking, turning the barrels of our weapons to any strange noises we heard, till we reached our destination.

We were alone, the space around us eerily quiet, the sun already setting, leaving a gray and ominous, overcast sky. The White House stood in front of us, but not how any of us had expected to see it. It didn't appear as it always had on TV and in the movies: front lawn stretching out like a sea of green, building standing regally, it's façade so bright white it almost sparkled: black iron, security gate surrounding the premises, each fence spoke, standing tall, sentry-like, in defense of the most important home in our country.

No, what we saw was a security gate that had been breached in several places: holes the size of railroad crossings, torn into the fence. The lawn had been ripped apart, riddled with craters, deep lines of tire tracks plowed across it from trucks and other military vehicles, now stalled: two jeeps in front of the White House—one turned on its side, and a pickup truck with a gun turret mounted in the bed, stood parked and unmanned on the south lawn. The columns were crumbling, the front of the building had been peppered with gunfire, both small and large caliber. Many of the windows were shattered, and through them and the open front doors, we could see small fires that were burning. And then there were bodies: scores of them, spread across the lawn, twisted and doubled over as though they had been dropped from hundreds of miles in the sky. The bodies were clad in black suits and shoes, or in army green, battle dress military uniforms: all of the clothes shredded by the gunfire that tore into the flesh of the dead.

We ran through the gate, over the lawn, Tornado barking furiously, leading us all, Greg glancing at me, a look of horror in his eyes: concern for what we might find. I felt the same dread.

Standing just outside the door of the White House, our bodies pressed against the walls; we were prepared to fight, not knowing what lay inside. Daniel, April and I stood on the right of the entranceway, Angie and Greg stood on the left, all of our weapons drawn.

I felt April breathing heavily at my side. She held the small 22. Caliber high in both hands how I had taught her.

"It's going to be all right, okay?" I said.

She took one of her hands from her pistol, wiped the tear from her cheek, nodded then gripped her gun again.

Turning back, I looked across the threshold to Greg and whispered. "We do this..."

"...on three," he whispered back.

I nodded. "Daniel...," I called, not looking back to where he stood behind me. "You ready?"

"Ready," I heard him say.

I set my eyes on Angie. She returned a steely stare and nodded her head, as if to answer the question I had just asked Daniel.

"One..." Greg counted off.

I drew my second weapon, the Walther, from my thigh holster, held both guns at shoulder height, pointed up, and took the two seconds to close my eyes, remember Mom, Dad and Sloane. They were the reason I was standing here about to lead my dearest friends—my new family—into a building where we might be ambushed, where we might be violently gunned down and ripped to pieces. The lives lost: my family, Angie's brother, Kendall, Beth, Potter, Jonny, and the billions of people all over the world who had been taken by the air: they were why we were there. We came all this way, toted Mom's notes to deliver them to Jenna, so a cure could be found someday. Be it tomorrow or five years from now, when all of us but April would've died, will not matter, so long as our race can be saved.

"Two..." Greg said, startling me out of my thoughts. "Three!"

Led by the barrels of our weapons, we pushed through the White House doors to find what I had prayed we wouldn't: holes blown through walls, the ceiling crumbling and threatening to fall, furniture on fire, everything blackened by smoke. There was blood on the floor: pools in some places, long smeared trails in others. And at the end of those trails, there were bodies:

"Hey!" Greg said, not to me, but to what seemed to be the only survivor in the building.

A girl, her back to us, she wore a white shirt, black slacks and shoes. The clothes were torn, dirty and bloodstained; her jacket missing, probably lost during whatever happened here. Across her back was the strap of an underarm holster.

"Turn around with your hands up!" Greg called to the girl again.

We all leveled our weapons on her.

"You heard him," I said. "Turn around slowly with your hands up."

She faced us, shoulders slumped, head down, hair falling over her eyes, a military issued Berretta pistol in her gloved right hand. She hadn't aimed it us, but the clatter of bullets being locked into the chambers of our weapons filled the room as we prepared to defend ourselves in case she had.

"Drop the gun!" Greg yelled.

"Drop it!" Daniel echoed.

She looked up, defeat in her eyes, and let the gun fall to the bloodstained floor.

## 48

Moments after finding Legacy Agent Ellie Burrows, she told us that the devastation before us: disabled and destroyed military vehicles, dead bodies lying on the floor around us, was the result of the battle that had gone on all night, and ended just hours ago.

"Battle?" Daniel said.

"After the air turned and our leaders died," Agent Burrows said, her face turned down, hands wringing around each other, as if to wipe off the dirt and dried blood, "We knew it was possible that someone might test our defenses, might try to take over the government by seizing the White House. We were always on high alert."

"Then how did this happen?" I said angrily, stepping through the foyer, kicking spent shell casings out the way. A dead agent sat on the floor, his back propped against the wall, his head hung, chin sunk into his chest, his white shirt dyed red with his own blood. He looked no older than me. "How, if you were so ready—"

"They caught us off guard, okay!" Agent Burrows snapped, finally looking at me.

"Who were 'they'?" Daniel said.

"Some radical militia, crazed fundamentalist, or maybe kids who got hold of some serious firepower and had a hard-on for taking down the U.S. Government. Who knows? But they accomplished it." Ellie stood, winced putting weight on her left leg. She hobbled across the room, shaking her head in disbelief. "Some time after midnight, all the windows imploded, there was an explosion so loud the ground shook, and then we were under fire from all sides. We held them off, kept them outside for better than four hours, then..."

"Then what?" April asked, her voice barely above a whisper.

Ellie turned, a grave expression on her face, looking as though there was more she wanted to say, but was afraid to.

"Where's the President?" I said, as if just realizing again why we'd come all this way.

"That's what I'm trying to say," Agent Burrows said.

"No, what you need to be saying is that the president has been locked away behind a cement door ten feet thick, somewhere twenty feet beneath this building," I said.

"We did our best."

"Best to what?" I said, raising my voice, marching over, stopping inches in front of her, Greg, Daniel, April and Angie crowding behind me, all of us waiting for an answer.

"As far as I know," Ellie said, her voice quivering, her eyes darting across the faces of my group. "I'm the only one left alive. And we—"

I snatched the Legacy agent by her ripped, bloodstained shirt and pulled her to me. "Jenna's dead?"

"No," Agent Burrows said, not resisting my hold on her. "It's the reason why whoever did this isn't here now. They didn't want The White House. They came for the president."

I pushed away, Agent Burrows stumbling back a few feet, nearly falling.

I walked over to Angie. "What are we going to do?" I asked her, then glanced at Greg, then Daniel for their input. Neither boy said a word. Angie didn't answer either, just shook her head, controlled fright on her face.

I readjusted the satchel with Mom's notes across my shoulder, comforted by the weight and the belief that as long as I still had them, and Jenna was alive somewhere, there was still hope for us: all of us.

"So the next move...what is it, Shea?" Greg said.

I shut my eyes, stood, feeling the room spinning slowly around me, as I tried to think. But there was nothing to think about; Jenna was the only person I trusted to give Mom's notes to. My belief was: we don't find Jenna, we don't live, and whoever trashed this the White House and killed all these people has won, and I can't allow that. I opened my eyes, faced my friends and said, "We go get her...wherever she is."

I started toward the doors, and without hesitation, what was left of our group, followed, past the bodies on the floor, the overturned chairs still burning and out beyond the threshold of the White House door.

"Wait!" Agent Burrows called. "You can't just leave me here. You can't just go!"

I ignored her cries, hoisted my backpack up, and prepared to take the first step in the countless it would take to find The President of the United States.

"You have no idea of where you're going," Agent Burrows cried. I heard the uneven falls of her steps as she hurriedly limped toward us. "You have no idea of who you're looking for."

I whirled around, yelled, "Do you know, Legacy Agent Burrows? Do you know what to look for?"

She jerked to a stop as if running into an invisible door.

"I know more than any of you. I can go with you. Let me help. I took an oath; it was my responsibility to protect the president. But I failed."

At the sound of those words, I was in my backyard again, my right hand raised, smiling, as Dad proudly pinned the sheriff's badge to my chest. Then I was in the gas station convenience store, the crack of the gunshot blasting through my ears, as the bullet exploded out of Dad's skull.

"Let me try to make up for this," Agent Burrows said, staring, pleadingly into my eyes.

I turned to Greg, and without a word, asked what he thought we should do. He said nothing, but took my hand, laced his fingers through mine, and squeezed, letting me know he would agree with whatever I decided. I turned to Angie, Daniel and April. "Can we find her?"

"No telling how long it will take," Angie said. "We'll need a place to stay."

"You can stay here," Ellie offered.

"Food? We'll need food," Daniel said.

April looked to Ellie.

"We're all out of that," Agent Burrows admitted. "But we can find some. I'm sure we can."

Tornado at my side, he stared devotedly up at me as we all gazed out at Washington D.C., its skies black with smoke, its horizon brightened by flames. We had made it. We were alive...for the moment. There was hope for us still, but so much further to go.

"Then we start tomorrow," I said.

END 4.22.15

If you enjoyed my latest novel—which I'm really hoping you did—let your fellow readers know what you think of Hate the Air by leaving your review on Amazon.com.

By doing so, you also let me know what works and what doesn't, which allows me to give you—my devoted fans—the stories you love most.

Thanks so much for your undying support!

RM

**RM Johnson** is the award-winning author of twenty novels. They include the bestselling Harris Men series, The Million Dollar and The Keeping the Secret series. He holds an MFA in Creative Writing and currently resides, happily, in Atlanta, Georgia.

Find more titles from RM Johnson

RM Johnson would love to hear your comments.

Email RM at **RMnovels@yahoo.com**

Friend him at **Facebook.com/RMJohnson**

Follow him on **Twitter @rm_novels**

www.ingramcontent.com/pod-product-compliance
Lightning Source LLC
Chambersburg PA
CBHW020745250626
47155CB00003B/921

*9780989511445*